When We Were Vikings

When We Were Vikings

A Novel

Andrew David MacDonald

SCOUT PRESS

New York   London   Toronto   Sydney   New Delhi

Scout Press
An Imprint of Simon & Schuster, Inc.
1230 Avenue of the Americas
New York, NY 10020

First Scout Press hardcover edition January 2020

SCOUT PRESS and colophon are registered
trademarks of Simon & Schuster, Inc.

For information about special discounts for bulk purchases,
please contact Simon & Schuster Special Sales at 1-866-506-1949
or business@simonandschuster.com.

The Simon & Schuster Speakers Bureau can bring authors to
your live event. For more information or to book an event, contact
the Simon & Schuster Speakers Bureau at 1-866-248-3049
or visit our website at www.simonspeakers.com.

Interior design by Michelle Marchese

Manufactured in the United States of America

1   3   5   7   9   10   8   6   4   2

Library of Congress Cataloging-in-Publication Data is available.

ISBN 978-1-9821-2676-6
ISBN 978-1-9821-2678-0 (ebook)

To Steven and Marta MacDonald

chapter one

The Viking my brother got me for my birthday was tall and had muscles. Even if you were not an expert on Vikings and had not read *Kepple's Guide to the Vikings*, you would say, that is a Viking. He looked like he could defeat hordes of villains and commit acts of bravery, like Beowulf, the most famous Viking, who defeated Grendel, who was not only a regular villain but also a monster.

But since I am an expert, I noticed many incorrect things. For example, the Viking's sword wasn't made of real metal, and his outfit was plastic instead of *brynja*, which is an armor made of rings to protect warriors from being cut with swords. His blond hair was not really blond. I could see that it had actually been colored.

After seeing the Viking, I chose a new Word of Today. The word ended up being *gargantuan*, a way of saying something, or someone, is amazingly large. It was a word that I had written on my list, with the help of my best friend, AK47, and since I remembered the definition, and since the Viking and the word went together, I decided I would put my other Word of Today (*eloquent*) away and make *gargantuan* the new Word of Today.

The Viking boomed through the door of our apartment, past Gert, and stood holding his sword. The first thing he said was: "WHERE IS ZELDA?"

He looked around the room, which was empty except for the couch, Gert's chair, the lamp in the corner, the coffee table, and Gert's TV, the most legendary thing we owned.

Gert pointed at me and made a sound with his throat.

"You," the Viking said, waving his plastic sword at me. "Are you Zelda?"

The Viking had already broken three of the rules that Gert and I have posted by the door to make sure our apartment stays clean and orderly and a good place for us both to live:

- Take off shoes to stop outside dirt from going all over the apartment.
- Do not stand in the doorway instead of closing the door and locking it as soon as possible, since people will try to rob us if they see the chance.
- Do not drop bags and things by the door, instead of taking them to the right place in the apartment.

The rules are written in big block letters that say: RULES OF COM-ING IN AND OUT, and there's a picture of the door and a person walking in that Gert and I drew together using the box of crayons I borrowed from the Community Center.

The Viking didn't see the rules, but when Gert made a noise and pointed to his own shoes, the Viking said, "Oh, shit," and kicked them off. "Sorry," he said.

(Even though swearwords are allowed, one of the House Rules is that we should at least try not to use them, which Gert finds harder than me.)

"The door too," Gert said, smiling.

The smiling was not a rule that we wrote down, but something we did for each other to show that we were happy with what the other person was doing without actually having to say, THANK YOU FOR DOING SOMETHING SMALL THAT I LIKED. That way we could save our Big Thank-You's for more gargantuan things.

"I have come to wish you a happy birthday," the Viking said to me. When he came closer he smelled like oranges sitting on the counter too long.

"*Góðan dag!*" I said to the Viking.

"Excuse me?" the Viking said.

"*Góðan dag!*" I said, louder and making sure that every sound of the words was clear and enunciated (Word of Today, June 4).

Góðan dag is the traditional Viking greeting, according to *Kepple's Guide to the Vikings*. Kepple's website has a video guide to pronouncing Viking phrases and words. *Góðan dag* is pronounced "go-than-dag." When you say words in Old Norse, you should sound like you're spitting. One of the things I did when I started trying to speak Viking was hold my hand in front of my mouth, so that I could tell if I was saying things properly by how wet my hand got.

He looked at my brother. "What's she saying?"

"*Góðan dag,*" I repeated, then said: "*Ek heiti Zelda! Hvat heitir þú?*" Which was me telling him my name and then asking what his name was.

"Tell her what I told you to say," Gert said to the Viking.

Gert was sitting on the arm of the couch, wearing a cone birthday hat with wrinkled fingers coming out of the top. The wrinkly fingers waved around from the balcony wind.

The Viking stared for a second, not knowing what my brother was talking about, and then his face got big with understanding. "Oh, right. One second."

The Viking closed his eyes and cleared his throat, like he was the President about to tell the world something very important. Gert turned down the drum music, which I had him download specially off the Internet from Kepple's website.

"Ack anne there," he said, stopping after each word and looking at me the entire time. "Ack anne there." The Viking turned to Gert. "Am I saying it right?"

"Is he?" Gert asked me.

"Ack anne there," I said.

It sounded like Old Norse, or sort of like Old Norse, only with less spitting. "Can you say it again, please? With more spitting?"

"Ack anne there." He coughed and took out a sheet of folded paper from his plastic underwear, which was shiny and gold (something a real Viking wouldn't be wearing). He handed me the piece of paper.

The words were in Old Norse. I sounded out each letter. "Oh," I said. *"Ek ann þér."*

Gert smiled. "Right?"

It was not perfect, but I told Gert that I liked the Viking very much with my smile.

⅂

Most Viking women stay at home and have babies and cook and clean. But that was never the type of woman I wanted to be. My favorite part of *Kepple's Guide to the Vikings* is the Valkyries, strong magical women who decide who gets to live and die in battles. They bring the warriors they choose to a place called Valhalla, a house where Odin and the other gods are that must be gargantuan to hold so many people. You can't become a Valkyrie, though. You are born one. Not like heroes, who become heroes by being legendary.

I am not someone people would think is a Viking. I am five feet and one inch and my arms are very skinny. My legs are not skinny because I play a lot of basketball with Gert, and basketball makes your legs strong.

I am a very good runner and can run forever, even though a Viking spends more time fighting than running. I was on the running team when I was in school. Our school mascot is the Crusader, who is almost like a Viking and also wears armor. But then I could not go to school anymore after I failed most classes.

Many people like me have big foreheads and small eyes. My friend Yoda has a face like that. But with me you would not know that I am not normal.

I have the element of surprise in battle.

Even though I liked Gert's Viking, I wish he would have asked a Valkyrie to come. Most people know a few things about Vikings, but not many people know things about Valkyries, who are more powerful than Vikings. If they do know anything, it's the song "The Ride of the Valkyries." It comes from an opera and was originally made by an old musician named Wagner.

Vikings like legends and since people still know about Wagner, even so long after he died, I like Wagner and respect his legend.

There were three other people I wanted to be at my birthday party. Mom was not alive, so I could not actually invite her, except in spirit in the way that Vikings can get the spirits of their dead family members and friends to come to parties invisibly, but I did invite AK47 and Marxy.

Our apartment building is in a crappy neighborhood, and Marxy lives in a very rich part of the city, so his mother, Pearl, never lets him come over, even for something as special as my first birthday since he and I fell in love.

Pearl also thinks that Gert is a thug. That is a stupid thing to believe, I think. Do thugs go to college on big scholarships to study about money?

No, they do not. They behave like villains and hurt others, instead of saving them.

My brother is good-hearted, but Gert scares a lot of people because of his shaved head and tattoos, especially the tattoo of the skull on his forearm that is laughing and has a big red tongue, and because he doesn't dress like someone who works at a bank or has a real job. He wears jeans and tight black shirts.

Those people, the ones who don't trust Gert, are shit-heels and fuck-dicks, because Gert is one of the smartest people I know, and the bravest, and if we were in the past, people would be writing legends about him, no problem. If villains attacked your tribe, you would want Gert there to defend you in battle.

I also missed AK47, though, and wished she was there. I knew that her and Gert still loved each other, even if she said she hated his stupid guts and he said she was never allowed to be in the apartment again.

AK47 would have liked the Viking. He was standing in his shiny gold underwear, making animals out of balloons. He said that his specialty was dogs. "But I can do some requests."

"What kind of animal do you want him to make?" Gert asked me.

I asked him for a dragon, since many of the oldest Viking sagas have dragons in them.

He blew up a balloon and in a second it was an almost-dragon. I held up the balloon and told him it looked good, even though it was more like a snake that had tried to tie itself like shoelaces.

"Another?" he asked.

The intercom buzzed. Gert didn't get up to answer it, the way he usually does whenever someone buzzes. That is a rule we have: whenever Gert is home and someone buzzes the intercom, he's the one to answer it and decide if the person in the lobby of the building is allowed to come in or not.

The intercom buzzed again. The Viking stopped his balloon and looked at Gert. I looked at Gert too.

"There is someone at the door," I said.

"I know. Do you want to answer it?"

"But the rule," I said.

Gert smiled. "I think this is a rule you can break today because it's your birthday. And because I think it's going to be someone special."

Normally we don't break rules, since we both like knowing how everything is supposed to work, and because I have trouble acting properly if I don't have rules to follow. But it was true, it was my birthday, and I was now an adult and twenty-one years old.

I stood in the middle of the living room, not sure what to do.

The intercom buzzed again.

"Seriously," Gert said. "Go answer it."

I closed my eyes and counted to ten, one of the things Dr. Laird told me to do whenever I felt all of the rules being broken.

"You can do this," Gert said.

"Okay," I said. "Let's do this."

I took the dragon balloon and went to the intercom box on the door and pressed the button that said TALK.

"Hello?" I asked the intercom.

"Is this Zelda?"

It was a woman's voice. I said it was me, Zelda. Then I heard Marxy's voice.

"Happy birthday," he said.

I looked at Gert, talking to the Viking. He smiled over the Viking's shoulder and gave me a thumbs-up.

He had made magic happen.

᛭

Marxy could not remember the traditional Viking greeting, but Pearl, who brought a smell of perfume with her, pointed to the sign so that he could read the House Rules.

"Remember your book?" Pearl said. "This is like a page from it."

At his house Marxy had a book of pictures that helped him get through the day, sort of like the House Rules.

Marxy is tall and when he walks he moves his head down, like he is afraid of his head hitting the clouds. He also talks slowly and does not like looking people in the eyes, except for the people he loves and trusts. Sometimes he picks up string he finds and rolls the string into tiny balls that he likes to chew on, which is gross but when you love someone you try not to be bothered by gross things they do when they can't help it.

A big problem is that he has trouble remembering a lot of the things he needs to remember.

Marxy was dressed very nicely, even though he was always dressed nicely. Today he was dressed like he was going to a wedding. He wore a shirt with a collar and buttons up the front. It was blue, my favorite color. His hair sat on one side and was shiny and combed.

"Gert," Pearl said, nodding at my brother, who was still with the Viking.

"Hey."

She looked at the Viking, her jewelry on her arm, gold rings, jangling. "And this is?"

"Thor," the Viking said. "King of the Vikings."

Pearl stared and then said, "Okay then. The stripper's going to keep his clothes on, right?"

"Only balloon animals for this Viking," the Viking said.

"You're a stripper?" I asked the Viking. "You take off your clothes?"

"I have many talents," he said.

"Well, keep it PG-13 for this party," Pearl said. She handed Gert a card and told him to call her if there were any problems.

"I'll be back in one hour."

"We'll try not to burn the house down," Gert said, which was a joke, since Gert is very careful about fire in the house and doesn't even like me cooking unless he's around, a rule we changed after I proved I could cook things for myself like pasta.

Pearl held Marxy's shoulders. "You can call anytime. Do you have your phone?"

Marxy showed her his phone. He bent over and she kissed his cheek.

⸙

Once Pearl left, the Viking made another balloon dragon and handed it to Marxy. I had been trying to teach Marxy how to speak Old Norse for months, but no matter how hard we both practiced, he couldn't remember.

He even had trouble remembering the Word of Today. I started keeping track of how long he could remember the Word of Today for and learned that with smaller words he didn't know, those words he could hold in his brain for three days. Even though his brain is probably bigger than my brain in size, there is something wrong with how it works, so actually he has less space in his brain than normal people.

For longer words, like *gargantuan*, he would forget the word in a day. We wanted to have a language we could speak together, one that nobody else could speak. That was why I tried to teach him Viking.

For my birthday Marxy had already given me a gift, a drawing he made of us as two Vikings. Marxy is not very talented at hands and feet and faces. I think he is very talented at showing that we are in love. And swords. Our swords look gargantuan and amazing in the picture he gave me for my birthday.

Marxy let the balloon dragon the Viking made float to the ground. The Viking scratched his hairless, sun-yellow stomach.

"Ack anne there," the Viking said to Marxy.

"What does it mean?" Marxy asked. He picked up his balloon dragon and was petting it on his lap.

"I love you," I said.

"I love you," Marxy said, wrapping his arms around me. "Eck anne pear."

I smiled at my brother.

"Should I keep making balloon animals?" the Viking asked.

"I don't know," Gert said. "Ask the birthday girl."

Marxy had another present for me: a French kiss. We had kissed before, but not the French way.

Since Marxy is the only person I've ever kissed, all I know is what the videos on YouTube tell me about kissing, and what AK47 told me about kissing, which is: not too much of anything. Not too much tongue, AK47 told me. Not too much lips. Not too much of anything.

Marxy's kisses are probably too much of everything, but that's okay. He put his tongue in my mouth and moved it around. We had talked about French-kissing before. We hadn't French-kissed yet, though, and Marxy thought that my birthday was the best time to do it.

He put his arms around me and then his mouth went on my mouth.

The kissing was in front of the Viking, who was standing by the stereo, looking at Gert's huge speakers. He watched for a second before calling out to Gert and saying, "I think you need to come in here," and when Gert came in from the kitchen he handed his cake to the Viking and pulled us apart.

"French-kissing," Marxy said, smiling and wiping spit that could have been either of ours off of his face.

"Yes," Gert said, patting him on the back. "Yes, French-kissing."

Marxy is tall like the Viking, but has less muscles. He's taller than Gert too. Even though he's almost gargantuan, Marxy is frightened of almost everything. I never tell him so, but he would be a terrible Viking warrior. Viking tribes have lots of people, not just warriors or heroes like Gert. Marxy could be a very good farmer because he likes being outside and in the sun, and he works very hard.

⇂

At the end of the night, after Marxy and the Viking left, Gert sat down on the couch beside me and stretched his arms and let out a deep yawn.

"Well, that went all right," he said, and he opened a can of grape soda, our favorite. He took a drink and handed the can to me. "Right?"

I told him it was a powerful birthday and even though I wanted to mention how it would have been better if he made up with AK47, I didn't. We sat on the couch for a while, drinking the can of soda. Then I sat up and remembered what I had wanted to do before going to bed.

"Can we watch it?" I asked.

Gert groaned. "It's getting late, and it takes forever to set up."

"Please?" I pinched the weird flabby skin on his elbow and gave it a twist.

He said we could, "but only once through," and put the can of soda on the coffee table, next to his pack of cigarettes and one of the Viking's balloon-dragons. He came back with a plastic bag with the VCR in one hand and the VHS tape in the other.

I helped him set up the VCR by plugging the cords into their holes in the TV, putting the red cord into the red hole and the yellow cord into the yellow one, while Gert balanced the VCR on top of the DVD player.

Then I sat on the couch and he put in the videocassette.

The TV was fuzzy at first and then everything became clear. Gert turned up the volume so we could hear the laughter.

In the video we are by the beach. Gert and Mom are wearing sunglasses and their blond hair shines in the sun. The wind makes the waves of the ocean lap against the sand. I am very small and wearing a pink bathing suit, and I have sunglasses on too—big green ones that cover half my face.

"Do your handstand," Mom says to me, and I am doing a handstand and Gert is holding one of my ankles, and Mom is laughing and holds the other and I am upside down. The waves splash into us, and then we are suddenly running down the beach, all three of us, and shouting as the camera follows us.

We are happy and wet. There are seagulls in the air and no clouds, so they look like letters of the alphabet flying through the sky.

"Where was this again?"

"Florida," Gert said. "Outside of Fort Lauderdale. We went here on vacation in—"

I closed my eyes. "Nineteen ninety-four," I said. "I was six years old."

"You got it."

The entire video is eleven minutes, then a TV show about the Amazon jungle comes on that someone accidentally taped over the beach video halfway through. The last thing the video shows is Mom laughing as Gert takes the camera and puts it right in her face, her teeth white and her lips wide and her hand pushes the camera away while she laughs like a famous person who does not want to be videotaped.

Then Gert hit STOP and the TV became black again. I had been holding my breath without realizing it and had to catch it.

"All right, time for bed," Gert said, taking the tape out and putting it into its case.

We did not talk about how Dad was behind the camera, the one who was running after us on the beach, or how the only time I can remember seeing him is when the camera looks down at his bare, hairy feet.

> ⇌

Vikings spend a lot of time talking about people who are dead, especially those who have died bravely in battle. Our mother died of cancer, not fighting other people, though when Gert tells it sometimes it sounds like a kind of battle: her fighting against a tribe of villains inside her body.

He told me that her hair fell out, that she became skinny and died because they were poisoning her. I don't remember her being poisoned with radiation, which is invisible. I don't remember much of anything about her. In the pictures around our apartment, she looks beautiful and blond, which is the hair color of all the famous Viking women.

Gert is blond, when he has his hair and doesn't shave it. I have dark hair, which is almost black. I do not shave it. Gert will not let me. At times I feel like I should have blond hair too, since I am the one who knows everything about Vikings, then I remind myself that hair color doesn't make anyone a Viking.

Deeds and actions are what will make a person great and legendary.

Our father named Gert Gert because it is a traditional German name. Gert does not know that I found his box of pictures of our father, which he got after our mother died. There is a photo of our father on a bed, without his shirt, smoking a cigarette. He has a shaved head and tattoos and a mustache and looks very much like Gert. There is another one of him on a motorcycle and Mom hanging on to his stomach, with her arms around him. He has a leather jacket and no helmet, even though riding a motorcycle without a helmet is against the rules and dangerous because if you crack your skull your brains could come out.

We do not know what happened to him. Gert says that he was arrested for breaking into houses and then when he got out of prison he did not come back to the family.

"He's probably six feet under," Gert said, meaning dead and buried under the ground.

We are not allowed to talk about Dad, and only sometimes allowed to talk about Mom. Gert does not like to talk about either of them very much.

I don't know very much about our mother, except what Gert told me. I make up stories about her and tell them to everyone. Vikings believe that telling stories here, on earth, will make a person in Valhalla very happy, and the best way to make someone happy is to make them into a legend that everyone talks about.

That is why I tell people my mother fought off fifty million boat-loads of cancers with a single sword.

"She was the bravest woman to ever live," I tell people.

Before going to bed, I took the photo of Mom that I had in a frame on my desk and, in my head so that I didn't wake anybody else, sung her praise. If you think about someone before going to sleep, sometimes you dream of them. In my dreams sometimes I think that Mom died and became a Valkyrie, that one day, when I am in a battle, she will take me with her to Valhalla.

chapter two

t is important to have a schedule to follow, so that everyone knows where you are and you know what to do.

For example:

On Mondays, I go to the library after breakfast to read the books about Vikings. Gert comes home from school and we have lunch together. I like to also play basketball on Mondays, on the basketball court outside of the apartment building.

On Tuesdays, I see Dr. Laird during the day for one hour, then I have Recreation Time at the Community Center.

On Wednesdays, I go to the library to read *National Geographic* magazine, to see if any new Viking pictures are in them. I also like to look at the pictures of animals.

On Thursdays, Gert and I see Dr. Laird together. Gert has no classes on Thursdays, so we go somewhere fun together on that day too.

On Fridays, Saturdays, and Sundays, I go to the Community Center for Recreation Time, Literacy Class, or Social Class.

My birthday party was on a Monday, and the next morning was Tuesday, so according to the schedule I would be seeing Dr. Laird.

Normally we leave the house at 11:15 a.m. in order to get to

Dr. Laird's by 12 p.m. Today, Gert said, our schedule was different. He had gotten a very important call and said we would eat breakfast earlier and leave the house earlier, because we had a place we needed to go first.

"Is it another birthday surprise?" I asked.

"More like an errand," Gert said, and he told me not to worry about it.

With Gert, I do not mind going to new places. If I am alone, I do not like new places, since it's easy to become lost and kidnapped and held for ransom.

I also like Gert's car, which he keeps very clean and shiny.

⩔

The place Gert took me to before Dr. Laird's was not a place I had been before. There were a bunch of houses with dead flowers and lawns that looked like they hadn't been cut in a long time. All of the houses were orange and yellow and looked very tired. Some had shrubs, and the leaves were brown and the grass on the lawns was brown and thirsty for water.

Gert pulled over by one of the houses, with a metal front door that had no screen. In front were two white plastic lawn chairs.

He parked the car and unbuckled his seat belt and turned the music off and the car engine grumbled until it was quiet.

"Where are we?" I asked. "These houses look sick."

"Nowhere. Just chill out and I'll be back in a couple minutes."

"One hundred and twenty seconds," I said. "Which is two minutes."

"I don't mean literally two minutes," Gert said.

"So then literally how long?"

He sighed. "Fifteen minutes. Tops. But if I take longer, don't freak out."

This is a problem Gert has: he likes to not be precise, a Word of Today that I use a lot because it helps me know exactly what to expect.

When you are the opposite of precise, imprecise or very general, people do not know when something is going to happen, or how.

I set my watch for fifteen minutes.

"Will that give us enough time to get to Dr. Laird's? Because he gets angry when you make me late."

"We'll be fine. Plenty of time. Now roll down the windows so you don't boil to death."

Gert walked up the sidewalk toward the house, to the door, and I smelled my armpits. He knocked and it opened, and he went inside. After rolling the windows down I took out my phone and texted Marxy and asked him what he was doing. He texted back and said **Nothing** and asked what I was doing, and I said waiting for Gert to come out of a house so we could go to Dr. Laird's.

He sent a smiley face that was kissing and hearts and said his mother told him to put his phone away. I sent him a picture of a smiley face and sunglasses, and also a fist emoticon to show that we were powerful.

Across the street, a woman in a green bikini sat in front of two young children who were splashing in a blue plastic pool. They started wrestling with each other and the woman in the bikini told them to quit roughhousing. They kept going so she put down her drink and got up and grabbed the child who had started the wrestling by the arm. She pulled him up and pulled down his pants and started hitting his backside until he started crying.

I did not want to keep looking at that.

In my opinion, parents should never hit their children. Uncle Richard used to hit Gert when he was younger. AK47 says it leads to emotional problems.

I turned away from the woman and watched the house Gert went into, which was number 334.

The time was 10:41 a.m. Eleven minutes had passed by. My appointment with Dr. Laird was always at 12 p.m.

We had exactly one hour and nineteen minutes to get there.

Since I did not know where we were, I could not do my problem-solving and minus the time it would take to drive from where we were to Dr. Laird's office, which is downtown.

Gert came out of the house and walked to the car. It had been twelve minutes.

"Come in with me," he said.

"But you said I should stay here."

"I know. But this is going to take a bit longer than I thought."

"We have one hour and seventeen minutes before we have to be at Dr. Laird's," I said, and Gert told me it would be fine, that we had plenty of time.

While walking I tried to take Gert's hand and he did not want to hold hands. "Not now," he said, and before we got to the door he told me to try not to say anything. "Just be quiet, and if you get asked questions, just answer them with as few words as possible. Okay?"

"Why are we here?" I asked.

"Got it?"

He took my wrist and squeezed it until it started hurting. I pulled my hand away.

"Got it, okay. Jeez. Hurting children causes emotional unstability as adults," I said, and the woman in the green bikini watched us, while one of the children cried. He would be emotionally unstable when he got older.

That was a fact.

Inside, the house smelled like cigarettes and marijuana smoke. There was the sound of a toilet flushing and a door opened down the hall. Then a large man with tattoos came out and opened his arms. Gert said that his name was Toucan and that he was very important, so I should be polite. Toucan had a cigarette in his mouth and didn't care when the ash fell off it and onto the floor.

"So you are the famous Zelda," he said to me, and he dabbed Gert and held out his hand to dab me.

I stared at his hand.

"Is my hand dirty?" he asked me, and looked at Gert. "Why isn't she dabbing?"

Gert said, "It's one of her things. Zelda, come on. Dab the man."

One of my rules is that I use dabs for people who I like, or who have earned my respect. Hugs are for members of my tribe only. I do not like being touched at all by strangers, and do not like being in places with a lot of people.

Gert gave me THE LOOK and so I held out my hand and dabbed Toucan's hand.

"I asked Gert to bring you in so we could meet," he said. "Plus it's hot as hell out there and I didn't want you cooking in the car. We're going to be seeing a lot of each other, so I'd prefer you weren't, you know, burnt to a crisp."

"I'm not *that* famous," I said.

Nobody took off their shoes, which meant that the Rules of the House here were different from those at home. Most houses allow you to wear shoes, and so I kept mine on.

"Mi casa es su casa," Toucan said. He stopped. "You know what it means?"

"My house is your house," Gert said.

Toucan took his cigarette out of his mouth and moved it around while he talked. "True. Now, do you know where it came from?" He was looking at me so I shook my head and said I did not know. Toucan continued explaining. "When Cortés first met Montezuma, the king of the Aztecs, Montezuma said, 'This is your house.' You know who Cortés was, Zelda?"

"He was an explorer."

Toucan nodded. "The right word is *conquistador*. And you know what they did to the Aztecs?"

"I don't know," I said. Toucan bent over until his cigarette was close to my face.

"He fucked them and took everything and killed them all."

I coughed from the cigarette smoke going into my face. It was quiet for a second.

Then Toucan laughed. Gert laughed too, not a serious laugh, but a quiet one. I did not know what was funny.

"He sounds like a shit-heel," I said. "Cortés."

"He was a badass motherfucker, is what he was. Now. Come, I need to talk to your brother about some things, so we'll set you up in here."

Toucan brought us to the living room, where there was a couch and a big TV. The carpet needed to be cleaned. We also have carpets in our apartment, and once a month Gert drives to the grocery store and rents a machine to wash the floor in our apartment, which gets very dirty after a while, even when we take off our shoes. Toucan for sure needed that machine.

At a round table in the living room some people were playing cards and smoking cigarettes. Toucan clapped his hands and they stopped playing their card game.

"Everyone. I am pleased to introduce Zelda, Gert's sister. Zelda, this is the gang."

I waved. "Hello, gang."

All of them turned to me and I felt like a stick standing around trees.

They started playing cards again. Toucan threw his cigarette so that it landed right in the middle of the table.

"She said, 'Hello, gang.'"

The gang put their cards down and each of them said hello to me. Toucan took out another cigarette and lit it.

"We've got some good games, Zelda," Toucan said, pointing to the TV. "Have a seat on the couch there."

I sat after Gert gave me a slow nod to show that it was okay. Toucan asked if I wanted anything. "Like a soda or something?"

I said I was thirsty and he asked one of the card players to bring me a Coke. "We've got the new NBA game. You like basketball, right?"

"We actually can't stay that long," Gert said.

I checked my watch. "We have one hour and twelve minutes until we have to be somewhere else."

"Relax," Toucan said, patting Gert on the back. "Plenty of time."

Toucan pointed to one of the people playing cards and told him to set me up. "Get her going on some *NBA2K*," Toucan said.

Gert told me he'd be right back. "I won't be long," he said.

And then he and Toucan went down the hall, talking in low voices. They looked like two large Vikings.

The person who was setting it up had low-hanging black Nike shorts so that you could see the top of his butt while he pulled out cords and untangled the controller. It was almost as bad to look at that as the woman who was hitting her child.

He handed the controller to me.

"Make sure when you play you do a new account," he said. "I don't want you fucking with my season."

He went back to playing cards with the gang.

I drank my soda and began playing. The game was very good. I had played older versions of it at the Community Center, during Games Nights, and I picked the Boston Celtics, who were my favorite team, even though nobody else liked them. Everyone else liked either the Lakers or the Warriors. People thought that the Celtics were boring.

I played for a while. I won one of the games, against the Denver Nuggets, and then lost to the San Antonio Spurs, who were the champions, so their team was very good. They are boring to watch on television but get things done on the basketball court. Gert likes that they do not get fancy and do things like behind-the-back passes or dribble too much. They pass a lot and are like a good tribe doing battle and working together instead of trying to do everything on their own.

The people playing cards drank beer and kept smoking. The house was full of smoke. I finished my can of soda and put it on the coffee table, next to the ashtray, which was very full. One of them got up and left because he had run out of money, and the others tried to get him to stay but he left anyway. After he left, another person left too.

After winning another game, I checked my watch. Twenty-one minutes. Gert had been gone for a while.

I put down the controller and I walked over to the people playing cards. I stood behind the person who had set up the *NBA2K* and watched the game. There were five people left playing cards and they all wore baseball caps and had tattoos.

There was money and cigarettes in piles in front of them. One was smoking from a vaporizer box. I knew that many people stopped smoking regular cigarettes and instead smoked from the boxes because they smelled better and looked like bathroom steam whenever it breathed out. The man was very large and fat and looked at me over his shoulder.

"Can I help you?" the Fat Man asked.

"I'm just watching," I said.

I had seen Gert playing poker before, in high school, and Uncle Richard used to play too. You put money in the middle and the winner who had the best cards got all the money. If you didn't want to put money in, you could also put cigarettes. That was what Gert did during high school. Uncle Richard liked playing for money.

The Fat Man I was standing behind ended up losing.

"Man, you're bad luck," he told me. "Go stand behind someone else."

"I got something you can sit on," said the poker player who had a red hat on. "Come on over here."

The Fat Man told him to shut his mouth. "That's Gert's sister."

The man in the red hat looked me up and down. "Doesn't look like Gert's sister to me," he said, and then patted his knee and said to come on over.

I decided to sit on one of the empty chairs, beside the person who had just won the last hand. He was thin and had his face hairs shaved into something called a Chin Strap that is thin and goes from your ears along the chin, like the straps you use to keep a bicycle helmet from falling off your head.

He stuck out his hand and said his name was Hendo.

"All right, Zelda," Hendo said. "You can help advise me. Could use a bit more luck."

"Pffft," said the Fat Man. "Your funeral."

We played poker together, like one team. Hendo liked to make jokes while playing. Nobody else laughed as much or made jokes like he did.

"So the chicken and egg are in bed together," Hendo said.

"Can you just deal?" the Fat Man said.

Hendo passed out cards and kept talking. "So the chicken is really happy. Big fucking smile on its face."

He finished dealing the cards and everyone picked them up.

"And then the egg, really frustrated, goes, 'Well, I guess we answered that question.'"

"Ha ha," one of the other players said.

"I don't understand," I said. "What was the question?"

The man in the red hat lit another cigarette and turned to the Fat Man. "Is she for real?"

I said that I was for real, but that I still wanted to know what the question was. Hendo said that the joke was that the egg and chicken just had sex, and that the chicken got off first and the egg was angry because it wanted to get off but it wasn't going to happen.

"Why wasn't it going to happen?" I asked, and was going to add, "and what is it?" but people do not like it when you ask too many questions at once.

"Is she retarded or something?" the man in the red hat asked, and the Fat Man punched him in the arm.

"That's actually not an okay thing to say," I said. "Like the n-word."

"Like the n-word," the man in the red hat said. "What planet are you from?"

"The planet where we keep taking your money," Hendo said, because we had won again. He made a smaller pile for me, where I got a little bit of money every time we won.

While we played I told him about runes and drew one for him on a napkin.

"It is supposed to protect you in battle," I said, and Hendo liked that.

"That's perfect. Poker is like a battlefield. Winner takes all."

Before the part of the card game where everyone takes turns and decides what to do, whether to bet more money or give up, he wanted to rub the rune for good luck.

"How much do you think I should bet?" he asked me, and even though I could not tell how good the cards in his hands were, I told him more or less. And he would always listen.

There was a break in the game when the Fat Man went to get more beer, and the man in the red hat went to the bathroom, taking all his money with him. The other two players went for a smoke. Hendo apologized for how rude the man in the red hat was being.

I told him that I was used to it. "People call me a retard all the time."

"Well, you don't look it," Hendo said, counting up the money in front of him. "I think he's just jealous because you're sitting over here and not with him."

Hendo stacked the five-dollar bills in front of him in one pile, the one-dollar bills in another. I helped him by putting the coins into piles, one for each number of cents.

"Like if you hadn't told me," he said, "I wouldn't have known you and Gert were related."

"Gert is more gargantuan than I am," I said.

"Yeah, but I just mean . . . you're a good-looking girl. And good frigging luck. Those runes are for real."

The Fat Man came out with a six-pack of beers. He put one in front of Hendo, one where the man in the red hat was sitting, and the rest in front of himself.

I thought about what Hendo said—how I was a good-looking girl, and how he could not believe I was Gert's sister. While we played poker I pretended I was not Gert's sister at all, and that I was a normal person playing poker. Things happened very fast in the game. I watched and tried to learn which cards were better than others. Hendo did not get mad when I picked the wrong cards or said what to do, and he high-fived whenever I told him to do something and he won.

This made the man in the red hat madder and madder, because even when we didn't win, the Fat Man won. The man in the red hat was the only person who wasn't winning at all.

"Why don't I get my own retard," he said, and turned to the Fat Man. "Do you think she fucks like a retard? Hey, do you swallow, retard?"

"You've got a rotten mouth on you, you know that?" Hendo said, putting his cards down.

"Swallow what?" I asked.

The man in the red hat started unzipping his pants. "You want to see? It'll be like sex ed—"

"Goddamn it," the Fat Man said. "Nobody wants to see that. Can we just play?"

"And you don't want to deal with Gert when he's pissed," Hendo said, holding his cards so I could see.

One of the other poker players got up and said he was leaving. But the man in the red hat told him to sit back down.

"Just because he's Toucan's new butt boy doesn't mean I have to suck him off like everyone else," the man in the red hat said.

"Gert is nobody's new butt boy," I said.

"Toucan tells him to jump, and Gert asks how high." The man in the red hat put another handful of coins into the middle of the table. "Raise."

A "raise" means that he believed he could win and wanted to bet more money to see if anyone else was just as confident.

Hendo threw in all of his bills, even the twenty-dollar bills, before I could even say anything. I knew that his cards were not very good cards, since there were no same numbers, and they did not count in a row like two, three, four, five, six. Altogether with the cards on the table, he had a four of diamonds, a king of hearts, a two of diamonds, a six of spades, and a seven of clubs.

"Put your money where your mouth is," Hendo said.

The Fat Man threw his cards down. "Well, I'm out."

"What about you?" Hendo asked the man in the red hat. "Going to spit or swallow?"

There was so much money in the middle of the table that I couldn't count it. But I knew that Hendo had at least fifty dollars in the bills from when we counted before. And then there were the coins and also the money that the Fat Man had put in the middle before giving up, and the money the man in the red hat put in.

I felt my heart thump in my chest. Hendo was smiling and did not seem to realize that he had bad cards that would not defeat anything.

Something incredible happened. The man in the red hat gave up too, throwing his cards down.

"That's what I thought," Hendo said, pulling all the money toward him. "Like a bitch."

Hendo and I dabbed and the man in the red hat stood up and started swearing. I said that the honorable thing to do was accept defeat with courage. That was when he flicked his cigarette at me.

Hendo stood up and they got in each other's faces and started pushing each other, the man in the red hat saying ugly things about me and Gert and how Gert probably fucked me every night, which was a gross thing to say.

Before they could fight, Toucan came in and asked what the fuck was going on, right when the man in the red hat was saying more things about me being a retard. Gert was with him, and when he heard the word *retard*, his eyes got wide and I knew that he was going into Berserker mode. Toucan put his hand on Gert's shoulder and went up to the man in the red hat.

"What did you just say?" Toucan said, pushing Hendo out of the way until he was almost nose to nose with the man in the red hat.

Gert stood in front of me so I had to stand on my toes and move my head to see. The man in the red hat looked down and said nothing. The Fat Man and Hendo were standing back, like they were worried a bomb was going to go off but weren't sure when and wanted to see anyway.

Toucan slapped the man's face. His hat fell off his head and Toucan slapped the man again and told him to apologize to me. The man in the red hat didn't try to stop himself from being slapped. He let Toucan hit him again and again.

He said he was sorry, looking at the ground.

"Louder," Toucan said. "I don't think she heard you," and the man in the red hat said sorry so loud that he was almost yelling, and Toucan held on to his head and made it so he was looking right at me while he said sorry for a third time.

Toucan asked Gert if he wanted to hit him. Gert started moving toward him but I held Gert's arm. "Don't," I said, because the man seemed very weak all of a sudden.

"I accept your apology," I told him, and told Gert it was time to go.

Gert told me to thank Toucan, and I held out my hand for a dab. He laughed and said we were going to have a special handshake, and he took my hand, opened it, slapped our hands together, tightened the fingers, and then patted me on the back.

I did not like being touched and stepped back as soon as he was done patting me.

"You and Gert can practice that," he said.

Gert gave me the keys to the car and told me I could get it started, that he'd be out in a minute.

As I was leaving, Hendo gave me a fist pound and told me I was the best good-luck charm he'd ever had. "You should come by every time I play. I'll be a millionaire in a month."

He told me to stay cool.

"I will. You stay cool too."

The man in the red hat stood by himself. As I walked by him he did not say anything to me, and when I took one last look at him I saw that he was crying.

I went outside and saw that the woman and her children across the street weren't playing anymore. The woman was inside of the house but one of the children was sitting alone on the front porch. I went to the car and got inside and turned it on. The air-conditioning whooshed in my face.

Gert came out from the house with a gym bag and threw the bag in the backseat. He said we were off like a herd of turtles, something he sometimes said as a joke. He pointed to the clock and said, "See? Plenty of time."

Gert started the car and we started driving. The little boy in the yard waved at me and I waved back.

"Are you Toucan's new butt boy?" I asked.

"Am I what?"

"That's what he said. That you were Toucan's new butt boy."

"I'm nobody's butt boy," Gert said. "And I'm sorry about that. If I'd known that piece of garbage was going to be there, I wouldn't have brought you." He sighed. "You know I'd never let anything happen to you, right?"

"I don't like those people," I said.

He drove for a bit. "Yeah, well. You're just going to have to trust me," Gert said. "You trust me, right?"

I stared out the window.

"Hey, come on. Have I let you down yet?"

"No."

"Because together we're unbeatable."

One of our favorite songs came on the radio, AC/DC's song "Thunderstruck," and he turned it up and started singing, and then I was singing, and I really did feel like together we could not be beat.

chapter three

t was 11:49 a.m. when we got to Dr. Laird's. Going upstairs took exactly eight minutes, unless the elevator was broken, but I could see from the car that it was working, because someone got out of it.

Gert asked me what our rule is.

"I know the rule," I said.

"I want to hear you say it."

"We do not talk about Gert's personal life."

He nodded. "Right. So, are you going to talk about the last hour?"

"Hour and eighteen minutes," I said. The clock changed. "Hour and nineteen minutes. And no, I will not talk about playing poker, or Toucan, or anything else."

"Good." Gert smiled. He told me to wait and got the envelope from his gym bag. "Give this to Laird."

ຊ

Dr. Laird specializes in development, meaning he works with children who are smarter than other children, and children who are not as smart as other children, and the kinds of kids like me and Marxy.

On his business card, which is stuck to our fridge with a magnet, he calls himself a "Developmental Psychologist."

Dr. Laird is not like other doctors. He doesn't take your temperature or give you medicine, at least not usually. Dr. Laird is more about asking questions and writing things down. Sometimes I go to the hospital where he has me lie down on a cold table and sends me into a machine that looks like a can of Pringles. A blue light shines across my entire body. It takes pictures of the insides of me, especially my brain, and every once in a while Dr. Laird lets me see my brain, all orange and pink and blue, which he says means those parts of my brain were working really hard when the picture was taken. Mostly we just talk, which I like because he is good at listening and asks me questions that show he is not just pretending to pay attention. There is a folder all about me, almost as long as *Kepple's Guide to the Vikings,* and Dr. Laird puts the notes he makes about me every week into the file.

After I sat down, he took out a piece of paper from the file, moved his glasses down his nose, to the pointy end, and started writing.

Dr. Laird is short and has a haircut that Gert says belongs in the seventies, longer on the top and in the back than on the sides. His office is full of books and papers and pieces of paper framed and stuck to the wall that show all the schools he went to. He has big forearms that have a lot of hair on them. Gert says those forearms also belong in the seventies, which I guess means he acts like we don't live in today, but back in time when people had hairy forearms and hair short on the sides and long everywhere else. Sometimes I thought he looked like the pictures of Vikings in *Kepple's Guide to the Vikings.*

He is very good at making you talk. He does not get weird and wiggly during silences but waits for you to feel weird and wiggly and talk, which he was doing to me.

Gert does not have insurance, so we have to pay Dr. Laird with our own money. If you have a good job they give you insurance and you don't have to pay for things like doctors or dentists. In Canada, for example, everyone has insurance. Since Dr. Laird knows we don't have insurance, he says we can pay on a Sliding Scale. Instead of making everyone pay the same, he makes rich people pay more, and poor people like me and Gert pay less.

This is an example of Dr. Laird being heroic, even though he does not fight actual battles with his fists.

Once Gert gets his degree and a powerful job, we will have insurance and won't have to pay anything.

Dr. Laird asked me how my birthday went. "Did you get any good presents?" he asked.

I told him about the Viking that Gert got me. "He was really cool. He wasn't a real Viking. I think he was a stripper who takes off his clothes, only he kept his Viking clothes on."

"A stripper," Dr. Laird said.

"Marxy came too, with his mother. We French-kissed."

"Ah. And how did that make you feel?"

"Good," I said. "Though it's kind of gross too. Because you put the tongues together. Have you ever French-kissed?"

Dr. Laird laughed and said he did, with his wife.

"Can you explain a joke to me?"

I told him the joke about the chicken and the egg. Dr. Laird listened until I was finished and didn't laugh.

"I didn't laugh either," I said. "It sounds like a stupid joke."

"I mean, it's all right but not *that* funny," he said.

"And what does 'spit or swallow' mean?"

Dr. Laird cleared his throat. "Where did you hear that?"

"Nowhere," I said, remembering that I promised Gert not to talk about Toucan's house.

Things were quiet, which happened a lot when I saw Dr. Laird. He always gave me time to think whenever I needed.

"Do you think I'm good-looking?" I asked.

"Did something happen with Marxy? Did he ask you about spitting and swallowing?"

"No, no, no," I said. "I just heard someone say it and didn't know what it meant."

"It's a very crude question some people ask about a particular sex act," Dr. Laird said, and he put down his pen. "Have you and Marxy done anything besides kissing?"

I shook my head and said no. "Just French-kissing."

"Have you thought about what it would be like to have sex with Marxy?"

I shrugged and said maybe, even though it was the first time I had actually said the words out loud. Dr. Laird said it was okay to talk about Marxy and sex, that it was natural for people our age, *adults*, he said, to want to express their love for each other physically.

"Gert does not like when I talk about sex," I said.

Dr. Laird looked around, his eyes touching everything in the room. He told me to look around, and then when I asked him why I was looking, he said, "Who else is in this room?"

"Nobody."

"Right. Gert's not here. It's just you and me."

"Yes," I said slowly. "I have thought about sex with Marxy, and what he looks like naked."

"Do you know about safe sex?"

"Condoms and babies and the penis." I nodded.

I like Dr. Laird. He is someone I would call "no-bullshit," just like AK47, just like Gert. A no-bullshit person will tell the truth, even when other people think you can't handle the truth. Dr. Laird said we would probably have to have a session to talk more in detail about what having sex with Marxy would be like.

"It's a bit complicated, and I'd like to talk about that a bit more," he said.

"I know that people are fuck-dicks about people like us having sex."

"To use the technical term, yes, fuck-dicks. But I am not one of those people. I just think that we should be as prepared as possible." He said that having sex was an important step, but that we should talk more about Marxy.

"What do you mean?"

"From what I understand, you're pretty different people."

I nodded. "He has a penis and I have a vagina."

Dr. Laird smiled. "Correct. But also in terms of where you are when it comes to who you are as people. Not just physically, but developmentally. Do you know what I mean by that?"

When Dr. Laird used the word *developmentally*, he meant the power of the brain.

"You're saying that Marxy and I have different brains."

"Exactly. And when it comes to things like sex and feelings, having different brains, as you put it, makes things more complicated."

I smiled, because Marxy always tells me how pretty I am. "Marxy is amazing," I said.

Dr. Laird asked what I liked about him.

I made a list of THINGS I LOVE ABOUT MARXY AND FIND SEXY:

- He has nice cheeks that squish when he smiles.
- Whenever he walks, his calf muscles get huge.
- His favorite color is red and mine is blue and when you put them together they make purple, another powerful color.
- He always smells nice and his clothes are never wrinkled.

- Sometimes he kisses too much with his tongue.
- He squeezes too hard because he is too big to show his love, which hurts but shows he loves you a lot.
- His impression of Sean Connery is very sexy.

Dr. Laird's egg timer went off, which meant that the session was over. "We should talk more about you and Marxy," Dr. Laird said, standing up. "Next time. But before you go, there's something I want to show you. Call it a birthday present, if you'd like."

He opened his desk drawer and took out some papers that were stapled together. It was an article he had printed off from the Internet about a famous Viking skeleton.

"Read the part I highlighted," Dr. Laird said.

I found the part he was talking about. "'Iconic Viking grave belonging to female wonder woman,'" I read out loud. "What does that mean?"

"*Iconic* means, like, very important. Inspires other people kind of thing."

"Oh. So this dead person is an icon."

"Just keep reading," he said.

The article said that DNA testing had shown that one of the most famous Viking skeletons actually belonged to a woman. Everyone thought it belonged to a man, and it was iconic, Dr. Laird said, because it was one of the oldest, most complete graves, and it was what a lot of archaeologists, who studied past peoples, used to talk about the past.

"Like your favorite writer, Kepple, for example," Dr. Laird was saying. "He probably thought like everyone else that this dead Viking was a man. But actually, since it's a woman, and she's a total badass with tons of weapons, now our understanding of Vikings will change. Right?"

"I'm following."

"And people like Kepple and scientists and historians will start talking more about Viking warriors who were women."

"Legendary," I said. "Whoa."

The grave was in a Swedish town called Birka and had lots of weapons and armor in it. The article said that this proved that the person buried was not just a normal person, but a "professional fighter."

I stared at the picture of the grave on the paper.

"Why did you show me this?"

"I'm showing you this," Dr. Laird said, "because I want you to start thinking about your own legend. Do you understand what I mean?"

Then I understood. Dr. Laird was showing me the Viking to show that I could be powerful. I said that, and he nodded.

"I think you have more in you than you think, Zelda."

There was no hugging allowed in Dr. Laird's office, because we were supposed to be professional. So I shook his hand.

We walked out of the office, into the waiting room where his secretary, Hanna, had his schedule. She told Dr. Laird that I couldn't leave yet.

"There was a bit of a problem with the last check Zelda brought," she said.

Dr. Laird frowned. "Did it bounce?"

That was when I remembered the envelope. I had put it in my pocket and took it out and gave it to Dr. Laird. "Gert told me to give it to you."

Dr. Laird opened up the envelope. There was money inside. He sighed and handed it back. "He knows I can't take cash, Zelda."

I held the envelope in my hands, because I wasn't sure what to do with it. Dr. Laird turned to Hanna and said to keep the same schedule next week.

"But can you get Gert to call me, Zelda?"

"I will tell him," I said, and Dr. Laird smiled and told me to take care.

⸾

Gert was parked across the street. I got in the car and gave him the envelope. I told him what Dr. Laird said, about the check and about not being able to take cash and to call him as soon as possible.

"What's the difference if it's cash or check?" Gert asked, and I told him I didn't know, and he said he was asking a rhetorical question.

I started reading the article Dr. Laird had given me.

"What's that?" Gert asked.

"There was 'a very monumental discovery that will change how we look at Vikings forever,'" I said, reading from the top of the page.

"Is that right?" Gert said. "You want to tell me about it?"

So I told him all about the female Viking warrior grave and the DNA tests, about the powerful implications and the small military planning figures they found in the grave, and I started to wonder what Kepple would think about the female Viking.

When we got home I went to my computer, turned it on, went to Kepple's website, where he has a Contact Form, and began typing him a letter.

Dear Dr. Kepple,

First, I am sorry for not remembering to call you a doctor on my last letter to you, but I thought that doctors helped sick people and then I learned that you can be a doctor if you know a lot about things like Vikings.

The reason I am writing is that there is an article I think you should read about a Viking grave in Sweden. Dr. Laird gave me the article to read (he is the kind of doctor who helps sick people, and also people like me who aren't sick but are different).

The article says that a famous Viking skeleton was actually a woman, and that she was a very high-ranking warrior. You should Google it to find out more.

Thank you and have a nice day.
Skál,
Zelda

I clicked SEND and the computer made a zooming noise, like an airplane taking off, and a message appeared that said: "Thank you. Your message has been submitted."

I had sent him five letters already and so far Dr. Kepple has never written back.

I hoped that this time Mom would tell Odin to make sure he did.

chapter four

thought all night about what Dr. Laird had said, about being the hero of my own legend. I stood in front of the mirror and did not see a hero reflected back to me at first.

According to *Kepple's Guide to the Vikings*, Viking tribes had four types of people: earls, free men, another kind called slaves which don't exist anymore, and warriors. Earls were leaders who had great hoards of treasure and had warriors who followed them. Most of the free men were farmers and people called merchants, who sold things. But warriors were free men too, and in order to become powerful, they went to do battle and defeated villains and found treasure.

When warriors defeat enough villains, act with a lot of bravery, win enough battles, and have enough treasure, then people sing songs about them and they become heroes. Gert was a hero for the football team in high school, because he was brave and defeated villainous teams who were supposed to be more powerful, and he won the biggest treasure in football, which is the State Championship. You can still go on the Internet and read *sagas* written about how Gert scored three touchdowns in the championship game, even though his knee was hurt.

His teammates were warriors and free men, but Gert was the hero.

Most people think that only men can be warriors. According to Dr. Laird's article, women can be warriors too, and powerful.

"If a woman warrior can achieve high status, we have to start questioning a lot of assumptions we have about Viking social conventions," the article said.

I read the article over twice to make sure I understood what it was saying. Before, people thought only men could be warriors who became legendary and heroic, and that women were not allowed to be heroes. But the Viking warrior in the article *was* a woman, and the things buried in the grave showed that she was also a hero and powerful in battle.

The Vikings called their legends *sagas*. According to *Kepple's Guide to the Vikings*, the term *saga* means "what is said." It also means "story." There are a lot of different sagas that are famous. All Viking sagas are about kings or warriors. My favorite Viking saga is a legendary one called the *Hrólfs saga Gautrekssonar*, since it has a powerful king who is also a woman, named Þornbjörg. She kicks many asses and is so strong in battle that people don't care that she is a woman.

My favorite part of the article was about the strongest kind of woman warrior, called a *skjaldmær*. They are not Valkyries, but are almost as strong. Women don't get chosen to be warriors very often in Viking legends. Girls at age twelve who were very strong and fit and could do battle with the same strength as the boys could become *skjaldmær*, which let them become warriors.

I was not a king, so I wondered if I could be a *skjaldmær*. But first I would need to have a legend.

Once Dr. Laird asked me why I liked Vikings. I told him three reasons:

One, they are brave.

Two, they are strong and people have to think twice before trying to hurt them.

Three, Viking heroes stand up for people who can't defend themselves.

I told Dr. Laird that I wanted to be all of those things. People look at me and do not think that I am brave or strong and that I am the one who needs protection. My legend will show people that, even if you are not gargantuan, you can still be strong and brave and help others in your tribe.

I opened up *Kepple's Guide to the Vikings* and began making a list of the things that all of the *sagas* had.

THINGS LEGENDS NEED

- ☐ A hero who is skilled in hand-to-hand combat
- ☐ A powerful weapon for the hero to use
- ☐ The hero must win the love of a fair maiden in danger
- ☐ Every hero needs a wise man
- ☐ Pillaging rival villages for treasure
- ☐ The hero must defeat a villain who threatens the tribe

Then I thought about what each thing meant.

A HERO WHO IS SKILLED IN HAND-TO-HAND COMBAT

Because I am not very big and powerful, I decided that in order to defeat villains I would have to become stronger. I had seen Gert doing push-ups and sit-ups in the living room and decided to add both of those exercises to my routine before bed.

I would also need to study martial arts. On the pad of sticky notes beside my computer I wrote, "GOOGLE GLÍMA," which is what the Viking hand-to-hand combat style is called, and stuck it on the wall so I would not forget.

A POWERFUL WEAPON FOR THE HERO TO USE

I did not have any weapons. All of the great heroes of the sagas had special weapons that helped them defeat the villains. For example, Prainn, the *draugr*, had a sword called Mistilteinn, which was always sharp, no matter how many heads it cut off. There was also Mjölnir, which was a hammer that belonged to Thor that always came back to his hand when he threw it.

I circled this part of the list.

The next legendary thing from the sagas is:

THE HERO MUST WIN THE LOVE OF
A FAIR MAIDEN IN DANGER

I looked up *maiden* and learned that it means "innocent woman" and added the word to my list of Words of Today, along with the definition. Most of the heroes of the sagas are men who saved fair maidens from villains and monsters, because the fair maidens could not save themselves. This was a problem. I did not want to be a fair maiden who needed to be saved. I wanted to be the hero doing the saving. Then I realized that I could win the love of a maiden who was not a woman but a man. And because I already had a boyfriend whose love I had won, I put a check mark next to this item on the list, which made me happy, since it meant I was already on my way to being a legend.

EVERY HERO NEEDS A WISE MAN

All heroes need a Wise Man or person to give them powerful advice. Dr. Laird was a Wise Man and he gave powerful advice as part of his job. I put a check mark next to this item.

PILLAGING RIVAL VILLAGES FOR TREASURE

Pillage was another word I had to look up, and I did not like the definition I found. It means "to steal, often with violence." Stealing isn't very honorable, and so I decided that I would need to find another way to get treasure. I put a question mark (?) next to this item on my list.

THE HERO MUST DEFEAT A VILLAIN
WHO THREATENS THE TRIBE

This was my favorite item on the list. Under TRIBE I wrote "Gert" and "AK47" and thought about adding "Marxy" but since he was already in the list as the FAIR MAIDEN whose love I had won, I left him off.

Next I made a list of VILLAINS:

- Uncle Richard
- Dad
- Cancer

I stopped writing. I thought of the poker game and added:

- The Man in the Red Hat

I put Toucan's name on the list too, but was not sure so I added a (?) beside his name.

There was one more item for my list that did not fit into any of the items from the sagas. I decided that the last part of my legend would be to get Gert and AK47 back together, in a relationship. If I am very good at my legend they will get married and have babies and our tribe will grow.

When I asked AK47 why she and Gert broke up, she said that my brother is a man-whore who needs to become an adult. When I asked Gert why he was a man-whore, and why he wasn't growing up, he knew that I had talked to AK47 and told me not to believe everything I hear.

I know that they broke up because Gert got her pregnant and she had an abortion without telling him. An abortion stops a baby from being born. Some people think that it is like killing a baby. AK47 says that it is more like stopping a cake from being baked by taking away the ingredients you need to make the cake.

AK47 is one of the people I love. If she was ever in trouble I would defend her with all my might. The problem is that I am usually the one who does something stupid or gets in trouble, and AK47 has to be the one to save me.

AK47 is a chaotic person, which is one of the reasons why Gert and her fought a lot. I started calling her AK47, and not her real name, Annie, after Gert said that when she's excited she talks loud and fast like a machine gun. Gert likes things to be clean and orderly, and even though he was kicked out of high school for breaking the rules, he actually likes when people follow rules. AK47 does not like rules. She is a free spirit who does not always act like women in movies and TV act, which is one of the reasons why Gert likes her. She used to run in high school on the track team so she has big muscles on her legs, and is almost as tall as Gert is and would be taller if she wore heels, which she doesn't.

‹›

Since it was Wednesday, I was prepared for the Community Center. AK47 usually comes late on a bus that makes a loud noise and a lot of black smoke when it enters into the neighborhood to pick me up from in front of the apartment.

After getting out of the elevator I went outside. Alf was smoking a cigarette. Alf likes to have his hair braided like noodles on his head. He is one of those people who is not a hero and not a villain either. He is just a regular person who likes smoking and works as a janitor at a school.

Sometimes he also likes to get high and smoke pot on his balcony, and the smoke comes to my window and I have to close it so that I don't get the air from him inside of me.

"Heard it was your birthday," Alf said when he saw me coming.

"It was."

He wished me a happy birthday and tried to give me a dab. I do not like dabbing with people who are not part of my tribe, so I did not dab with Alf. He put his hand down. Alf is also in love with AK47 so when she comes to pick me up he is usually outside, smoking, so that he can say hello to her and try to convince her to go on a date with him, something he would never do if my brother was around.

He asked, "How's your brother?"

I said Gert was fine.

"Cool," Alf said. "Still doing the college thing?"

I said that Gert was defeating college by getting good grades.

"I went to college. Lasted one and a half semesters."

The smell of Alf's cigarette smoke made me cough. One of my weapons is that people forget I am there, since I am not gargantuan. In fact, I am the opposite. AK47 always says that a good warrior turns weaknesses into strengths, and people who are almost invisible, like me, can sneak around enemies. The bad parts of being invisible are that people like Alf blow smoke on me accidentally and do not notice.

I wondered if I should add Alf to my list of villains.

He held out his cigarette and made the ashes fall on the sidewalk.

The bus pulled around the corner, past the other apartment building across from ours. It was a weird-colored bus. Most buses are yellow. The bus that AK47 drove was the color of mouthwash, since it used to belong to a hospital and was so old that it was only a little green.

Alf quickly threw the cigarette on the ground and covered it with his foot.

It was 8:55 a.m. The bus stopped and the front door opened.

"I know, I know," AK47 said. "I'm late. I know."

In the windows I could see my two friends Yoda and Hamsa waving. I waved at them. Yoda had his face pressed up against the glass. He looked like a pancake with a mouth.

"Hey, Annie," Alf said. "Was just keeping the birthday girl company."

He patted my shoulder.

"She doesn't like being touched, you boob," AK47 said.

AK47 has short hair like a man, almost buzzed, and doesn't wear dresses or skirts. She is also half black, which makes a lot of people nervous, since Gert and I are white and all of Gert's old tribe, from high school, didn't like black people.

She waved at me. "Come on, Zee."

I told Alf to have a nice day.

"Let me know when we can have some dinner together," Alf called to AK47, who shook her head and closed the door.

If he continued trying to steal AK47 from Gert, he would *definitely* be added to the list of villains.

☡

I got on the bus and went to sit down in the back with Yoda and Hamsa, who were in seats across from each other. We always sit in the back, since that's where all the legendary people sit in high school. Gert used to sit in the back with his friends, and they were the coolest people, so we sit there too. We were never the cool kids on regular buses, so now, on AK47's bus, we were allowed to be cool.

AK47 told me to sit up front, so I sat on the seat next to AK47.

"And wipe your hands on this." She pulled a piece of Kleenex from the box between her steering wheel and the big glass window. "That sweaty motherfucker creeps me out."

Hamsa and Yoda both wished me happy birthday. They didn't get up from their seats, since getting up while the bus is moving is against the RULES OF THE BUS.

"Happy birthday!" Yoda shouted, and I yelled, "Thank you!" and then Hamsa yelled the same thing, and then they wished each other happy birthday, even though neither of them were born on the same day I was.

I didn't mind that. Part of a good birthday is sharing it with the people you like, members of your tribe, and so I did not mind sharing my birthday strength with them.

"Yes, it's everybody's birthday," AK47 said. "Whoopee."

"How was it?" she asked. "Good?"

I told her that Gert got me the Viking, who was actually a stripper. "But he didn't take off any of his clothes when he came to my birthday."

She shook her head and said, "That idiot brother of yours."

The bus started rolling down the street. Another car came around the corner and AK47 didn't even slow down to go around it. She is a better driver than anyone I have ever seen, even Gert, who can drive fast and never gets into accidents.

AK47 said, "Okay, are you ready for your gift?"

I said I was. She told me to look under the seat. There was a box and I pulled it out. The wrapping paper had Christmas trees and Santa Claus on it.

"Sorry. Ran out of birthday paper."

"It's okay, I like Christmas a lot."

She told me I could open it any way I wanted, and so I opened along the taped parts, since I don't like tearing things.

"Did you get a present?" Hamsa said from the back.

"Mind your own beeswax," AK47 said.

I took off the Christmas paper. The box wasn't very big. That didn't mean it wasn't a powerful gift, since small things can be strong, like AK47, who was only a little bit taller than me.

"Holy crap," I said. Inside the box was a Viking sword.

"I know it's not very big, but I figure it's a start."

She stopped the bus in front of the Community Center. To go with the sword, she handed me a piece of paper that had RULES OF THE VIKING SWORD on it.

"Since I know you like having rules, I thought this would help."

I read the paper.

RULES OF THE VIKING SWORD

- You are not allowed to use the sword for evil.
- When you're not using the sword, it must be put in its box and left there.
- Nobody else is allowed to use the sword.

AK47 said that the exceptions to that rule were her and Gert.

"But I'm going to hold on to it for you today. And when we hang out, you can play with it."

"Vikings don't play," I said. "Especially not with weapons."

AK47 nodded and said that was true, that weapons were not toys. Yoda and Hamsa ran to the front of the bus.

"Holy crap," Yoda said. "Is that a real sword?"

"It's real metal," I said.

"Can I see?" Hamsa said.

I told them it wasn't allowed out of the box until AK47 said it was okay. They looked at AK47, who had turned off the engine and took out her key.

"Everyone but Zelda off," AK47 said.

Hamsa and Yoda got off. AK47 gave them both fist pounds. They had seen AK47 and I do the fist pounds and had started doing them too.

"Have a good day, you goons," AK47 said.

That was another thing they liked. They liked the weird things AK47 called them, like *goons* or *critters*, which means something small, even though they are bigger than her, and bigger than me, and adults and not small animals too.

"Can I have a sword?" Hamsa said when AK47 and I shuffled off the bus.

"Or a lightsaber," Yoda said, meaning a sword made of light from the movie *Star Wars*.

"Those don't exist," AK47 said, patting him on the back.

I took the sword out. It was not very big. I held it in my hands, trying not to touch the metal of the blade. I didn't want to cut my hand. Viking swords are always really sharp. *Kepple's Guide to the Vikings* says warriors spend a lot of time sharpening their swords before a battle.

The little Viking sword was shorter than a ruler. I held it in my hand in front of me and imagined that the bus was moving quickly toward a tribe of Vikings. Their swords would be bigger, but it isn't how big your sword is, AK47 is always saying, it's how you use it.

"I asked them to make sure the stuff on the handle was Viking," she said.

The markings on the handle were runes, which are small symbols that have a lot of power.

"They're supposed to be authentic. *Pur*, or whatever, is on there. I guess that means Thor. It's a replica of this Thurmuth sword," she said.

The sword had some very powerful runes. According to *Kepple's*, those two runes combined to make the person using the sword a gargantuan warrior.

My favorite rune is called *Dagaz*, only you say it like "thaw gozz." It looks almost like an H.

Dagaz means to become awake or to transform. That is what I want to do in my legend: I want to go from a normal Viking to a hero.

I asked AK47 if we were going to battle, if that was why she gave me the sword.

"Every day's a battle, sweet pea," AK47 said. "It's not full-size, but be careful."

I gave it to her. Even though a Viking is not ready to defeat villains without a weapon, I knew AK47 would keep it safe, and she said she would give it back to me at the end of the day.

Because AK47 had given me a sword, I realized that I could now cross that off of my list of THINGS LEGENDS NEED. I now had three things that all Viking heroes need: a fair maiden, a powerful weapon, and a wise man.

chapter five

Every day the Community Center has two hours where everyone like me and Hamsa and Yoda and Marxy can talk and play in the gymnasium if they want. These are people who are "retarded," which is a word I do not care about, but is one of the words that nobody is allowed to say, like the n-word Gert used to say before he and AK47 got together, and which I cannot even say out loud, even though this is my legend.

Sometimes at the Community Center we use the art room and do paintings. At night, twice a week, there are also literacy classes where we practice reading and writing and making sure our brains get exercise.

I go to the Community Center for half the day and eat lunch there, and then AK47 drives me home on the days that Gert can't pick me up because he's at school.

"The birthday girl," Big Todd said when I walked into the Community Center. He gave me a high five instead of a pound.

"Big Todd, my man," I said.

"Did you have a good birthday?"

I told him about the Viking stripper and the sword AK47 gave me. He asked me if I had it with me, since weapons weren't allowed in the Community Center.

"Having a special weapon is one of the most important parts of being a hero," I said.

"It's not a weapon," AK47 said, coming over. "And I'll be holding on to it for today."

"Does Gert know?"

"A Viking's weapon belongs to the Viking and is nobody else's business," I said.

"Exactly," AK47 said.

Big Todd is the person who runs the Community Center programs and gets us organized. He is tall and skinny and gay. His boyfriend, Noah, sometimes comes by to play basketball with us in the gym. He and Big Todd met playing basketball in college. Once I said to Gert that he should play basketball with Big Todd and Noah, since he was almost as good at basketball as he was at football, but Gert does not like faggots, a word that means gay but in a bad way, and is one of the words that AK47 told me never, ever to use.

Todd was the only gay person I had ever met in real life, and he was also one of the nicest people I had ever met, gay people or other people. I didn't really understand how he had sex, since neither him or his boyfriend had vaginas. AK47 told me not to worry about it.

"They do just fine," she said, and I know that when she says things like that, it's time to stop asking questions.

The Community Center has big windows in front, and brown squares up the side that make me think of the Jenga game. A lot of different kinds of people go to the Community Center. There is a big gymnasium in it, and machines that can help you build muscles. Originally Gert used to go in there to work on his muscles while I was with Big Todd and Hamsa and Yoda and Marxy.

Inside of the classroom there are a bunch of orange and blue chairs, the plastic ones, and a whiteboard that used to be a chalkboard. It smells good. Everyone likes to smell the board, especially when someone uses the markers. Big Todd keeps an eye on who smells the markers for the board too long.

There are always a bunch of parents and brothers and sisters who wait for the class to start. I used to wish that Gert waited for class to start, like the other parents and brothers and sisters. Now, especially after my birthday, I felt like heroes needed to do things without parents and brothers and sisters. Also, people like Hamsa and Yoda and I did not have people waiting for us, since we came on the bus, which means we're poor compared to other people. We do not have to pay for the bus or have cars, because it is a free service.

The people who were not part of the class left when Big Todd clapped his hands and asked us to get into pairs.

Yoda and Hamsa chose each other. I looked around for Marxy, but he had not arrived yet. Usually Hamsa, Yoda, Marxy, and I trade with each other, since we are all friends and we don't do many weird things, so practicing isn't very hard. It was hot in the room and the air conditioner in the window shot wind into my face as I went around, trying to find someone who was not weird.

Everyone had paired up except for me.

"Do you have a partner?" Big Todd asked.

"I am waiting for Marxy," I said.

"Well, we can't wait any longer." Big Todd looked around. "There's Sarah-Beth. Sarah-Beth, do you have a partner?"

Sarah-Beth shook her head. She was standing away from everyone, by the window but not looking outside. Even though she has been to the Community Center a hundred times, she is still afraid of everyone and acts weird. She is the worst person to be social with. She has Down syndrome like Hamsa, but is two years older than him. She has long hair that she plays with all the time. There are places on her head where the hair is gone and she is bald like an old man, only her hair is very long in other places.

Big Todd told Sarah-Beth that I was going to be her banking person and to join the others, who had already started sitting down.

"Okay," I said to Sarah-Beth. We sat across from each other at the table. "No being weird and putting things in your mouth. Okay?"

"Okay," Sarah-Beth said. She sat down on her hands to show me that they weren't going to put her hair in her mouth.

Big Todd told us to pretend that we were in a bank and that we wanted to give them a check, which is a slip of paper that has money in it. Not actually in it, but when you give it to the bank, the bank puts money into your bank account. The last few times we practiced being social we talked about money and bank accounts, and how important it is to understand money if we all wanted to be independent adults.

"Think about banks as the place where all the money you make gets held for you," Big Todd said. "That way you don't always have to carry it around with you."

I raised my hand. "So it's like a treasure hoard," I said.

"A what now?"

I explained that whenever Vikings defeated other tribes or monsters, like dragons, in battle, they took the treasure and kept it locked up in a hoard. "They don't carry around the treasure, but if they ever need it, it's there."

Big Todd snapped his fingers. "Exactly. It's like a treasure hoard. And debit cards let you take out some of the treasure from your hoard, your bank account, without having money with you all the time. Now, checks are pieces of paper where you promise to give some of your treasure to someone else."

"And what happens if a check bounces?" I asked, since Dr. Laird had said that Gert's check had bounced.

"It means you promised someone treasure from your hoard but you didn't have as much as you promised in the check."

So that meant that Gert's hoard did not have enough money to pay

Dr. Laird, which was why the check promising treasure to Dr. Laird so that he could help me bounced. I put my hand up again.

"Last one, Zelda," Big Todd said. "Things'll become clearer as we go along."

"Where do you get more treasure for your hoard?"

"From jobs, dummy," someone said from across the room. "Can we bank now?"

Big Todd shot over a dirty look.

Sarah-Beth stared at the piece of paper in front of her. It was supposed to be the check. There was a plastic box with a bunch of plastic cards that were supposed to be fake debit cards. Sarah-Beth and I had to share a debit card, which was bad because I knew she would start chewing on it. So I got the card first.

When I pretend-asked her to give me money from my bank account, using the plastic card from the basket, Sarah-Beth did not answer. Her mouth was full of her orange hair.

"I would like to deposit this check, using the bank account with my debit card," I said, and showed her the check, and also the plastic card.

Instead of being a banker, she closed her eyes and plugged her nose like she was going underwater.

That wasn't what people did in banks, I told her. Her eyes popped open.

"You don't know everything," she said. "My sister plays with her hair, and there's nothing wrong."

I raised my hand and tried to wave to Big Todd, who was going around listening to the banking happen.

"Good," Big Todd said to another pair at the other end of the table. "Good banking, everyone."

My hand waved like crazy until he saw me and came over. "Who is working for the bank, and who is bringing in the check?" he asked.

"Sarah-Beth just eats her hair."

Big Todd asked Sarah-Beth which she wanted to be, the banker or the customer. Her hair was covered in spit, and her hands were covered in spit too. If I worked in a bank, I wouldn't want to touch a check with spit on it, and if I was bringing a check into a bank, I wouldn't want spit to get on my check. I said that and Big Todd said to take it easy.

"Give her a chance." He pulled up an extra chair and sat beside Sarah-Beth. He put a piece of paper, the fake check, on the table in front of her. He spoke really slowly to her. "So, this is a check. Remember what a check is?"

She nodded and pulled her hair straight.

"What is it?"

"Money," she said.

"Right. And if Zelda's the bank, what do we do with the check?"

"We bring it to Zelda, who will put it into our bank account."

"Good." Big Todd looked at me. "Well, Zelda? You're the bank. What are you going to ask Sarah-Beth for?"

I sighed. "The check, and for her to sign the back of it, and to give me her plastic card."

Big Todd smiled and asked Sarah-Beth if she had those things, and since we were pretending he gave her a fake plastic card. She signed the back of the check. It wasn't a very good signature. We had been practicing signatures and hers didn't look like it had any letters in it, except for the *S* and the *M* of Sarah-Beth's last name, which I didn't know.

"Great signature," Big Todd said. His smile was gargantuan. "What do you think of that, Zelda? Pretty cool, right?"

Sarah-Beth had stopped chewing her hair. She was looking right at me. It was okay, I said. "But I don't know how it says her name."

Big Todd shook his head at me and asked if he could talk to me and we went to have a talk while Sarah-Beth kept chewing her hair. He took me by the window.

"Why were you being like that with Sarah-Beth?" he asked.

I shrugged. "I didn't want to be paired with her. I wanted to be paired with Marxy."

᛫

Marxy came late, after the first people who had been bankers had switched and become the people with the cards and the checks. Sarah-Beth asked me for my identification card.

I waved to Marxy.

"Can I please have your identification card?" Sarah-Beth said.

Marxy waved to me from across the room and said my name.

"I am talking and I need your identification card," Sarah-Beth said again. Big Todd went over to Marxy and pointed him to the person he had been partnered with, whose name was Michael but everyone called him Carrot, because he liked eating them more than anything. Carrot had come late and so Big Todd had to work with him.

"Take my spot," Big Todd said. "We're doing banking."

Marxy liked banking, so I waved my hand and said he could bank with me. "And Sarah-Beth can go with Carrot."

That was an example of Problem Solving, which we had learned about two months ago in Social Class.

Big Todd said that Marxy and Carrot were going to work together, and that was that. "And don't call him Carrot."

Sarah-Beth was trying to make her signature on the back of the fake check better. I told Big Todd that, fine, I would help her by being a better banker.

"Why do you like Vikings so much?" she asked.

"Because they're powerful."

"In Japan they have samurai and ninjas and people who know karate."

"A Viking could defeat all of them."

She shrugged. "If Vikings are so strong, why are they all dead?"

"They're not all dead. I'm a Viking."

Sarah-Beth shook her head. "No, you're a girl."

"If you're so smart," I said, "why do you eat your hair?"

Sarah-Beth stared down at her signature, which looked nothing like the letters of the alphabet. She put up her hand and waved to Big Todd.

"How's it going over here?" he asked.

"Zelda made fun of me for eating my hair."

"She started it."

I walked outside of the room with Big Todd and he shut the door. As we walked by people said, "Oooooh," and Yoda said, "She's in trouble."

Outside, Big Todd asked what was going on. I told him about our argument about Vikings and samurai.

Big Todd crossed his arms. "Okay, so if I'm following, you just had a disagreement. Right?"

He was right and wrong at the same time.

"She is trying to make me mad."

Big Todd leaned against the door. "A lot of times in life you have to deal with people you don't like, or who try to make you mad. That's why we have classes like this. To give you practice not losing your cool. Would a legend lose her cool over something as silly as a disagreement?"

I shook my head and said no.

"Okay." He opened the door and put his hand on my shoulder. "Besides, when you're here, Sarah-Beth is as much a part of your tribe as Marxy is." I looked back at Sarah-Beth, who had stopped trying to practice her signature and was now making drawings of animals. "Go and apologize."

Big Todd led me over to Sarah-Beth.

"Sorry I made fun of you for eating your hair," I said, holding out my hand.

She shrugged. "It's fine."

Big Todd cleared his throat, a sign that I should say more things in apology. So I added, "Samurai are strong warriors too."

She looked up from her paper. "Maybe Vikings and samurai are both just as strong as each other."

I said that maybe they were. In my brain, I said to myself, *There is no way a samurai could defeat a Viking in combat,* but I did not say that, because one rule of apologies is that you make them and even if you don't mean them, you have to pretend that you do.

～

When I got home from the Community Center Gert was reading the Book of Macroeconomics at the kitchen table. He had his head tilted and since he had no hair it was wrinkling and turning red and veiny, which means whatever was going on inside his brain was bubbling to the surface. He was chewing on his pencil and when I asked him if he was stressed out, he held up one finger to tell me to be quiet, and with his other finger he covered up parts of a sentence, word by word, the way Dr. Laird had taught me to do whenever I had trouble understanding how words came together.

Once I tried to read one of Gert's books, but the types of books Gert read for school were filled with math and numbers, which I am not good at.

The big times for Gert's classes were in the middle of the semester and at the end. Midterms and Final Exam season. On the school schedule he kept on the fridge, Gert had those days circled and highlighted yellow and surrounded by ten or fifteen stars that looked too little for someone as big as my brother to have drawn.

His Midterm was the next morning. I took off my shoes, following the RULES OF THE HOUSE. I had my Viking sword in my backpack, in its case, which AK47 had given me on the bus ride home, and I went and hid it in my room. Then I took out the money I was saving in my jar.

When I came out I sat across from Gert and set the money down on the table.

"I would like to begin contributing money to the tribe's hoard."

He looked up from his Book of Macroeconomics. "What?"

"All tribes have hoards, which they use to pay for things. And I would like to add my own treasure to the hoard." He wasn't understanding, so I added, "Your check bounced with Dr. Laird because we don't have enough money."

"The check bounced because it was a mistake. Now, if you don't mind, I need to study. Okay? I have the big midterm tomorrow."

I went to my bedroom to review my list of things that a hero needs and put a check mark next to "A powerful weapon" and underlined "treasure." Then I did push-ups and sit-ups, and after that I went on YouTube to learn about how to properly fight with a sword.

Gert stuck his head into the room and said he was going out to his study group and would be back in a few hours.

"There's dinner in the fridge," he said, and saw the YouTube videos.

He asked what I was doing and I told him preparing for battle.

chapter six

Now that I had a real weapon, I could learn to defeat villains more skillfully. But I was not very good at sword-fighting yet. According to the sword-fighting videos on YouTube, there are three ways to attack using a sword.

1. Thrust: Poke the sword at your enemy.
2. Parry: Stop your enemy from stabbing you.
3. Slash: Not poking, but trying to stop your enemy by cutting them with the sword.

I practiced each of them in the basketball court outside of the apartment until it got dark, pretending that Grendel, who is the most monstrous villain in the Viking story *Beowulf*, was in front of me. One of the things I've learned is that Grendels can hide inside people, pretending to be human beings until they decide to attack.

All of the VILLAINS on my list probably had Grendels inside.

For example, Uncle Richard, who Gert and I used to live with, was a complete shit-heel, and Gert defeated him in combat and could have probably ripped Uncle Richard's head clean off, but I asked him to be a hero and he did not rip Uncle Richard's head off, even though Uncle Richard was a villain who deserved it.

Uncle Richard was the first person I met who had a Grendel inside. He looked like a regular person, but sometimes, especially when he was drunk, he became villainous. When he was the most villainous, he hit Gert with a beer bottle and cut the top of his head.

The other villains on my list were also Grendels. I practiced defeating the man in the red hat from the poker game, and also Toucan, and also Sarah-Beth, but I stopped battling her, because I decided she wasn't actually a villain. She was just annoying.

Dr. Laird once asked me to describe the Grendels. He told me to talk about them in whatever way was most helpful.

"What they look like, what they sound like, what happens when they come. Whatever."

He even gave me a pad of paper to draw them. The problem was most of the time I could only hear them grumbling. Sometimes they came in my dreams, or I would turn very fast when bad things were happening and I could only see their tails or hairy legs.

In high school, before he dropped out, Gert read a book called *Grendel*. He said it was the one book he actually liked in English class.

"I'm familiar with the novel," Dr. Laird said. "Is that the first time you read about Grendel?"

I nodded my head and told Dr. Laird that Grendel is a villain and gets what he deserves. Dr. Laird asked me what I meant by that.

"Grendel attacks the Vikings and eats one of them, like a villain," I said.

"Did you read the novel?"

I shook my head. "Gert read it and told me about it, and then I read *Kepple's Guide to the Vikings*."

"Well," Dr. Laird said, "it's sort of a backward interpretation."

He told me that you're supposed to read the book and feel sorry for

Grendel, even though he does bad things. "He can't help it. It's in his nature."

I did not like that version of the story, because it made the Viking hero a villain and the monstrous villain a hero.

"Sometimes good people do bad things," Dr. Laird said. "And sometimes things aren't as simple as good and evil."

"The Grendels are evil," I said.

"Well," Dr. Laird said, "maybe the Grendels you're talking about are pure evil. But regular monsters are more complicated."

‡

After vanquishing Grendels with my Viking sword on the basketball court, I went back home and turned on my computer and began typing.

Dear Dr. Kepple,

I have more questions.

First, I know that Beowulf defeated Grendel in the most famous Viking epic. But are there more than one Grendel? Dr. Laird says that whenever I hear Grendels coming they aren't the real Grendel. Is it possible the real Grendel survived Beowulf's attacks and hid for all these years?

Second, I was recently given a Viking sword for my birthday. It has powerful runes that I would like your opinion on, but the Contact Form on your website does not allow me to attach pictures like an e-mail. Is there a way I can send you a picture of the sword?

Skál,

Zelda

I clicked SEND and saw that it was getting late in the evening. I texted Gert asking him where he was and what time he would be home. We have a rule that if he is going to come home late, he texts to tell me.

I made myself dinner using a very special Waffle Pizza recipe that belongs to Gert and me. First, you have to take the can of tomato sauce, pour it into a bowl, and microwave it for one minute. While it is microwaving you put frozen waffles into the toaster. If you do it correctly, the sauce and the waffles will be ready at the same time. Then you put the tomato sauce onto the waffles, and then cheese slices onto the tomato sauce, and meat onto that.

Gert texted while I was making the Waffle Pizza to say that he would be home very late and to not wait up. It was getting late and I began to worry about his Midterm. A warrior needs to be rested before facing a challenge that big.

After Waffle Pizza I did my routine of brushing my hair, brushing my teeth, and changing into my pajamas. I smelled under my armpits and decided I did not need a shower.

Before going to sleep I made sure I set my alarm clock so that I could wake up early and wish Gert *happ* on his Midterm.

I had not been asleep for very long when a noise outside of my room woke me up.

I always know when Gert is drunk because he runs into things and makes a lot of noise. Lying down in my bed, I could hear him laughing, and then laughing in a weird way until I realized that his weird way of laughing was someone else.

A woman who was a stranger and not AK47.

The Vow, which in Old Norse is called a *heit*, we have is that whenever one of us wants to bring someone the other one doesn't know into the apartment, we tell the other members of the tribe, which right now is Gert and me but it used to be AK47 too.

After Gert and AK47 broke up, Gert was bringing all kinds of strangers into the house late at night. I couldn't sleep and many times the strangers and Gert were very drunk. I do not like people who are drunk in general and especially not Gert, since Mom was drunk when I was in her stomach and that is why I am different, which is a better way of saying *retarded*. Gert did not drink very much when he and AK47 were together.

Now he drinks a lot.

It was 1:23 a.m., even though it was less than five hours since I had gone to sleep and sent Marxy text messages about kissing videos on YouTube.

I walked to my door, turning the handle really quietly until a line of light came in.

From my bedroom I could only see half of the living room. The other thing I could see was the hallway and the bathroom door. Gert was in his jeans and his sweatshirt, falling around, going from the kitchen to the living room and saying things under his breath.

Then I saw another person, who had a lot of long black hair and a short skirt and before long those ingredients added up and there was a woman standing in our living room.

Gert handed her a glass of something yellow. She drank a big gulp. He drank some too. They kissed and Gert whispered something in her ear and she laughed.

I watched him walk by my door and into the bathroom. The woman ran a hand through her hair and took out her phone. She pressed the buttons and her face got bright from the screen. She was wearing a lot of makeup.

She also broke the rule that said she had to take off her shoes.

I could hear Gert peeing in the bathroom.

This was the time to confront the intruder to the house, while she was alone and did not expect to be confronted. This was a battle tactic that Vikings employed—attacking at night so that they caught their enemies unaware. I jumped out from the hallway and stood behind her and said, "WHO GOES THERE," in a booming voice.

She dropped the glass that she was holding and said, "Oh my God!" The glass bounced on the ground and spilled all over the carpet.

"Identify yourself," I said.

"Jesus," she said, and called out Gert's name, putting her hand over her heart.

"You cannot pass!" I told her.

The toilet flushed and Gert came in, pulling up his pants. He saw us, me and the woman, standing on the other side of the living room from each other.

"Sorry," the woman said. "I just, she scared me and I wasn't expecting—"

"No, it's fine." Gert turned to me. "Zee. What are you doing up?"

"You have been drinking," I said. "And you have your Midterm Exam tomorrow."

The woman bent down and picked up the glass. "I'm sorry," she said. "I can clean this up," and Gert told her that it was fine and not to worry about it.

"It's not fine," I said. "You are breaking the rules."

The woman's mouth opened and then it closed. "Maybe I should go," she said.

I told her that was exactly what she should do. Gert did not ask permission and what's more he was drinking and the longer he stayed up the less sleep he would have. In order to be your strongest you need to be rested.

"Hold on a second," Gert said. He turned to me. "What's the problem here? I had a couple drinks. Big deal."

I crossed my arms over my chest. "You have to get up early tomorrow for your test."

"My test isn't early. And it's my test, not yours."

The woman was standing behind Gert. She was touching his arm in a way that AK47 used to touch it, moving her hand up and down his arm, which I could not stand to look at.

I turned and walked back to my room to show him that I was angry.

Once I got into my room I sat there and crossed my arms, waiting for him to come and apologize. Instead of that happening, I heard them talking more and then they started laughing, and then they got quiet. I knew that they were going to have sex, so I turned on my Viking music as loud as I could. The person who lived above my bedroom in another apartment bonked on the floor, which made the ceiling shake. I put my head under the blankets and closed my eyes and wanted it to stop.

⅂

I had seen Gert having sex before, when we were living with Uncle Richard in his house. Gert had a girlfriend named Charlene who came in through the basement window very late at night and Gert took her to our room. I was asleep when she came in and thought that I was dreaming and that she was a monster. We slept in a bunk bed. Gert's bed was on the bottom, since he was so heavy and would probably fall through the top bed if he slept there. I slept on the top bunk. I liked being up there. I could see everything and if something wanted to get me it had to go up the metal ladder.

Gert told me to be quiet when I woke up and asked who was out there in the dark. The night-light was on the ground and did not show enough light for me to see properly.

"It's okay," Gert said, standing on the edge of his bed so his head was where my head was, on the top bunk. He put his hand on my mouth and when he took it away I asked what was going on.

"Nothing. Go back to sleep."

I asked who was in the room. The smell had changed from Gert's deodorant and Uncle Richard's cigarettes and the pot Gert smoked to perfume of girls at school.

"Charlene," Gert said.

"Hi, Charlene," I said. I turned on the clip-on lamp that stuck to the wall beside my head, and when the light came on it was so bright that Gert told me to shut it off.

Charlene looked at Gert and said it was too weird, doing it while I was in the room.

"She doesn't care," Gert said. "Right, Zee? She can sleep through anything."

I asked what I was going to be sleeping through and said that, actually, I do not sleep very well if I know something is going on in the room and that a person who is not me or Gert can see me sleep.

"I don't like to be watched either," Charlene said. "Maybe this was a bad idea."

Gert came over to my bed again and whisper-asked if I would go to the bathroom for a little while. "Or the living room."

"But it's my bed," I said. "And my room."

"It won't be for that long."

"Oh yeah?" Charlene said. She was leaning against the desk, her arms crossed against her chest. She was tapping the back of her heel against the wall. Gert put his hands on my shoulders. "Better be longer than that."

"Ha ha. Very funny." Gert put his chin on my mattress and whispered, "Please? What do you want? I'll do anything."

"It's getting late." Charlene was chewing gum and made it snap in her mouth.

"Anything," Gert said to me.

There was nothing I wanted that Gert could give me. For example, I wanted Mom back alive, and I wanted to be more than I was, and I wanted to go to regular classes in the school, like Gert could.

"Can you tell me more stories about Mom?" I said.

"Right now?"

"Tomorrow after school. For at least an hour."

Charlene's gum snapped again. "I don't have all night," she said. "I've got kids too."

"Fine," Gert said.

"Pinky swear?"

He looked back at Charlene, who was picking cat hair off her tank top and letting it fall to the carpet. Gert stuck out his pinky and our fingers wrapped around each other before snapping apart to make the promise unbreakable.

In the living room I put the pillows under my head and pulled the blanket up to my chin. Uncle Richard's house was not very clean and the food from dinner that he hadn't eaten was still on a plate. Sometimes he slept on the couch after watching TV and going to work, his stomach sticking out and his legs spread apart. If this happened we were supposed to shut off the TV and put a blanket over him so that he would not be angry when he woke up in the morning, or be too tired from being cold and waking up in the middle of the night to find a blanket.

He was not on the couch so I made myself into a burrito and squished my pillow under my head, making it twice as powerful to sleep on. The television was on mute and I flipped channels. There weren't many. Uncle Richard thought that cable was a rip-off and used antennas to try to get more channels. Sometimes the channels worked but mostly they didn't.

The only channel that worked was a show from a long time ago about a family from the frontier who drove in wagons and raised cows.

The women looked like nuns and had big dresses and the men were always shooting things and getting into fights before drinking beer at the end on the front porch of their house, in chairs that rocked back and forth.

I had just started falling asleep in front of the settlers on TV when I heard footsteps coming from Uncle Richard's room down the hall.

"What are you doing in here?" Uncle Richard asked. "Shouldn't you be sleeping in your room?"

I pretended to snore and not hear him. He said he saw me move a few seconds ago and that he knew what fake snoring sounded like.

He pointed at the TV. "I can't believe this is the best we can do."

On the TV, the settlers were in Church. Uncle Richard went over to the TV and moved the antennas around. He was very used to the antennas. Uncle Richard did not work very much, since he had hurt his leg after getting hit crossing the street by a postal truck. They gave him a lot of money after and he bought the house and opened a bar for a while, until it closed from the people working there cheating him out of money.

The TV got fuzzier and he changed the channel to sports, which hadn't worked when I first turned the TV on. He moved my feet out of the way and we started watching boxing.

"I think I know how this one ends," I said.

"Well, don't spoil it for me."

One of the fighters was a lot better at first. I already saw the end of the fight and knew that the fighter who looked crappier ended up winning by knocking his opponent out three times in a row, very fast.

Uncle Richard scratched his chest and said he was going to get a beer. "Do you want anything?"

"No thank you," I said.

He came back and sat down. We continued watching and some-how while the fighters punched each other, Uncle Richard had put his arm around me and was touching my shoulder with his fingers. I could feel him drawing something with his pointer. Then I recognized the shape. It was a letter *Z*. I started to wiggle, and he asked me what was wrong.

"You need to lighten up or you'll end up like your brother," he said, and I did not like that and wanted to yell at him, but I also did not want to get Gert in trouble. Gert and I had made a pinky swear, which was like a Viking pact, only then I did not know that I was a Viking and did not call it that. I did not learn I was a Viking until Gert gave me *Kepple's Guide to the Vikings* for Christmas. Gert and Uncle Richard were always fighting about something, ever since Gert got bigger than him. Uncle Richard used to slap Gert and call him "boy" and say that if he lived under Uncle Richard's roof, then he would live under Uncle Richard's rules too.

Even though we were related by blood, we were not the same tribe because of how he treated Gert.

While sitting on the couch, I tried to watch the television and prayed that Uncle Richard would not hear Gert.

Some sex noises came from the bedroom and to hide them I made a coughing noise and said that I was starting to get a cold.

"It's going around," Uncle Richard said. He told me to wait right there while he got some brandy. "An old family remedy," he said, coming back with the small bottle that smelled sweet but also very strong.

He poured a little bit into the cap that he took off the bottle and handed it to me. "When we were sick as kids, me and your mom, we used to take a nip of this and it would heat us right up." I told him it smelled bad, and he said that was sort of the point. "Trust me," he said. "Just make it all go down in one gulp."

I did what he said and the brandy went into my stomach, where it did warm it up. I made a face.

"It doesn't taste very good," I said.

"Yeah, but it feels good. Right?" Uncle Richard smiled, showing his teeth, which he had gotten whitened so that they were not so yellow anymore from the coffee and the cigarettes.

He put his arm around me again, and this time I felt his finger go from my shoulder to my arm and then his hand was between my arm and my body. Gert sometimes put his arm around his girlfriends like that. Then I felt his hand touch my chest, and I froze.

The sex noises got louder from Gert's and my room, and this time I forgot to cough. The fingers stopped. Uncle Richard had heard them.

"Motherfucker," he said, and got up to go to Gert's room. I tried to hold him back and he pushed me down. "Not the time to be fucking around," he said.

I threw off my blanket and ran and tried to stand in front of the door.

"Move," he said.

"No," I said, and like Gandalf in *The Lord of the Rings* said, "YOU SHALL NOT PASS."

Uncle Richard pushed open the door. The lights were off in the bedroom but the light from the living room made everything bright. Gert stood behind Charlene, who had her arms on the chair at Gert's desk. They were both naked.

Her face turned away and she ran to the bed and Gert asked what the fuck was going on.

"Get out of here, you little whore," Uncle Richard said, throwing clothes at Charlene. "Your mother would be ashamed of you."

There was a lot of shouting and Charlene started putting on her shirt. Gert stood up to Uncle Richard, who was wearing clothes while Gert had no clothes on.

"What's the matter with you?" he said, and Uncle Richard slapped him across the face.

Charlene screamed and ran by me in her underwear, holding the rest of her clothes.

"You're a piece of white trash, just like your father," Uncle Richard said.

When Uncle Richard said that about our father, Gert punched him. It was the first time Gert had ever hit Uncle Richard, while Uncle Richard had hit Gert a lot. They started wrestling and I didn't know what to do to make them stop. They knocked into the desk and knocked over a light. Uncle Richard's leg bent in a weird way, and for the first time, Uncle Richard could not be more powerful than Gert.

So I started shouting, as loud as I could, until they stopped wrestling. Uncle Richard pushed himself off of Gert and stood between us, breathing fast and hard.

"Stop it," he said.

Gert wiped blood off of his mouth. "Don't yell at her," he said.

And Uncle Richard threw up his hands and walked out of the room, saying that he regretted the day he ever took us in. Once he was gone I stopped screaming. Gert put on his underwear and sat on the bed, holding a T-shirt to his face to stop the blood.

"Fuck," he said, hitting his knees. "Now everyone at school is going to hear about this. Why did you tell him?"

"I didn't tell," I said. "He heard you being loud."

"Fuck," Gert repeated, and threw the shirt on the ground and grabbed a sock to stop the bleeding.

We sat together on the bed.

"We need to get out of here," Gert said, turning the sock inside out so that he could use the clean inside part to wipe his nose again. "By any fucking means necessary."

chapter seven

The next morning, the morning of the Midterm Exam, I meant to wake Gert up and make him a powerful breakfast before his test, even though I was pissed at him for drinking and having sex all night with someone not AK47.

But he was gone and so was the girl. His door was locked and his shoes weren't there, and the house was silent. Outside the day was getting loud with cars and people going to work.

"Crap," I said.

The Word of Today was *incongruity*, which is when things do not fit together. It is a very old word, the Dictionary said, and can also mean "disagreement."

Last night Gert and I had incongruity about who was allowed in the apartment.

"We will have to stop our incongruity," I would tell Gert when he came home from his test, to make sure that he knows I do not appreciate strange people in our home.

After practicing the Word of Today, saying it in three sentences to help me remember, I remembered that I wanted to help Gert for his test. I checked my watch to make sure I would have enough time to perform a sacrifice in Gert's honor before taking the 11:15 a.m. bus to the library to read.

Kepple says that animals can be sacrificed, and humans, and also objects to show the gods how much you respect them, and to ask for things. For my sacrifice, I wanted to ask that Gert succeed and prove to everyone that he is not a thug or dumb.

For the sacrifice to work, the object has to be important. That is what the word means: to give up something that you like. I went around the apartment, trying to find something important to sacrifice in the coffee container.

The most important objects to me were:

- The picture of Mom and Gert and me as a baby.
- The video of Mom.
- The letter that Marxy wrote for me, saying he loves me.
- *Kepple's Guide to the Vikings*, which Gert gave me for Christmas.

I took a deep breath. I did not want to sacrifice any of these things. The thing that I loved the most was the picture of us. It had the most power, even though it was very small and could fit into my pocket.

"Okay," I said, taking out the picture from the plastic. "This is my sacrifice for Gert."

I was proud of Gert for going to college, since nobody thought he could do it. Or almost nobody. AK47 and I thought he could do anything. He didn't have a high school diploma. If he had a high school diploma, he could have gone to the school that said they would pay for everything if he played football for their team.

It was AK47 who convinced Gert to go to college. He had blown out his knee during his last year of high school, meaning he ripped part in a way that made it hard to walk. He got a job at a gas station and started getting a big roll around his stomach. You couldn't even see the veins in his arms anymore.

Some days AK47 and I would go to visit him. She would drive her car to see him and have him pump gas into her car. She thought it was funny, making him do that, but after she would always complain that the gas where he worked cost too much. She did not approve of him working at the gas station. She said that it was bullshit, that he was wasting his talent and she thought that he could be a hero again, even though she didn't use those words exactly.

Gert is the leader of our tribe, and when people thought he was a thug and not smart, it was like they were talking about the rest of our tribe. Gert had protected me in high school from people who called me a retard, and now people thought that he was stupid and would never become a hero.

One day AK47 brought him a piece of paper that she had seen posted at the Community Center. It was for a scholarship at the college for people like Gert, who were in financial need and had experienced something called "Hardship."

"If you actually meet the deadline, I'll do that thing you like," AK47 said, slapping the paper down on the kitchen table in front of Gert.

"What thing you like?" I asked her, but they were staring at each other and not listening to me, and finally Gert said, "For a week," and AK47 smiled and said they had a deal.

Every night after he came home from the gas station he worked on his essay.

AK47 wouldn't tell me what the essay was about. She wouldn't let me read it either. "It's up to him to tell you."

"So why did you get to read it?"

"Because I'm a hypocrite and you're just going to have to get used to it. Okay?"

Hypocrite is one of the ten words on my Favorite Words list, along with words like *bloom* and *pedigree* and *cursive*. I don't use any of those words, and nobody ever really uses them around me, so when I hear them I get excited. A hypocrite is basically someone who says one thing and goes ahead and does the other while expecting everyone else to do the first thing. So if I told you to not run on the deck beside a pool and then ran on the deck later, I would be a hypocrite.

Gert ended up getting the scholarship and quit his job at the gas station.

In order to keep the scholarship, Gert needed to have high grades, which is why he studied Macroeconomics so hard. His scholarship gave us money for food and for his car and things like Dr. Laird.

The essay he wrote in order to get the scholarship was powerful. He did not allow me to read it, though.

"Why not?" I asked.

"When you're older," he said, but even when I was older he said no, that it had things that were private and I would not like.

"Try me," I said.

He did not want to try me.

When I went to the kitchen, I saw that Gert had forgotten his special graphing calculator, which cost him almost one hundred dollars. It was on the kitchen table. It was a critical weapon for defeating the tests he studied for.

"Holy crap," I said.

Without the special calculator, his test would go disastrously.

He did not answer his phone when I called to tell him that he had forgotten it. I looked at the clock. Then I went to his schedule on the fridge and looked for the box that said MACROECONOMICS.

His test was coming up and I did not know if he would have time to come back for his calculator.

My heart began racing around in my chest.

I sat down and took ten breaths. AK47 did not answer her phone. The photograph of Mom and Gert and me stared at me and everyone was smiling in the photo. It was like they were trying to tell me something, even me as a baby.

There was a rule that said I could only take the bus to places that Gert and I went to together at least once, so that I knew the right way to go and didn't get lost, and to make sure that they weren't dangerous places. I had never been to Gert's college except once, when me and him and AK47 went to visit it, before he agreed to go. Kepple would call the college foreign territory, and it was a place that I hadn't conquered. I found the address on the schedule, then I went on Google Maps and found out what bus to take to the college.

I did not like breaking the rule about the bus, but Gert would be defeated without his calculator, and fail his test and lose his scholarship, which will take treasure away from the tribe's hoard. And sometimes the heroes of legends have to break the rules in order to save the people they care about.

I got my bag and put the special calculator in it. I whispered a prayer to Odin to bless me on my quest.

ᛉ

The bus stop near our apartment has a lot of graffiti on it and usually smells like pee. I made sure not to sit on the bench, because that is where a homeless man sleeps at night, on the seat with food that people leave for him on the ground.

Someone must have left him Burger King. There were a bunch of wrappers from the hamburgers and fries.

I brought my map to show the bus driver. "I need to go here," I said. "Do you go there?"

He nodded. I paid the fare, which was three dollars, and sat down next to him on the bus, the way I would next to AK47 while she drove.

The bus driver had a large beard. At first he did not want to talk and just stared straight ahead through big sunglasses that showed what he was looking at like a movie screen.

When I started talking to him, he turned down his radio so he could hear me. I told him that I needed to go to campus in order to save my brother.

I said that Gert saved us from living with Uncle Richard, who was a gargantuan fuck-dick. Uncle Richard's house was always full of villainous people who got angry with Gert and sometimes fought with him. Gert got his college scholarship and moved us to the apartment we were living in, which was very far from rich people, but also not so close to really bad people like Uncle Richard.

"Sounds like your brother needs to save himself," the bus driver said.

"I have a son like that," the woman across the seat from me said. "He doesn't listen to nobody."

"Is your brother bad news too?" another woman in a yellow raincoat said.

I shook my head.

"He's really smart, but even really smart, strong people need help," I told her.

"Amen to that," the first woman said.

"My mom was an alcoholic," I said. "She was drinking when she had me in her stomach and that's how I became the not-normal way I am. A lot of people say I am retarded, but that is not an okay thing to say."

"Huh," the bus driver said. He scratched at his neck with his fingernails. It sounded like scrubbing a toilet.

"I can use the word *retard* if I want to," I added. "It's okay. I am taking the power from the word and using it for good, like when black people use the n-word."

Once I had heard AK47 use the n-word, which was a word she made sure Gert never used, and that was what she told me: that sometimes you can take an ugly word people have for you, like *retard*, and let the air out of it like a balloon. But she also said that only someone who had been hurt by the n-word could use it that way.

"Every other way it hurts people," she said, and I did not understand until I thought about the word *retard* and how it was used to hurt people, and how I could make it not hurt me.

The other thing is that a lot of people get weird when I talk about Mom and how she accidentally poisoned me.

Dr. Laird has a lot of pamphlets, and there are websites too, that explain what happened when Mom had beer and other things while I was a baby inside her.

For example, people like me can have "abnormal" faces, which I do not have, and smaller heads. They are short like I am, and can have trouble sitting still and thinking, which is something Dr. Laird has helped me with. They can also have weak bones and need a lot of calcium, which builds bones, in order to stay strong.

"My fair maiden gets called retarded a lot," I said. "It bothers him, so whenever I hear someone call him that I make them apologize."

"Your fair what now?" the woman across from me asked.

"My fair maiden. His name is Marxy."

"Maidens can only be girls," the woman said. "That's what the word means."

"Well, I don't care what the word means, because it's my legend."

She stared at me for a long time. "Well, anyway," the woman said. "Sometimes people need help. My son, we all got together and told him how much we cared about him. You know. How he has children to look after. Maybe that's something you can do with your brother?"

That sounded like a good idea. I thought of the people who could help me. There was AK47, who said she hated Gert, even though she loved him. I could also ask Dr. Laird. Those were the only friends of Gert's that I knew and liked.

The bus turned a corner really sharply and the bus driver told me that we were going to be on campus soon.

"You going to be okay?" he said.

I said that I was. He stopped the bus and I showed him the special Viking handshake, where you grab the person's wrist. Then at the end we made a fist dab.

"Good luck," he said.

"You too," I said. "*Happ.*"

Happ means "good luck" in Viking, along with *gipta*, which I said after, since I didn't know what the difference between the two types of luck was.

When people started getting on the bus, coming in like a gargantuan wave, the bus driver held out his hand and said in a booming voice: "WAIT YOUR GODDAMN TURN."

And the people, who were mostly young and students with books and backpacks, stopped trying to get on the bus. I felt like a hero who had just defeated hordes of bad warriors. They moved out of the way and let me walk off the bus.

"Middle building," the bus driver said before letting all of the people back on. "The tall one with the bells."

౽

The campus of the college is gargantuan and reminds me of pictures I have seen of Viking towns, with lots of people walking around. Nobody has swords or axes or hats with animal bones sticking out of them, though. Students don't look anything like Vikings. They do not have a lot of muscles, or most of them do not. Some of the students I saw were big and could do well on the battlefield. But the battlefield they were on happened in the brain.

When Gert first got into the college, Gert and I and AK47 all went together to walk around. AK47 whistled and said, "Not bad, for a state college," and Gert shrugged and scratched his elbow. He was wearing his baggy clothes and some people walking toward us made sure to walk really far away from us as we passed on the sidewalk.

That happens a lot with Gert. It's like he is not only big, he is bigger than he really is when he walks.

AK47 rubbed his shoulder and told him not to worry. "All that matters is your brain," she said. "Let the rest of these idiots be shit-heels."

While walking through the college, holding on to Gert's calculator and the printout of his class schedule, I started to get nervous, since there were so many people around and I was not with anyone I knew. My heart felt like a bird, bouncing against its cage inside of me. In my brain I told the bird to stop going crazy, that it was time to be a Viking bird and not a coward.

I rubbed the sides of my head and closed my eyes and counted to ten.

"Are you all right?"

I opened my eyes and there was a girl standing in front of me. She was holding a large book and wore sunglasses, which were not as shiny as the bus driver's and sat on the end of her nose.

"I am fine," I said.

"Lost?"

I nodded. She asked me where I wanted to go. I showed her the schedule from the fridge that had Gert's classes. People were walking by and someone hit me with their bag accidentally.

The girl pushed the person and said, "Dick, watch where you're going."

She read the information on the piece of paper and said where I wanted to go wasn't far. I told her that the bus driver said it was the building with the tower.

"No. Here. Come on," she said, and started walking.

I followed her. While we walked she asked me about what I was doing on campus and who I was and I told her I needed to save my brother.

"He needs his special calculator in order to write his test."

"Midterms are a bitch," the girl said.

"His name is Gert. Do you know him?" I asked, and when I told her his name she said she didn't, but that it was a big campus. We went up the hill.

"Lots of people go here. But that's a pretty weird name."

At the top of the hill she pointed to a building with a flag sticking out of the top. It was big and metal with a lot of windows.

"That's where the Econ Department is. Your brother's class should be there." She handed the paper back to me. "Second floor."

I thanked her and told her to stay cool, and we dabbed and she added a move to the dab, where she pulled her hand away after our fists touched and made the sound of an explosion.

ᚢ

I ran up the stairs of the building to the second floor and walked down the hall and read the numbers by the doors, which were very small. Inside the rooms the students all had their pencils in their hands and were using them to do battle with the sheets of paper in front of them. Many of them had the calculators that Gert used.

This told me that I was in the correct building.

The door to the classroom on the sheet of paper had a small window in it. I could not see Gert, and the window was not big enough for me to see the entire room, which looked like a movie theater, with students sitting in chairs and a Professor standing at the bottom. A computer shot pictures up on a screen at the front.

The screen had numbers and things on it that I did not understand.

I put my ear to the glass of the door so I could listen to the teacher at the front of the room, who was talking very loudly.

"The image projected will correspond to question seventeen," she was saying.

The projector changed pictures and showed another one that was even more confusing.

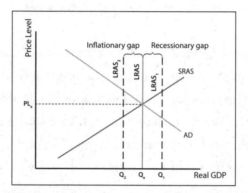

"This is the time," I told myself. Closing my eyes, I pushed the door and it made a loud metal sound as it opened.

The teacher stopped talking at the front of the class. The students in their chairs all turned to look at me too. All of them got really quiet, like instead of dropping a bomb that exploded I dropped one that sucked up all of the sound.

"Can I help you?" the teacher said.

I took out Gert's schedule and read the name under MACROECO-NOMICS. Dr. Gillroy was the name of the professor who was teaching Gert's class.

"Is your name Dr. Gillroy?" I called to the woman.

The students sitting down started whispering to each other and laughing.

The woman was older, with gray hair that was crimpy and stuck out. When I asked her for her name the second time, the students turned back to her to see what she was going to say. People pointed their phones at me.

"I am, and you're interrupting my exam." She folded her arms across her chest.

"I am trying to find my brother," I said. "He is in this class. I need to give him this." I opened my bag and took out Gert's special calculator. "For his exam."

She opened her arms and said to the class, "Does anyone here know this young woman?"

I made my eyes jog across the classroom, looking for Gert. I said his name aloud. Nobody put up their hand to say they were Gert.

"Does anyone here know a Gert?" she said.

That was when a hand went up. It did not belong to my brother. It belonged to a girl who was sitting in the last row, with blond hair that was pulled back in a ponytail. She had glasses and skinny arms.

She said, "I think I know who she's talking about."

"And?" the Professor said.

"May I be excused?" she asked the Professor, who looked at the clock.

"The exam's already late to start."

The student asked if she could come up and talk to the Professor. She came down the stairs of the classroom and to the front. The girl and Dr. Gillroy talked quietly, and then the girl walked up the steps to me and said that she knew Gert and that we should probably talk outside of the class, since we were disrupting everyone else.

⇗

We went to the cafeteria. She said that her name was Jenny and that she knew Gert, only she said it in a weird way and then asked me how he was doing.

"Good," I said. "We should try to find him if he is not in his exam. Maybe he got lost."

"Somehow I don't think so." Jenny smiled. "You two look a lot alike. I can see the resemblance."

"I need more tattoos."

And Jenny laughed and said that was true. She picked at her fingernail. "So you're looking for him, and he told you he was in this class."

"And that he has an exam."

"We did know each other," Jenny said. "I mean, we weren't best friends or anything. But we hung out outside of class." She chewed on her nail again.

I asked if that meant they had sex. Her face got red. Most of the girls who knew Gert had had sex with him.

"It's okay," I said. "Gert has sex with a lot of people."

"Yeah," she said. "I got that impression."

She told me they had been part of the same study group for their Economics class, the one with the big test. I told her that he had gone to the study group last night.

"Last night," she said.

"He came home very late and was drunk. Sometimes he likes to go out and have beers after studying, even though he knows I do not like when he gets drunk."

For some reason she did not want our eyes to meet. Usually people do that when they know something and they do not want to tell you.

So I gave her THE LOOK that AK47 taught me, staring right into her face and her eyes.

Jenny sighed. "Okay, it's probably none of my business, but I don't think he's doing well in class."

I frowned. "He hasn't said anything."

She said that Gert had not been coming to class for a while, and that this was not the first time he had missed a test. "Gert missed his Stats test too. And I haven't seen him in class for weeks."

That was impossible, I said. Gert had been studying and going to class. "He is not a person who lies," I said. "He is not dishonorable like that. And we do not lie to people in our tribe. That is a big rule."

Jenny saw someone walking with a tray of food and called him over. "Karl, can you come here for a minute?"

Karl was short and shaped like a ball, with a big stomach. He also had red hair, just like Carrot from the Community Center. He sat in the free chair, putting his tray down. He had soup and a tuna fish sandwich on it.

"What's going on?" he asked, and then he looked at me and back at Jenny.

"This is Gert's sister, Zelda," Jenny said.

"Hey," he said, and we did a funny handshake. "Cool. Where the hell's he been? I'm almost out of hash." Karl unwrapped his tuna sandwich, pulling all the plastic off. "It's been dry as shit on campus."

Jenny made a noise with her throat.

"What?" Karl said. When Karl talked I could see the food in his mouth. Then he looked at me and put his hands over his mouth and apologized.

"What does Gert have to do with being out of hash?" I asked. "And what is hash?"

Karl looked at Jenny. "Oh. Well, he's sort of—"

He stopped and bit more of his sandwich.

Jenny said, "Zelda came all the way here to bring Gert his graphing calculator, for Econ."

The rest of Karl's sandwich disappeared into his mouth. "I heard he's going to fail, like, mathematically," he said. "Maybe academic probation. Right?"

"I didn't hear that," Jenny said.

I put my hands on the table and spread out my fingers. "Okay," I said. "What does that mean?"

"It means that he's either not going to class or failing his tests. Maybe both." He nodded his head. "I don't think he got busted for dealing, so it's probably not that. Anyway, if you end up talking to him, can you get him to give me a call? It's Karl. He's got my number."

❧

When I got home I was very angry and decided to take action. I had gone all the way to the college to bring him the calculator. If Karl was correct, Gert was in big trouble.

He is very serious about me not going into his room when he is not home. I have always respected his wishes. But I had to find out who was telling the truth and who was lying. If Gert had lied about going to his test, that was one lie. But if he had stopped going to classes and was failing, he should have told me.

I knew Gert had books and papers on his desk that he said were from school. I put down my bag in my room and went to Gert's room. I knocked on the door and said it was me, to open up.

If he was not at school, he should have been home.

Everything was quiet.

Gert's door has a lock on it, but I knew that if you took a pen apart and used the plastic tube inside, you could stick it into the round hole of the lock and press around and the lock would sometimes open.

AK47 showed me how to do it.

So I found the pen and opened the door.

Gert was not hiding in there from his test.

His room was not very clean and smelled like his underarm deodorant and also cologne, and dirty laundry and his armpits. The poster of Al Pacino from *Scarface* stared at me and said SAY HELLO TO MY LITTLE FRIEND.

Gert likes to keep everything clean and orderly. His messy room was weird. I did not know where to look, so I started at his desk and looked at the papers there. It looked like homework and things from college. They would not help very much.

I checked under his bed and also in his desk, and in the table beside his bed, where he kept his condoms for having sex and also bundles of socks.

His room has a bigger closet than my room. I went into it and moved all of the shirts that were hanging up out of the way. It was like being in a jungle and being attacked by all the plants. At Uncle Richard's he kept his important things in our closet, behind a lot of clothes.

I saw the gym bag that Toucan gave him.

I put it on Gert's bed and pulled open the zipper. There were two envelopes and one of them was empty and the other one had money in it. All of the bills were for twenty dollars and I counted them twice and there were twelve bills. The envelope also had a piece of paper inside, folded up, from a notebook. Gert had written names on the paper and a number beside the name. Some of the names were crossed out.

I put the money and the paper back in the envelope. Then I put the gym bag back into his closet. There was another box hidden behind the gym bag that I had not seen before. It was metal and had a key inside the lock.

I turned the key and the box opened.

There was a gun inside.

chapter eight

"Shit-heel!" I shouted at the gun, even though it was made of metal and couldn't hear me. I also shouted, *"Níðingr!"* a word from *Kepple* that means "scoundrel or person who can't be trusted."

The problem with guns is you can make them go off by accident, and the television always shows people getting shot and dying. Sometimes even children and babies get shot. Before AK47 allowed me to call her the name of a gun, she made sure I knew that guns were dangerous and that people who used them to hurt others were cowards. I did not like the idea of Gert being a coward who used guns like a villain and stopped touching the gun.

"Shit-heel," I said, because if Gert had a gun it could go off by accident and kill a baby. "Shit-heel, *níðingr*, shit-heel, *níðingr*!"

Vikings did not use guns. They stopped being powerful and vanished in 1050 AD. The first cannon used in battle was in 1250 AD. So they were late to inventing guns.

During high school, when Gert was still playing football, one of his friends on the football team got shot on the street. Gert was not there, but everyone in the school had to go to a meeting in the gymnasium to talk about how the friend got shot and how guns were very dangerous.

There was a picture of the student from the yearbook on the wall and people were crying. I also cried, even though I did not know the football player who had died. Crying is like yawning. If one person cries, then everyone starts crying. Gert did not cry in the gymnasium but he did cry when we were back home at Uncle Richard's. After the shooting there were metal detectors and police officers in the school, which made everyone angry and nervous at the same time.

I thought of the THINGS LEGENDS NEED list. A sword needs skill to use and is a powerful weapon in the hands of a master. Many cowards and villains use guns. As a hero, Gert should not have a gun.

While I was in Gert's room, cursing the gun, I heard the door of the apartment open.

"Zelda?" Gert called, and I started to panic.

Before I knew what I was doing, I had the gun in my hand, which I did not mean to do. I meant to leave the gun in his room and never think about it again. But now it was in my hands, and I did not want to be holding it anymore.

Gert called my name again.

The panic continued inside me and I put the gun back into the box and locked it, and as fast as I could put it behind the gym bag in the closet. I just made it out of his room by the time he came down the hallway.

"What were you doing in my room?" he asked.

"Why were you lying to me?" I said.

He stomped past me and looked in his room and asked why his clothes were all over the place, if I wasn't in his room. He looked in his closet where I had found the box with the gun. He rooted around in there and came out and said, "What is the rule about our bedrooms?"

"What is the rule about lying to me about writing your Midterm Exam?" I said back.

"What are you talking about?"

I went into my room, got the calculator and held it up, and said, "You forgot your calculator."

"Oh." Gert took the calculator. "This test isn't one that needed the calculator. Stats needs the calculator. Not Macro. But I was looking for it."

"But you use it for your studying," I said.

"This was all word problems. You don't need a calculator for that, do you?"

"No," I said.

"And can we agree, once and for all, that you stay out of my room and I stay out of yours? Isn't that about respect?"

I nodded. It was a RULE OF THE HOUSE we had come up with together.

He asked if I was hungry. Before I could answer he walked to the kitchen, went to the fridge, and took out ingredients to make a sandwich.

He started cutting some tomato. "What? You're looking at me weirdly."

"You did not do your test today," I said.

The knife he was holding went through the tomato, over and over and going *clunk* on the cutting board. "Is that right? Then where was I for the last two hours?"

"Lying to me."

He sighed and put down his knife. "All right. Out with it." When I asked him out with what, he said, "Whatever it is you're talking around. Just say it."

I told him I knew that he skipped the test because I had gone to the classroom on his schedule on the fridge. He had forgotten his calculator and would fail the test without it. That was when I met Jenny and Karl and learned that he was on academic probation, which was very bad news and meant he would get kicked out of college if he didn't smarten up.

"And Karl is out of hash," I added.

As I talked he started putting the mayonnaise on two slices of bread that jumped out of the toaster. There wasn't much mayonnaise in the jar and the knife bonked around.

"We are also out of something," he said, holding up the mayo jar. "Have you been drinking this stuff or what?"

"I am not in the mood for making jokes," I said. "You haven't been going to class."

He put the jar down. "Okay. You want the truth?"

I said that I did. "We are truth-tellers and part of the same tribe."

"I've dropped Macro. The class. That's all. I have no idea why they think I am on academic whatever."

"Probation," I said. "Which means you are in trouble and if you screw up more you get kicked out of school." I had Googled what it meant and put it next to *incongruity* on my list of Words of Today.

"Yeah, I know what it means."

I asked him why he was pretending to study for the test when there was no test. He said that he knew I was serious about him being in school and he didn't want me to get mad. "I didn't want you to worry or anything," he said.

I became a bit less angry.

"So you haven't been kicked out of school and will need to start working at the gas station again?"

"No. I won't be doing any of that."

He came over, holding a plate with a bologna sandwich cut in half, in triangles. I took one of the sandwiches and it tasted very good. We ate our sandwiches for a few bites and then he remembered something and put his sandwich back on the plate.

"I almost forgot." He reached into his backpack and took out an envelope. "You've got mail."

He handed it to me. My name was on the front and the stamp was of a Viking helmet.

"I don't get mail," I said. "Except from boring things like the government."

Gert bit into his sandwich. "Go on. Open it."

I tore the envelope open and inside was a card from Marxy.
It said:

DEAR ZELDA,
    YOU AND GERT ARE CORDIALLY INVITED TO
HAVE DINNER AT MY HOUSE ON FRIDAY AT 5 P.M.
PLEASE RSVP IF YOU CAN COME.
MARXY, esq.

I asked what RSVP means. "It means get back as soon as possible to
let a person know if you can come," Gert said. "Why?"

I could not help smiling. "We have been invited to dinner."

"Is that right?"

"With Marxy and his mother."

"Sounds awful. Can we say no?"

"NO," I shouted.

"I know. I was just teasing you." He finished eating one of his sandwich halves and licked his fingers. "When is this fancy dinner?"

"Friday."

"Friday. I think I have plans."

I gave him THE LOOK.

"Joking. Okay, we'll go. All right?"

"And you have to behave yourself and be the perfect gentleman and
wear nice clothes. You must represent our tribe well."

"So many demands. Anything else, Captain?" He smiled at me. "I
can't believe you went all the way to the college yourself. That's pretty
impressive. I'm proud of you."

I picked up my sandwich and took a big bite and suddenly the
graphing calculator and academic probation or anything else didn't
matter anymore.

chapter nine

All week I had been thinking of the dinner with Marxy. We had texted back and forth about it a million times. He didn't come to the Community Center because his father and Pearl were fighting over him and couldn't decide where he should stay.

His father wanted him to go to a special school during the day where experts like Dr. Laird could show him extra attention.

I hate it, he texted me. I miss you and Yoda and Hamsa and Sarah-Beth and Big Todd and Annie.

I texted back and told him we missed him too.

On Thursday, AK47 helped me decide what to wear. There was a dress Uncle Richard had bought me for Gert's high school graduation, which I never got to wear. It was white and blue and had flowers on it. There were no sleeves and you could kind of see my boobs squished in my bra underneath it.

I also had a pair of shoes that were nice and hurt my feet. AK47 said that was how you knew something was fancy. It ended up feeling crappy to wear.

On Friday, at exactly 4:30 p.m., I was wearing the dress and shoes, waiting for Gert to pick me up in front of our apartment building. When it became 4:31 p.m., I texted him that he was late.

He texted back: Two minutes.

Marxy texted me saying: I am excited to see you!

Gert pulled up in his car. It was sparkling from the car wash and he was wearing his nice clothes.

"You look good," I said, and did AK47's frying pan finger sizzle, which she used to do when she thought Gert looked sexy.

He wiggled his shoulders and adjusted the seat belt. "It's itchy as hell." He pulled on the knot of the tie. "Are you nervous?"

"A little."

"Don't be. This'll be fine." He put his arm around me and gave me a squeeze.

We drove a little bit. On the other side of the window was the city, with all of its tall buildings sticking up. I could not tell which one of them was our apartment. They were far away, not just in distance. They also felt far away because the air felt different. They were like gray teeth in a giant blue mouth.

"I wish that we could do this all the time," I said.

"Do what?"

"Wear nice clothes and go to dinner."

Gert was quiet for a while. "You know, you look a lot like Mom wearing that dress. She used to wear dresses like that."

"Really?"

He nodded. "Not all the time. But we used to go to Church. You were still in the stroller."

I asked him to tell me more. He scratched the part of the neck that stuck out near his tie's knot. He said that he hated going to Church because he didn't like sitting still, but he liked going with Mom. "She was so beautiful," he said. "Man. Everyone stopped to talk to us."

He told a story about how someone once tried to steal me, while I was in a stroller.

"Really?" I asked.

Gert laughed. "Yeah, we turned around for two seconds and someone was pushing your stroller away. An old woman. I guess she thought she was still young and you were her baby."

"Holy crap," I said.

"Yeah. I'm glad you didn't get stolen, though. Even if you are a knucklehead sometimes." He smiled at me and I said I was glad I didn't get stolen too.

⩔

Marxy's house was in the suburbs, and when we came to the door, Gert had a bottle of wine that I didn't know he'd bought. He got it out of the trunk, wrapped in a brown paper bag.

"It's what people do when they have dinner parties, right?" he said, showing me the bottle. "I think it's red with dinner. But I'm not sure."

"I don't know. I've never been to a dinner party."

I added it to the list of rules in my head: for dinner parties, bring wine, probably red. "Are we going to drink wine?" I asked.

"We don't have to," Gert said. "I know you have a rule about that stuff."

Because of what happened to Mom and how she drank too much, I decided I was never going to drink, ever. It was a rule for myself. But Vikings drank, especially when happy and at a gargantuan feast, and I was feeling happy and going to a feast. Maybe there are different rules for feasting at dinner parties.

Vikings always drink mead and wine at powerful feasts, but they do not drink mead and wine at any other time. You cannot do battle if you have too much. I asked Gert if that was one of the rules of dinner parties—that you needed to drink mead.

"I mean, it's what happens a lot. Not mead. Nobody drinks that anymore."

"Then we can have wine. But only while eating."

We walked up the stones in the ground in front of Marxy's house, through the metal gate, and past flowers and a large tree.

Gert rang the doorbell and Marxy answered the door. He had a nice shirt on, dark blue, and nice brown pants, the kind with the line in the middle which is called a "crease."

"Hello," he said. "Welcome to my house."

Pearl came up behind him. She was wearing a yellow dress and a gray cardigan over it. "Right on time. What's this?"

Gert handed over the wine. "I wasn't sure what to bring, so I got this merlot stuff."

"Gert isn't a big wine person," I said. "He likes beer."

Pearl smiled and stepped aside. "Well. It was thoughtful. Come on in. Kick off your shoes."

"We have that rule too," I said, closing the door behind us.

I had only been to Marxy's house once, when neither of his parents could drive him to the Community Center and AK47 had to pick him up. That time I stayed on the bus. Now that I was inside, I saw pictures of Marxy as a baby on the wall, wearing a sailor's outfit, and also his family. There was a painting on the wall of a ship at sea, and the house smelled very nice and soft, like laundry that comes right out of the machine.

The dinner table was already set up. Pearl was serving chicken and mashed potatoes. We sat with Pearl at the head of one side, and Gert on the other. Marxy and I were across from each other. Pearl asked if I wanted some wine. She opened the bottle with a corkscrew and poured herself some.

"Yes, please," I said.

"Me too," Marxy said, and Pearl told him he could have a little bit but not more than a glass. "He got into some coolers I had in the fridge one time, and let me tell you," Pearl said, "that was a handful."

"I puked all night," Marxy said.

"Lesson learned," Pearl said. "Is anyone religious here? We're atheists, but I'm happy to say grace if that's what you do."

"We're fine, right?" Gert said.

Marxy turned to me. "Zelda can say the Viking thing."

I cleared my throat and closed my eyes to remember the Viking blessing from *Kepple's Guide to the Vikings*. "Odin and the other gods, bless this bounty set here before us and have some yourself and enjoy it."

Pearl smiled. "Odin, huh?"

"I used to go to Catholic school," Marxy said, poking the chicken with his fork. "But I hated it."

"The teachers there were puritanical. Here, honey. Use this." She handed Marxy a sharper knife with the crinkly end, the kind you use to cut power meats like steaks.

Marxy turned to Gert after cutting up his chicken. "Did those hurt? The writing on your arms?"

Gert had rolled up his sleeves before dinner and you could see some of his muscles and tattoos. "My tattoos?"

Marxy nodded his head. "Is it like drawing with a pen?"

"No. It's more like a needle."

"I'd like a tattoo, please," Marxy said.

"Ha." Pearl nearly spilled her wine. "Fat chance of that. Though Marxy's father has one."

"It's a name on Dad's arm, right here," Marxy said, patting his own arm between his shoulder and elbow.

"And not mine." Pearl sighed. "Young love."

Gert wiped his lips on his napkin and started cutting up more of his chicken on his plate very loudly.

"Marxy tells me you've started calling him something," she said to me. "What was it, Marxy?"

"Fair maiden," Marxy said.

I nodded. "All Viking heroes have fair maidens," I said. "And before anyone says that only girls are allowed to be fair maidens, I think that those rules are old and we need new rules where anyone can be fair maidens."

Gert laughed.

"I think it's cool," Marxy said. "Why are you laughing at me?"

Pearl reached over and patted his arm. "Honey, it's okay. Nobody is laughing at you. Right, Gert?" She gave him THE LOOK.

"I'm sick and tired of people laughing at me," Marxy said.

I kicked Gert under the table and he put up his hands. "Okay, hey, I wasn't laughing at you. It's just not something you hear guys called a lot. That's all."

"Well, Zelda can call me it if she wants," Marxy said, picking up a bite of chicken with his fork.

Nobody said anything for a little while. I decided to fill the silence with my announcement.

"And another thing is that I want to have sex with Marxy, because Dr. Laird says it's normal for people our age to express our love for each other physically," I said. "I have also got my period."

"Jesus," Gert said, putting his fork down. "Can we not talk about fucking periods, please?"

"I know all the rules about sex," Marxy said.

Pearl poured herself some more wine and laughed. "Well, hello there, awkward dinner conversation topics." She turned to Gert. "But I'm glad the subject came up, Gert, because this is the reality. They're not children anymore. They have functioning reproductive systems, sex drives."

"You're talking about me like I'm not here again," Marxy said.

"And me," I added.

Pearl smiled and dabbed her lips with her napkin. "I apologize. To both of you. Feel free to add anything."

"We're in love," I said, and reached and held on to Marxy's hand from across the table, almost getting my arm in the bowl of mashed potatoes.

Pearl nodded. "Marxy knows about sex. He masturbates."

"Mom!"

Pearl shrugged her shoulders. "It's nothing to be ashamed of. We all masturbate."

"I do," I said. "Dr. Laird says the same thing. And Gert does too. I caught him once."

"Jesus Christ," Gert said, his face getting red. "I think I'm going to be sick."

I wondered if all dinner parties ended up with people talking about important things. Gert did not like talking openly about things the way Pearl did.

Pearl continued talking. "I assume you aren't comfortable with the two of them exploring their sexuality in your apartment."

"No," Gert said. "No goddamn way."

Pearl nodded. "I agree. It probably isn't ideal anyway."

"Why not?" I asked.

She pressed her lips together and looked like she was thinking. "We'd want to make sure that your first time has as few complications as possible."

"This whole thing is complications," Gert said. "He can barely tie his shoelaces. There's no way he should be having sex with anyone, especially not someone like Zelda."

"I can tie my shoelaces," Marxy said.

"And what do you mean, 'someone like Zelda'?" I asked.

Pearl didn't raise her voice. She put her chin on her hands and her elbows on the table. "Yes, what do you mean by 'someone like Zelda,' Gert?"

That was when Gert's phone buzzed.

He crumpled up the napkin on his lap and rolled it into a ball and put it on the table next to his plate, which still had a lot of food on it. "I need to take this," he said, holding up his phone.

He pushed his chair back and walked out of the dining room. I watched him go, and once I turned back to the food I saw that Pearl was watching me.

"Mom," Marxy said, "you're doing the thing where you have a staring problem again."

"I'm not staring. I'm just curious. Can I ask you a question, Zelda?"

I nodded. "You *may* ask me a question."

I did not get to hear what she was going to ask me because Gert came back into the room and said we had to go.

"Now?"

Gert said that our time was up.

"I am enjoying dinner," I said. "We never have food like this at home."

Pearl smiled. "I'll take that as a compliment, Zelda." Then she addressed Gert. "If this stuff is making you uncomfortable, then maybe it's time for you to grow up. Marxy and Zelda are comfortable talking about sex."

"I'm putting on my coat and then we're gone," Gert said to me. He nodded at Pearl before he walked out.

"I love talking about sex," Marxy said.

Even though Gert is part of my tribe and we always have each other's backs and are loyal, I didn't want to leave with him. I wanted to keep eating dinner.

"He's wound up pretty tight, isn't he?" Pearl asked.

I nodded. "Very tight."

Pearl asked Marxy to go to the kitchen and get some Tupperware containers, and to start clearing the table.

"Already?" he asked.

"And take your time," Pearl said. "I'd like to talk with Zelda for a minute."

Sighing, Marxy tucked in his shirt and started to pick up one of the plates.

Pearl touched his arm. "And start with the chicken, please. Do you remember how to put on the plastic wrap?"

He said he did and went to the kitchen. Gert called from the other room and said he'd see me in the car. I sighed.

"Can I ask you a question, Zelda?" Pearl asked.

"Shoot."

"What was it like before you and Gert moved out on your own? It's my understanding, from the things Marxy has told me, that your mother passed."

"Battling cancer," I said. "She was very brave."

"I had a cancer scare myself. Breast cancer. You should get screened for it regularly, by the way." I blinked and asked what that meant. "It means having a doctor check to make sure. Do you know how to examine yourself?"

I shook my head.

"If you ever have a lump. Here." She touched her chest. "You need to go to a doctor."

Marxy came to take more of the food away and asked why we were touching our boobs.

"Nothing. Girl stuff," Pearl said.

"Mom drank alcohol when I was inside of her, and then she got cancer and we had to move in with Uncle Richard."

"Uncle Richard."

I nodded. "He and Gert were not friends. They fought a lot."

"And you and Uncle Richard?"

"I didn't like when he hurt Gert."

Marxy brought in Tupperware containers and started putting food in them. She asked Marxy to get a plastic bag, and when he came back she put all the Tupperware containers into the bag and spun the top, then tied the arms of the plastic bag.

"How do you know how to do those things?"

Pearl laughed. "My mother was pretty strict when I was a kid. I learned every kind of domestic thing you could think of." She paused. "*Domestic* means—"

"About home and family. It was one of my Words of Today."

"Exactly."

I hugged Marxy and said I was sorry about Gert again, and Marxy gave me a kiss on the lips but didn't French.

"Have a good night, Zelda," Pearl said, handing me the plastic bag. "And tell Gert we should talk more. Seriously."

❧

Gert was sitting in the car, the window down, smoking a cigarette. He threw it on the ground when he saw me coming.

"Thanks for being a total fuck-dick," I said, getting in the car and slamming the door.

"Yeah, well." He started the engine. I reached over and turned the engine back off. He looked at me and threw up his hands. "Look, I'm sorry. That all just came out of nowhere. You should have told me. What happened to the rule about telling each other important things?"

"What about not telling me about school? You broke the rule first. Also I didn't know we were going to be talking about me and Marxy having sex."

"Can you stop saying that?"

"Sex?"

Gert said that the conversation was over. "I don't know what kind of perverted bullshit Dr. Laird says to you, but I'm going to have a talk with him."

"I am going to have sex."

"We'll see about that." He turned the car on.

"It's my legend."

"Not under my watch. No way, nohow."

We started driving. It was very dark on Marxy's street and even when we got out of his neighborhood it was hard to see the city now. I did not like how Gert was acting. He was looking out the windshield, even though it was being a mirror and you had to look through your own face to see the other cars. The way he was looking gave me the feeling he didn't want to be with me. It was not one of our rules—giving a silent treatment. Even if he wouldn't see me, I tried to make THE LOOK.

"I'll get my own apartment," I said. "With Marxy."

"And where are you going to get the money?"

"I'll get a job."

"Doing what?"

I crossed my arms. "I can do whatever I want."

"You don't have a job, you don't have any references. Do you even know how much having a place costs? Do you know how to pay the bills?"

"I can learn."

Gert snorted.

"Why did you do that?" I said.

"Do what?"

"Make that noise. You don't think I can learn."

While we drove, his phone started buzzing, and before he could grab it I got to it first.

"Gert's phone?" I said.

"Don't fuck around," Gert said, trying to grab the phone away from me. We stopped at a light and it changed and he had to start driving again.

"Five ten," the voice on the other end of the phone said.

"Gert is an asshole," I said to the person on the phone. "Did you know that?"

"Zelda, I'm serious. Give it."

Gert got the phone away from me.

"I think the person hung up," I said.

"What did they say?"

"Some numbers."

Gert pulled the car into the parking lot of a Dunkin' Donuts. He was dialing a number on his phone and then put it to his ear, waiting for someone to answer. Nobody answered. He said I needed to tell him what the numbers were.

"I don't know," I said. "Five something."

"Five what?"

"I'll tell you if you turn the car around and drive back to Marxy's."

"Five what, Zelda? This is important. Five eight? Six? What?"

His phone buzzed again. Gert picked it up and listened. He reached across and opened the glove compartment and took out a pen. Then he pointed at my feet, where garbage from McDonald's was in crumpled balls.

I did not know what he wanted.

"Napkin," Gert said, covering up the phone with his hand. He wrote some numbers on the napkin, and hung up the phone.

Gert spread the napkin on the dashboard with one hand while he drove with the other. He dialed a phone number, reading off of the napkin. He put the phone to his ear, told the person on the other end, "Five minutes," and told whoever it was to be ready.

We started driving again. "You've got limitations," Gert said. "It's a fact, I'm sorry to say, but it's true. Do I wish things were different? I do. But, Jesus Christ, Zelda. If you got pregnant, what would happen then?"

"I'd have a baby," I said, not very loud. "That's what would happen."

⌇

Gert parked on a street behind a school that was closed up, with boards in the windows. Gert would not tell me why we were there, or who we were waiting for. He just told me I had to stay in the car and then went outside.

Before he did he clicked the button to lock the doors so that I couldn't get out. These are called child locks, and because I am not a child I know that there is a secret way for me to get out if I need to, which is the button on the driver's door, beside where Gert's knee goes when we drive.

He walked out toward a playground. I could see Toucan, and the Fat Man.

When Gert came back he had one of the gym bags. He opened the trunk and threw the bag in. He got back into the car and turned it on.

"Why do you have to keep doing what Toucan says?" I said. "I think he's a villain."

We drove away from the school and back toward home.

When Gert got mad he always drove fast, and I could tell he was mad because he went through stop signs without stopping fully. He had no right to be mad. I was the one whose dinner he had ruined.

That was when a police car came up behind us. The sirens shouted at us and Gert looked in the mirror. The police car stayed behind us, the lightbulb on top of it spinning around and around. Gert pulled over the car.

"Fuck," Gert said. He hit the steering wheel with his hand before turning the car off. "Motherfucker," he said.

The police car parked behind us. I turned around to see it better and Gert told me not to turn around. Gert closed his eyes and took a deep breath. He hit the steering wheel again with his hands. The policeman stayed in the car and did not come out right away.

"This wouldn't be happening if we were still at Marxy's having dinner, instead of fuck-dicking with Toucan."

The policeman got out of the car and started walking up to our car.

"Just," Gert said, rolling down his window, "just don't say anything. Okay? Be quiet."

The policeman was tall and skinny and pulled his belt up a bit when he walked.

"I'm serious," Gert said one last time while the policeman walked toward us. "Just don't say anything."

The police officer leaned over the car. His flashlight made my eyes hurt. He asked if Gert knew why he had been pulled over. Gert said that he didn't know.

"You went through at least two stop signs," the officer said.

Before Gert could say anything, I said, "My brother is a shit-heel who doesn't like to talk about sex."

The policeman stared at me. Then he asked Gert to step out of the car. Gert reached across from me and took out some papers from the glove box.

I was so mad at the way he behaved during dinner that when Gert got out of the car, I got out of the car.

"Miss," the police officer said.

"He thinks he is the king of everything, but he's not."

Turning to the police officer, Gert said, "She has cognitive issues."

The officer kept chewing his gum and said, "Is that right?"

The policeman took the papers from Gert and flipped through

them. He told us to go back into the car, and we both did, and he went back to the police car with the papers. Gert got mad and asked what the fuck was I thinking.

"I told you not to say anything."

"And I told you dinner was important and you ruined it."

We stopped shouting when the police officer came back and handed Gert his papers. He said he would let us go with a warning. After the policeman drove off, Gert did not start the car right away. Then he opened the car door and got out.

I asked him why we weren't going home.

Gert took three steps toward the side of the road and stopped.

After a while he bent over and threw up.

chapter ten

did not want to talk to Gert for the rest of the night. It was a silent protest, like what Gandhi did to the British people. Vikings can use their swords to defeat enemies, but there were other ways too.

Before bedtime, Gert knocked on the door of my bedroom. I told him he couldn't come in but he opened the door, just a little, anyway. I spent all night sending apologies to Marxy, who did not respond.

"Can we talk for a second?" he asked.

"No."

"Well, too bad."

He came in and sat down on the spinny chair at my desk. "I'm sorry. I already said it ten times."

"Say it a million times, see if I care."

I turned away from him and faced the white wall. There was a piece of old tape stuck there and I scratched it off. Gert did not leave the room. I kept scratching even though the tape came off very fast.

"Can you stop that?"

"No."

He sat on the bed. The springs that lived inside of the mattress creaked. "You know, I spend so much of my time making sure you have everything you need." I could smell his armpits. His deodorant had stopped working. He said, "You think this stuff comes with a rule book? I have no fucking idea what I'm doing half the time. Can you cut me some slack for once?"

He touched my back between the shoulders, which gave me an electric shock and made me even madder for the way he screwed up the dinner with Marxy.

"You stink and are a villain and you lied to me and acted dishonorably," I said, and without looking I grabbed something off the table beside my bed and threw it at him. The something ended up being my alarm clock. He must have not been watching, or maybe the room was so dark that he couldn't see it, because the alarm clock hit him in his face and bounced off the bed and onto the floor.

His hand went up to his face and he turned away.

"Screw the shit-off," I said.

"Fuck," he said, holding his face. He kept his hands there so that he looked like he was wearing a mask made of his fingers. Then he took his hand away and the fingers had blood on them, and his nose had blood on it too.

I did not mean to make him bleed and tried to tell him that.

He was gone and slammed the door before I could get all the words out.

I turned on my "Sounds of the Ocean" music that lets you think you're at sea. The music has dolphins and whales and birds and the waves crashing, so it's easy to imagine being on a boat with Vikings, rowing somewhere under the sun. If I imagine hard enough I can almost smell the ocean.

I didn't mean to throw the alarm clock at Gert's face. I just meant to throw it somewhere.

After a while I opened my door, very quietly, and stuck my head out to see what was going on. Gert's door wasn't closed all the way. I went into the hallway and stood outside his room.

The bedside lamp was on, and Gert was hunched over on the edge of his bed. Sweat made his head look like he'd dipped it in a bowl of water. His tattoos were now a very weird green color in the light and made his arms and chest look dirty. I couldn't see my favorite tattoo of his, an eagle, a very powerful bird, that he has on his chest. Even though he was getting fat, he still had muscles on his shoulders and arms, big muscles with veins that reminded me of worms just under his tanned skin.

I thought maybe he was thinking about how he was going to get mad at me, for throwing the clock and hurting his face. Then I heard him. He was crying. Not just normal crying. He was crying very seriously. His body started shaking. The green tattoos crinkled as the muscles under them got big and then small.

He looked up and I saw that his nose had a bandage taped onto it with Scotch tape. The air was thick and felt like it was about to rain.

"Góðan dag?" I said quietly, opening the door a little bit more.

Gert made a throaty sound and said, "Close the door."

I opened my mouth and started to say words that I didn't know wanted to come out, sorry and things like that. He stood up and said, "CLOSE THE DOOR," in a really loud voice that Gert only uses when he's very serious, so I closed the door and ran to my room and put my pillow over my head.

⇗

The morning after our fight, I woke up and remembered that I had been a shit-heel. One of the rules that Gert and I had was that he would never hurt me, and I would never hurt him, in combat. We could say villainous words, but fighting with our hands or other weapons was not allowed. I had broken a very important rule by hitting him with the alarm clock.

The Word of Today I picked was very powerful, since I looked it up especially and did not use the special calendar that tells you what the Word of Today is supposed to be.

It was supposed to be *collateral*, which was okay but not the right word. I wanted to find a special word to say sorry, and so the Word of Today was *contrition*, which means feeling bad about something you did and feeling "contrite."

"I am contrite for hitting you in the face," I said to myself. "I feel contrition for hitting you in the face. People who hit members of their tribe who they love should have contrition."

I went into the kitchen and Gert was making breakfast. He had a Band-Aid on his face.

"Morning," he said. There were eggs in the frying pan.

"Good morning," I said. "I have contrition for hitting you in the face with the alarm clock."

"You have what?"

"Contrition. That's a special Word of Today. It means—"

"I know what it means." He cracked another egg onto the pan and scooped up the first egg onto a plate.

"I'm sorry I hit you with the alarm clock," I said.

"I know you are," he said. "And I'm sorry for what happened, that I messed up your dinner."

"*You didn't* mess up *our* dinner," I corrected. "Pearl and I had a very good talk."

He brought over the plate of eggs and put it in front of me, with some toast on it.

I asked him a question I had been thinking about asking him all last night. "Why are you friends with Toucan? He is a shit-heel villain."

Gert wiped his hands on a paper towel and sat down across from me. "Yeah. He kind of is. And I wouldn't say we're friends."

"He's not part of our tribe."

"No. Definitely not."

"So? Why did you have to go see him?"

He put down the knife and fork. "Look. He helped us with some money, when we moved from Uncle Richard's. That's the truth. Okay?"

"I don't like him," I said, cutting open the eggs and watching the yolk spill out. "He's a thug."

"People say that about me." He dipped his toast into the yolk on his plate. "How are the eggs?"

"Good," I said. "Yellow. And you're not a thug. You are a hero."

"Well." He sighed. "Okay. Toucan got us out of a bad spot."

He said that I might not have noticed, but things were not good with Uncle Richard. Gert said that Uncle Richard acted nice sometimes and was angry for no reason other times. And that he was creepy.

Gert said, "Remember the time he walked in while you were in the shower?"

"Yeah," I said. "He said it was an accident."

"I call bullshit on that." Gert took a sip of his water. "Remember how I started doing your laundry?"

"I thought you were being nice."

"Yeah, and I didn't want him touching your underwear."

I thought about being on the couch with Uncle Richard, the night of the big fight with Gert, and how he was touching me.

"Is that why you didn't like talking about sex at Marxy's house?"

"I didn't like talking about sex because you're my sister and it's gross, that's why. Anyway, what I'm trying to say is that I needed to get us out of there, and borrowing money from Toucan was the only way we could do it fast."

He got up and said he would do the dishes.

"I accept your contrition," he said, giving me a dab.

I got ready and thought about him owing money to Toucan, which I did not like. I took out the jar under my bed where I have been saving money and counted it out.

I had thirty seven dollars and fifty cents.

Before going down to catch the bus, I asked Gert how much money he owned Toucan.

"It's owed, not owned. And why?"

I gave him the money I had been saving. It was a lot of bills and a few coins. He looked at the money in his hand. "I already told you to keep it," he said.

No, I told him. "I will help you pay off our debt to Toucan. I would like to put it in our bank account. This time you are not going to say no."

"It's not our bank account, it's mine, and what you've got won't even make a dent. This is your hoard." He put it back in the jar and shook it. "You don't need a bank account, Zee. If you need money, just ask."

chapter eleven

Even when Gert was working in the gas station, before his scholarship and before the money helped us get a place far away from Uncle Richard, he made sure that I could go to the library and the Community Center. We did not have very much money, but Gert is powerful at surviving life's battles.

I knew that people do things they do not want to do to contribute to the hoard. It is like a sacrifice, only instead of lighting things on fire, or killing animals to make Odin and the other gods happy, you sacrifice yourself and instead of doing the things you want to do, you have to do things for other people.

According to my list of THINGS LEGENDS NEED, I needed to get money to make the tribe more powerful and to protect Gert against Toucan.

Gert had always sacrificed so much. Now I wanted to make a sacrifice for the good of our tribe, which right now had me and Gert and AK47, even though she and Gert were not a couple at this time. Also, Gert did not believe I could contribute to the tribe's hoard, and I wanted to show him that that was not right.

On Monday, on the bus to the Community Center, I went and sat down next to Hamsa, putting my backpack on the ground. It was a day off for AK47, so another person was driving the bus. He did not return my dab as I got on. He just said, "Good morning," and did not say anything else.

"Yoda usually sits there," Hamsa said. "You'll need to move when we go to his house to pick him up."

I told him I knew about their rule and would move. I just wanted to ask him about his job, which was cleaning dishes at a restaurant.

"Oh," Hamsa said. "It makes my hands look like prunes." And he held up his hands to show me that the skin was all wrinkled.

"Like prunes," I said, and Hamsa nodded and went back to looking out the window.

"I have another question," I told him.

"We're almost at Yoda's," he said, tapping the glass of the window.

I told him I would be quick with my question. I asked how he got the job, since it is hard for people like us to get jobs, and in this economy, Google says, it is hard for everyone to get work.

"My uncle owns it," Hamsa said. Then he saw Yoda, standing on the sidewalk, and waved. "There is Yoda. You'll need to move," Hamsa said.

The bus stopped and I picked up my bag and stood up. "Can I get a job there?"

"You should talk to Big Todd," the driver said as I was getting out of the seat. "There's a program for that kind of thing, I think."

"You aren't Muslim," Hamsa said. "You have to be Muslim to work at the restaurant."

Yoda got on the bus and I moved to another seat. He was right. I was a Viking, not a Muslim.

〉

At the Community Center, Big Todd rubbed his face. We were in his office, which was small and had a desk and a chair and books on a shelf.

There was a basketball game going on in the gym, but getting a job to help Gert was more important and I told Big Todd that I needed his help.

"Hamsa has a job, so why can't I have one?"

"You never acted interested before," Big Todd said.

"I want one now. All Vikings have jobs, even if the job is fighting."

"Well, I probably can't get you a job fighting."

He took out a binder from a drawer in his desk. It was gargantuan, with papers and plastic sheets hanging out. It flopped open like an accordion on the desk.

"Okay. So, we're a bit late in the season. What type of stuff are you interested in? I mean, besides Vikings. We have partnerships with a few places."

I thought about what I could say. "I like movies," I said. "And reading *Kepple's Guide to the Vikings*. And running and basketball." I almost said, "Thinking about Marxy," but that was not a job.

Big Todd wrote things down on his pad of paper, then started flipping through the book. "Okay," he said. "Let me put in some calls. Does Gert know?"

"Gert is not part of this quest," I said.

Big Todd nodded. "Okay. Fair enough." He stopped flipping through the pages and made a teepee out of his hands. He blew out his cheeks.

᛫

Big Todd gave me papers to read with questions I was supposed to answer while he tried to figure out where I could work. The paper was called "Ten Things to Know Before Your First Job Interview." The things to know were:

- Don't lie on your résumé (which is pronounced res-oo-may).
- Find a job that interests you. (I wasn't interested in working at

Hamsa's uncle's restaurant, but Vikings have to do things they
don't want to do for their tribes.)

- Read about the company. (I would take notes on a piece of paper
before an interview.)
- Dress for success. (The article said to make sure I dressed like I was
a professional person who the company would want to hire.)

There was also a list of questions that an employer would ask in an
interview. The article said I should know how to answer the questions
before I tried to get the job. I made sure to practice what to say, which
was what the "Ten Things to Know Before Your First Job Interview"
article told me to do.

Question One: Why are you applying for this job?
I wrote that it was time I began contributing to the well-being of my
tribe and that having a job will help me repay the tribe's debts.

Question Two: What are your strengths as a worker?
Being a Viking, I am powerful and defeat enemies. I don't give up
during battles. I am a hard worker.

Question Three: What are some of your weaknesses as a worker?
I wasn't sure what to say. I am not a very big person, but Gert says
that I am a warrior.

Big Todd came in and told me that he had found me a job interview
at the library, which was actually a perfect place for me to work.
"They said they *might* have a position."
I looked up. "Really?"
Big Todd said that I should probably dress nicely for the interview.
It was going to happen in two days.

"A real interview? Not practice?" I asked.

"Yes, ma'am. As for what to wear, it doesn't have to be super fancy," he said. "But it can't be what you usually wear either. It's important to dress for success." When I asked what that meant, he said, "Think of when warriors go to fight. They have to wear armor. It's what people who do battle wear, right? Well, people who go to job interviews wear skirts and nice blouses. Do you have any of those?"

I did have a skirt, but I had no blouse, which is a fancy shirt. "You should talk to Annie," Big Todd said. "She can probably help."

⌁

I called AK47 when I got home and almost forgot to take off my shoes.

"Hey, buttercup. What's going on?" she said.

I felt like I was going to explode so I shouted into the phone, "I HAVE A JOB INTERVIEW AT THE LIBRARY."

"Easy, homie," she said. "I know. Big Todd called me. You have, what, a day and change until your interview?"

I counted. "Forty-three hours and forty-seven minutes," I said, since the interview was early in the morning. She said that she had already cleared some time that afternoon to go shopping with me, since it was her day off.

Before she came I made sure to write a note saying to Gert that I was going to the mall with AK47 and stuck it to the table, where we usually stuck our notes. Then I shut my door and looked at the Word of Today, which was *consultation*, meaning to meet and discuss and "consult" with someone about a topic. I consulted myself about my closet. I had never had a job interview or a job before. The nicest clothes I had was a skirt that AK47 had lent me and forgot about and did not fit either of us anymore.

⌇

AK47 picked me up in her car and we went to the mall. The store she wanted to go to was The Gap.

We went inside and AK47 showed me three skirts to try on. The first two were black and loose and they did not fit. The third one was fancy and did fit.

"All right," she said. "Let's see you move in this thing."

I walked out of the changing room and it was hard to walk. The fancy skirt was very tight. I told AK47 that it was definitely not for doing battle in.

"You got that right." She came over and turned me around. "It looks good, though. It makes your ass look nice but not slutty."

"We don't want slutty," I said.

"No. Definitely not for a job interview at the library."

She also made me try on a bunch of different shirts, the kind that button up in the front. I liked the bright-pink one. She said blue was probably more professional.

"The funky colors, save those for special occasions. Strip shows, funerals, things like that. Here. Try this one."

I started to ask why I would go to a strip show and then realized she was joking and laughed. Once we had picked out a skirt and blouse, she also got me a pair of pantyhose, which are like socks only they go all the way up your legs and you can kind of see through them. They make your legs look smooth.

"Which is what you want. You don't want to have to be shaving your legs all the time."

"I don't shave my legs very much," I said.

"Me neither. But if you're going to be doing public work, you sometimes need to. It sucks, and pantyhose, whether you like them or not, are the things professional employers like the ones you're after want to see."

She showed me how to put them on. Then she showed me how to tuck the blouse into the pantyhose so that they smoothed out the blouse, and how the silver clasp above the zipper in the back made the skirt stay on. Once we were done, she stood back and looked at me.

She whistled.

"Not bad, not bad," she said. "What do you think?"

The skirt was tight around my waist and the pantyhose felt like someone was squeezing me. AK47 said that was good, that was how it was supposed to feel.

"It's the burden of our sex," she said.

As a treat, AK47 paid for the clothes and said it was a loan when I tried to tell her that I had my own money in my hoard. "But if you really feel bad, you can pay me back with your first paycheck."

"It's a deal," I said. "Vikings always pay their debts."

We walked out with the shopping bags, and instead of leaving the mall AK47 took me to another store. It was a special place, she said. It sold underwear only, which was confusing, since I did not understand how you could have a whole store for something that nobody ever saw.

"Well," AK47 said, "that's not entirely true. *Some* people see the underwear, besides just you." She said to trust her. "Come on," she said, pulling me past naked mannequins who had only bright-colored bras and panties on. "We're going deep."

⇗

I had never been to a fancy underwear store. All the clothes were in small stacks. Pictures and posters of beautiful women in their underwear hung on the walls. It was weird, since the people shopping acted like they didn't actually mean to be in there. Why did they act like they were in the wrong store? If you wanted to buy nice underwear, why would you pretend you don't?

"Because people are afraid of sex," AK47 said.

"I'm not."

"No, but you're not a complete Puritan either."

"Marxy's mom said they weren't puritan-something at dinner."

"It means prude. As in, uncomfortable with sex."

"Like Gert."

"Ha. In no universe is Gert a prude," said AK47. She held up some underwear. They were bright red and lacy, which means you can see through them, sort of. "What do you think of these?"

She handed me the red lacy underwear. I stretched them and I could almost see my fingers right through them.

"Why would someone want to see through your underwear?"

"Because it's sexy," AK47 said.

"Did you wear sexy underwear for Gert?" I asked, and she laughed.

"Zee, your brother didn't like me wearing *any* underwear."

"Oh."

She folded the underwear and put it back on the table. There were so many stacks of underwear and bras and other things I didn't understand how to wear. It was like a zoo of underwear and sexiness.

The saleswoman came over and asked how we were doing. "Are you finding everything okay?"

"We're not Puritans," I said. "But we don't want underwear we can see through."

The saleswoman looked at AK47, who shrugged. "We're looking for something not too slutty, but kind of provocative."

She showed me a lot of different panties. I was surprised at how many types there were. At home, Gert had boxers, and I had panties that were either white or blue or green. Nothing lace or red or sexy. I could not imagine Gert finding any sexy underwear while doing our laundry. He would be very confused.

I took the underwear we found into the changing room.

I stared at myself in the mirror. The light above me was powerful and shone down on me like the sun. I patted my stomach. It was very hard from my Viking training. All of the women in the advertisements of the underwear store were tall and had big breasts. I tried to make my lips like theirs, pushing them out. Then I put on one pair of the underwear that the store woman gave me and the bra that was the same red. I turned around and around. Using my hands I tried to make my hair flat and turned to show the mirror my sexy pose.

"How's it look?" The saleswoman knocked on the door. "Need a pair of eyes?"

She meant did I need someone to see. I opened the door and stood in front of her and told her I felt powerful.

"You look great," she said.

AK47 was standing beside her and nodded. "A bit on the marm side," she said, "but I like what I'm seeing."

When we left the store, we decided to go to a movie together, to celebrate shopping. The movie was about a soldier who is not in a war anymore and has a lot of secrets that the Army doesn't want the world to know. The Army kills the soldier's family and he gets revenge. There was a lot of action and shooting and I did not like watching it and had to leave the movie theater.

AK47 found me in the parking lot outside of the theater. She sat down next to me on the curb, where it was quiet.

"Hey, I thought you liked action movies?" she asked.

I shrugged. I did. "Why do people buy guns if they aren't going to do battle?"

"It gives them power, you know?" She put her arm around me. "Hey. What's going on?"

"Nothing," I said. But she gave me THE LOOK and I started crying, because I remembered about Toucan and Gert and the gun and the Midterm Exam and everything.

"Something's going on. You're doing the thing you do when you're stressed out." She touched my hand. "Come on. You can trust me."

AK47 gave my hand another squeeze, and I felt like if I didn't tell her I would explode.

chapter twelve

blurted it out. I didn't mean to. I said Gert had a gun and hadn't been going to class and was a liar. AK47 lost her shit and got very angry, which for her meant becoming quiet. In many ways this is scarier than when someone gets angry loud. You do not know what a person who is quiet and angry will do next.

When we got in the car, AK47 drummed the steering wheel and didn't start the car.

She was giving me THE LOOK.

AK47 is fearless. When it comes to Viking things, she is the person most like the Valkyries. That was one of the reasons why Gert fell in love with her. She could take his shit. Other people are afraid of him, but he is afraid of AK47, especially when she gives him THE LOOK.

"She's giving me THE LOOK, Zee," Gert would say. Or: "I know that look."

THE LOOK is like a missile, which actually didn't exist in the time of Vikings. A missile goes from one place to another and explodes the villains. AK47 does THE LOOK and like a missile it explodes whoever she shoots it at. Gert is not a villain, but sometimes he does villain things and she needs to explode him back to normal.

I have tried to learn how to do THE LOOK. It is a good way to become powerful in battle, where you have to use every weapon you have.

I liked to practice my own LOOK in the mirror. One of the things
that makes AK47 good at sending THE LOOK like a missile is her
eyebrows, which are very black and like caterpillars. They bend in the
middle when she is angry, and when she is really angry and wants to de-
stroy whoever she's looking at, they actually bend in a lot of places. Her
eyes are brown and sometimes I think when she's doing THE LOOK
they become black.

Even when she did start the car, she was doing THE LOOK the
entire ride home, giving it to the road, to the other cars, to the steering
wheel.

While she drove I worried that I had done the wrong thing and betrayed Gert. But AK47 was someone I knew I could trust, and I knew
that she loved Gert and Gert loved her.

She parked in front of our building, in a place you couldn't park in
for a long time. She didn't even turn the blinkers on that she used to
show people that she was not going to stay long.

She shut off the engine. She didn't let go of the steering wheel,
which she was holding on to like she was hanging off the edge of a cliff
and the steering wheel was the only thing she could grab to stop her
from falling.

We sat there for a second.

"I'm so frigging pissed, Zelda," AK47 said. "You have no idea. A
freaking gun. In the apartment. Do you have any idea how dangerous
that is?"

"I know, which is why I told you."

"Right. Yeah. You did the right thing." She patted my leg. "Good
work. And this school crap? He has to keep a full course load to keep his
scholarship. He can't just drop a class like that. Especially not a prereq."

Prereqs are things you need to do before you can do anything else.

We went upstairs, carrying our shopping bags, to our apartment door. I got out my key but AK47 was already unlocking it with hers, which I did not know she still had.

Gert was inside watching TV and eating cereal on his lap.

"Hey, how was the movie?" he said to me. And then he saw AK47. "What's she doing here?"

"Shut up," AK47 said.

He ignored her. "Zelda, why is this person in the apartment who I said I never want to see in the apartment ever again?"

When she started giving him shit, Gert told her to mind her own business, which was when I said, "It is her business, because it's my business too. I am passing her all of the business."

"Guns, Gert. Seriously?" AK47 shook her head. "And these gang-bangers you've been hanging around with?"

"Stop being melodramatic," Gert said.

"You don't think I hear things?" AK47 said. "Everyone knows you're dealing."

I did not know what this meant and asked if someone could explain what was going on.

"I'm not your rescue project," Gert said. He put the cereal bowl down and got up and went to the door, walking past us and opening it. He told AK47 to get the hell out.

AK47 said she wouldn't leave until he gave her the gun. When Gert said there was no gun, AK47 pointed at me and said, "She said she found a gun. In the metal box. Are you calling her a liar?"

"Sounds like one of her Viking fantasies," Gert said.

"Shut up!" I said. "You had a gun in the metal box and two hundred and forty dollars in the envelope in the bag and you lied about the study group!"

AK47 got right in his face and then pushed him.

"You motherfucker," she said. "You want her to get shot?"

By now she was yelling and pushing him and he was trying to stop her from hitting his face. Gert told her to stop being hysterical and AK47 said, "Oh, you want to see hysterical?" and started trying to punch him. He turned her around and held her in a backward bear hug. Then she bit into his hand and he said, "MOTHERFUCKER," and then blood came out of his hand.

He pushed her away and held up his hand, while she flew into the wall with a thump.

I could not see the Grendels, but I could hear them, making their noises and clawing from inside of the walls.

I realized that I was crying because suddenly their faces became blurry and snot came out of my nose in a river.

"Stop it stop it stop it," I kept saying.

Everything was moving very quickly, and I did not like watching them.

I went into the hallway, where it was quiet and where two people I loved from the same tribe weren't fighting. I closed our front door and sat against the wall. I stayed there and held my head.

Alf had come out of his apartment and asked me what was going on.

"It sounds like goddamn downtown Iraq in there," he said.

I told him that Gert and AK47 were fighting, and then there was a loud boom and before I could tell him not to go inside, Alf opened the door.

I got up and followed him. He clapped his hands to try to get their attention and to be quiet.

"You guys need to chill the fuck out or I'm going to call the police," Alf said. "Especially you, Big Man."

Big Man was Gert.

"What?" Gert said.

"Chill the fuck out," Alf said, and he stepped between Gert and AK47, who were now on opposite sides of the apartment. AK47 was in the kitchen and Gert was in the living room, and Alf went and stood in the space between them.

That was a bad idea. Gert doesn't like when people get in his way and he was already getting close to becoming a Berserker.

Berserkers are special Vikings who are savage, meaning they are like robots whose only job is to win battles and kill their enemies. They are also called *Úlfhéðnar*, a word I didn't know how to pronounce, even with the Google speaking program on the computer. The problem with Berserkers is that they are so mean and angry that when they fight you can't talk to them, so sometimes they get so angry that they become villains themselves.

Gert pushed Alf off. Alf bounced against the wall and tripped over the coffee table. Then Gert wasn't arguing with AK47 anymore. He was ready to fight Alf, who was walking backward and holding his hands up.

"Gert," AK47 said, and tried to grab him.

Things started moving very quickly, like a basketball spinning on a finger with the person slapping the ball to make it go faster and faster, until the lines on the ball disappear.

Gert hit Alf very fast and hard, and then Alf fell down. And in a second Gert sat on top of Alf, whose little arms tried to stop Gert from punching.

It did not take very long before Alf's face turned red and he started bleeding out of his mouth and nose.

My head started squishing even more then, because my brother was being a very ugly villain and going Berserker.

Gert kept holding Alf by the neck but he turned and saw AK47, who was pointing at me and shouting for him to stop. He blinked and then he was not a Berserker anymore.

"Fuck," he said.

Alf coughed when Gert let him go, holding his neck. He was having trouble breathing.

Gert walked backwards. His stomach went in and out very quickly. "Fuck," he said again.

AK47 bent down and touched Alf's shoulder.

"Get out of here," AK47 said, helping Alf up. "Please. Just go."

The Grendels were so loud now that I could not hear anything else, and the sounds they made made it hard for me to see.

❧

One of the things I have trouble with is when Gert acts villainously. Even though Alf should have minded his own business and not tried to act like a warrior in front of AK47 to try to impress her, he is also a lot smaller than Gert, and older, and is not a very good warrior.

AK47 and Gert made a tent around me with their arms, so that the only thing I could see was their shirts. With them around me the world slowed down and got quieter.

"It's all right," Gert said. He was whispering to me, in my ear. "It's all right, Zelda. It's okay."

AK47 was kneeling down next to us and helped Gert lift me up. The Grendels were still growling, but not as loud. I opened my eyes.

"There we go," Gert said.

"I should—" AK47 pointed at the door. "I should get going."

Gert reached out for her. "Can you stay a minute? Please?"

I brought my knees up to my chest and pretended I was a gargantuan stone and inside of me was calm. The more like a stone I could make my arms and legs and head and body, the calmer the inside parts of me could get.

"Okay," Gert said. "Are you okay?" He was walking around in circles and couldn't sit still. Some Berserker was still inside of him.

"No," I said.

AK47 told Gert to sit down and stop stressing everyone out.

"Sit," she said, and Gert came over and acted like he didn't know where to sit down. "It doesn't have to be next to me," AK47 said.

I was sitting in the leather chair, the one with the legs that go up, though we couldn't make the legs go up, since something in the chair was broken and the legs would get stuck.

"We shouldn't have fought like that," AK47 said to me. "Let's get that out of the way. Right?"

She said that to Gert, who was walking around shaking his head. "Right?"

"Right," he said.

"And Gert shouldn't have kicked the crap out of that old man. So you need to apologize for that too."

Gert turned to me and said he was sorry. "But he had no business coming into our apartment."

I told him that Alf was weaker, and that heroes protect the weak, not fight them. Gert said that he knows that.

"You should be in school," I said. "Why aren't you in school? And what about the gun?"

"The billion-dollar questions," AK47 said.

Gert shook his head. He didn't like to be asked questions by people. He was the question-asker. He scratched his bald head, which wasn't as bald as it usually was. Little hairs were trying to poke through and were a shadow on his head.

"Look," Gert said, "the gun isn't loaded. Okay? It's just for show. For protection."

AK47 folded her arms across her chest. "So there *is* a gun."

"See?" I said.

"I keep it locked up, and in the metal box."

"So how did Zelda find it then?"

Gert turned to me. "My room was locked. What were you doing in there?"

My face became hot, until AK47 told me it was okay, nobody was mad. So I said that everyone at the college said that he was kicked out of school, and that he was telling me he was going to school, and that I went to look for proof.

I felt like we were not talking about the most important thing, which was Gert not being in school. "You are supposed to be in school," I said. "Because you are smart and want to get a good job and ride in nice cars and go on vacations on the beach."

AK47 made a snorting sound with her nose. "Okay, Scarface," she said. *Scarface* is Gert's favorite movie, even though Al Pacino dies at the end after getting shot a hundred times and has a nice car and takes nice vacations.

"She's right, though. How many classes are you failing?" AK47 asked.

Gert sat down on the chair across from hers. He looked at his hand, which was purple from punching. "Just a couple."

"Fuck that," AK47 said. "Sorry, Zelda. But it's definitely a swearing time."

"I think so too," I said. "Fuck that not going to school."

"Can you go back?" AK47 asked.

He stood up and said he needed water. He went to the kitchen, and AK47 said she was sorry too. I asked her for what, and she said, "For coming here like Rambo," which was another one of Gert's favorite movies. When Gert came back with a glass of water, he said that he should have told me that he wasn't defeating school.

"I could have helped," I said.

"No offense, Zee, but this is above your pay grade," he said.

"I thought you were doing okay," AK47 said. "And we could always study together, even if we're not talking. I don't mind helping. And who the hell is Toucan?"

Gert stared at me. "Nobody."

"Gert."

Gert stretched out his fingers and wiggled them. "He helped us move."

"Like rented a truck?"

"Like lent me money. He's a friend. An old friend. From when I played football."

Gert didn't smile like I thought he would. He looked like he had just suffered a major defeat in battle. AK47 went to the fridge and got a bag of frozen vegetables. She gave it to Gert to put on his hand.

"Now, let's get this gun bullshit taken care of."

We went to Gert's room, and he went into his closet and took out the metal box and opened it.

AK47 said she would get rid of the gun. Gert tried to argue and then his hand started hurting and he didn't have the energy to argue anymore.

"Fine, take it."

Even though there was no sound after that, it was like a bomb was exploding. AK47 was wearing THE LOOK and when she stopped wearing it her face was the face she gave him when they were boyfriend and girlfriend. Gert had on a face like that too.

I did not like how angry and quiet the air felt. "Can someone say something?"

AK47 put her bag down. She kicked off her shoes.

"I'm still pissed off at you," she said to Gert.

"I am too," I said.

Gert said that he knew all that. He got up and walked over to AK47 and they stood looking at each other for a long time. Then AK47 said, "Zelda, can you go out and play for a little while?"

"You are going to have sex," I said. "Aren't you?"

AK47 took Gert's not-hurt hand and said, "It appears that that's the case."

"I'll put on my headphones," I said.

We walked down the hallway, Gert and AK47 holding hands and

walking first, and me walking behind them. When I got to my room, I closed my door. I was victorious for one part of my legend: Gert and AK47 were in love with each other and having sex, even if Gert was still not in school, like I wanted him to be.

I took out a pen and put a check mark next to GET AK47 AND GERT BACK TOGETHER from my list of things to do to be legendary.

It was a very powerful moment. I decided to share it with Dr. Kepple, so I went to my computer and clicked on his website, which I had bookmarked.

Dear Dr. Kepple,

Hello again. It's Zelda. You still haven't answered my last e-mail, but that is okay, since you are probably busy studying Vikings. I am becoming very skilled at using my sword and would say that I could defeat most of the villains I have read about in your book. I mentioned my Viking sword, if you remember. And I have succeeded in getting Gert and AK47 back together, an important part of my legend.

However, I have some questions about Viking hoards that Kepple's Guide to the Vikings *does not answer. On page 174 you say that Viking tribes went to war with other tribes and pillaged, which means to take treasure from other places that you have defeated. Are there any ways that Vikings get hoards, other than pillaging? I also have an interview at a library for a job. (I don't know if Vikings have libraries, so that is another question you can answer.) Thank you for reading, and have a good day.*

Skál,
Zelda

chapter thirteen

That night, after Gert and AK47 went to bed and I sent my letter to Dr. Kepple, I set my alarm clock so I could wake up early, before Gert and AK47, and make them a feast of a breakfast to celebrate her coming back to the tribe. They had sex a long time, I could hear them, and I started to wonder about having sex with Marxy and fell asleep and wanted to dream about it but didn't.

When my alarm clock went off Gert's door was open, he was still asleep inside on the bed, lying down face-first. AK47 was at the front of the apartment, putting on her shoes to leave.

"Where are you going?" I asked.

She put her finger to my mouth to shush me. "Let him sleep," she said.

I lowered my voice and asked where she was going. AK47 stood up and whispered, "No offense, Zee, but this isn't a happy ending."

"But you and Gert had sex."

She put her finger to her mouth again and pointed to the hallway so we could talk there.

"Yeah, we had sex," she said, closing the door behind us. "And?"

"And you love each other."

"I know you think all stories have to end in a perfect way," she said. "Life is complicated. You can love someone and they can be bad for you, or not right. I'm just not sure."

"But you can always be perfect for each other and help each other become strong," I said back.

She sighed. "Zelda. He doesn't want help. Okay?"

I ran in front of her and put up my arms and said, "YOU SHALL NOT PASS." She tried to walk past me and I kept standing in front of her.

"Come on, move," she said, and I told her I was moving, and jumped in front of her again.

She stopped trying to get around me. "Are you hungry?" she asked. "A little."

"Well, I'm hitting McDonald's before work. If you want, you can come plead your case. But I'm too hangry to be human on an empty stomach."

ᛉ

We waited in line at McDonald's and she explained why she didn't trust what Gert was saying, about getting on the right track and changing.

"As much as I'd like to think he's changed, after the last time we broke up, I can't throw myself headfirst into this shit. I just can't."

"He said he will not be involved with Toucan anymore."

"I don't know this Toucan asshole, but I know people like him. And if your brother owes him money, that's bad news."

"But that's why you should stay! You can be his fair maiden!"

"Honey, I'm nobody's fair maiden. Gert has to learn to take care of himself."

We got to the front of the line and ordered our food. AK47 liked the McMuffins and I liked pancakes.

"Look. For whatever reason, I have a soft spot for that asshole in my heart. Maybe it's because of poor role models growing up and I feel the need to save birds with broken wings."

"What if we make him go back?"

"Make him? The point is he has to start doing things himself. This was his chance."

"He can take courses again if he failed," I said. "You have to give heroes the chance to face defeat and then rise above it."

She put her McMuffin down. "Zelda."

"You are always talking about how I need to be given the chance to take care of myself and be my own legend, and you helped me pick out clothes for my job so I can be my best Viking self."

"It's not the same thing." AK47 didn't say anything for a few seconds. She stared out the window at a van that was trying to park into a space that was too small for it. "I just, I love him, I do. And I want things to work. But it's not so simple."

Then I thought about things that helped me in my legend, and I realized what Gert needed more than anything. "I think we should make rules for Gert to follow," I said. "We need a RULES FOR LIFE FOR GERT."

AK47 laughed.

"He's a grown man, and I don't know if you noticed, but your brother is very much against rules."

"I am a grown woman and rules help me," I said. "And these will be rules for the tribe. If he loves us, he will agree to follow them. Do you trust me?"

AK47 took a drink of her juice. "It's not about trusting you, it's about—"

"Do you?" I asked.

"Yeah, of course."

"Then I'm asking you to trust Gert and give him a chance to be a hero again."

AK47 put her juice down and wiped her mouth. I could tell she was thinking. Her brows were wiggling.

"Okay, but if he screws up, that's it."

"We will give him his rules and if he breaks them then that's it."

She smiled. "You're a good sister, you know that? He's lucky to have you."

"Us," I said. "He's lucky to have us, because we will keep him in line."

I dipped my hash brown into the maple syrup container until it was almost all covered with syrup and put it in my mouth. If Gert was here he would probably tell me to use less maple syrup and be less messy, even though it was me who ate the hash browns, not him. I wanted him to stop doing things like that. I was getting tired of rules that other people made for me. I wanted to make my own rules.

"When things are my business," I said, "I want them to be my business. I want to have my own business. Like the sex."

We talked about how Gert had gotten so angry about the idea of me and Marxy having sex. AK47 actually thought that Gert had a point, though she didn't agree fully with him.

"By point I mean, it's probably normal for him to feel weird about it. On the other hand, Marxy's mother is right. You do need to talk about it. And he needs to not get weird when someone says 'period.'"

"Maybe that should be one of the things on our RULES FOR GERT. No getting mad about sex and periods."

She nodded. "Good start." The rest of the McMuffin went into her mouth. She used one of her fingers to wipe extra cheese off her lips. After two chews she swallowed all of the food in her mouth. She pulled a pen out of her bag and clicked the tip out.

She flattened the receipt from the food on the table and stared down at it. She tapped the pen against her chin.

"I mean, we don't want to be too harsh," she said.

"I want you to be back together," I said. "Why would I make it harder for you to get together again?"

"Yeah, but I have him by the balls, and with your brother that almost never happens. I figure we can put our heads together and maybe get the most out of this, while he's ready to make concessions."

A concession could mean a stand, where hot dogs and soda are sold at basketball games, or it could mean giving something you don't want to give to another person, so that you can get something you want back.

AK47 and I were trying to figure out which concessions Gert would want to make so that he can get what he wants, to be back together with AK47. And actually, she wanted to get back together with him too, but for her it was backward. Her concession was getting together with Gert, since there is a lot of crap that is part of being together with my brother.

"He needs to cut the bullshit," I said. "Right?"

AK47 started writing on the receipt.

"Good. We have to make sure they're specific enough, you know? So that if he gets pissed we can have ammo to fire back at him. We need them to be demands. I've already confiscated the gun, so we can cross that off the list."

"What does *confiscated* mean?"

"I've taken it from him and will be getting rid of it. So we can cross that off our list of demands."

Demands are the opposite of concessions. When warring tribes meet to decide what happens next, if they don't want to fight with swords, they fight with words to figure out who gets what. They fight with demands.

AK47 had four demands to getting back together with Gert. They were "deal-breakers." She would not make concessions about any of them. They were:

1.   Gert would have to begin going to see Dr. Laird on his own again, which he'd stopped doing.

2. He would not sell pot anymore or be friends with people like Toucan, who is almost for sure a villain, AK47 said, since she asked around and apparently a lot of people believe he is a "shady motherfucker." Shady motherfuckers are worse than fuck-dicks and shit-heels combined, according to AK47.

3. Gert would do summer school in order to make up for the credits he lost when he dropped courses.

4. He would throw away his gun.

We put a check mark next to Number 4, because AK47 had taken away the gun.

I asked her why she didn't have another deal-breaker about Gert having sex with other girls.

"That goes without saying," she said. "Actually, it doesn't go without saying. Good call."

She wrote "Don't have sex with other people" on the receipt.

My demands were that I wanted him to stop telling me what to do all the time. For example, when it comes to having sex with Marxy, he cannot stop me. I had also decided that I wanted to have my own job.

"And I would like his support," I said. "And I am going to open my own bank account and contribute to the tribe."

AK47 smiled and said we could do that without him. "You can just go into the bank and open an account. Though you should probably get someone to go with you before you sign anything."

We continued writing our RULES FOR GERT.

On the ride home, I thought of a different demand. It wasn't just for Gert. It was for AK47 too. And it wasn't a RULE, it was something I wanted.

She had the radio on and turned down the volume. "Okay, I'm listening."

"I want to see the essay," I said. "The one that got him the scholarship."

She did not say anything. I asked her what was going on in her brain. She said that she didn't know if I wanted to read it.

"I mean, I know you think you do, but it was written for a particular audience. It wasn't written for you to read."

"Gert wrote it, and it's about me. I want to see."

It started to rain. The sun was mostly gone behind clouds and rain spat on the windshield. AK47 turned on the wipers. I watched them go back and forth for a while. I had made a demand of her and I realized that I did not have any way to force her to show me the essay. Also Gert would not want to show me either.

"Like I said," AK47 said, turning toward our apartment building, "that's his call."

⁊

It was very official when we brought Gert our list of RULES FOR GERT. We sat around the kitchen table. Each of us sat at a different corner. We were in a business meeting. AK47 had rewritten our demands on a piece of paper with two rows: one for her demands, and one for my demands. We wanted to make it more official-looking than the receipt and the napkin.

"You got to be kidding," he said, holding the paper up. "What is this, the Second World War? Which one of you is Poland?"

"Deal-breakers," I said. "That's what those are."

"Why do *you* have deal-breakers on here?" he said to me.

"I'm negotiating on her behalf," AK47 said. Gert shook his head.

"Two against one. How's that fair?"

Gert went through the list. He said he was fine with everything, even seeing Dr. Laird.

"You can't go Berserker."

"I'm fine."

"The sex thing, though," Gert said.

"It's her body," AK47 said. "Her life."

"It's my body and my life," I said. "And when you love people, you show them your love by touching each other in ways that are nice. I love Marxy."

Gert frowned, but he didn't say no, didn't say anything. He just stared at the list.

After, to show he was ready to follow THE RULES, he went and knocked on Alf's door and told Alf he was sorry. Alf had bruises on his face and answered the door with a steak knife that he held in front of him. He said he would cut Gert up badly if Gert tried anything.

"He's here to apologize," I announced.

Alf's eyes were puffy and narrow and he didn't put the knife down. "Is that so?"

I gave Gert a little push. He looked at me, then at AK47, who had her arms crossed.

"It wasn't right, what I did," Gert said finally.

"Goddamn right," Alf said.

"What else?" AK47 said to Gert.

"I was also wrong to put my hands on her," he said. "And to scare my sister. It probably looked real bad, what was happening."

"You put your hand on a girl like that, I'm not just going to stand by," Alf said.

"And I appreciate it," AK47 said. "Don't we, Gert?"

He didn't say anything. AK47 gave him THE LOOK. "I was wrong," Gert said finally.

Alf put the knife down. "Well. Fuck you anyway," he said, and shut the door.

"Well, that went well," AK47 said.

chapter fourteen

I t was the day of the library interview. Wednesdays are perfect because they are my reading days at the library already. But Big Todd told me that my interview was not at the library by the Community Center that I went to.

"It's a bit off the beaten path," he said, an expression that means a place that people did not go to and beat down with their feet to make a path.

"Oh," I said, and Big Todd gave me a weird look.

"You're okay with that? We can cancel if you want."

"No," I said. "Part of a hero's legend is doing things that are off the beaten path."

Big Todd smiled. "That's what I'm talking about," he said.

He drove me to the library and gave me bus schedules and directions, driving the exact way the buses would go. I followed along with my finger on the map, while reading the directions out loud.

"You look good, by the way," Big Todd said. "Very professional."

"Thanks. AK47 helped pick this out. And fancy underwear for Marxy."

"Oh boy," Big Todd said. "TMI on that one."

He meant "too much information." He laughed and I asked him

if he wanted to know a secret. "If it's about you and Marxy doing the dirty, please, no thank you."

"It's not. Gert and AK47 are back together."

Big Todd looked over. "Yeah? Like officially?"

I shrugged. "She stayed over the last two nights. And they've been having sex."

And then we both said "TMI" at the same time and laughed. "Well," Big Todd said, "as long as they're both happy and he treats her right, and you right, I'm okay with it." He pointed ahead at a small building that looked like a red-brick house that had eaten a lot of glass windows and metal. "That's it. Up there."

⁊

Even though I didn't have any work experience, Big Todd helped me make a résumé that made it look like I could be a good library worker. The library woman, whose name was Carol, chewed on the end of the pencil. Big Todd crossed his legs. He was nervous and kept making his legs bounce up and down.

We were sitting in an office with the glass windows. All around were shelves of books and people reading at tables. A giant fake palm tree was tall over everything. Big Todd said he would come with me for moral support, but also to answer any questions the woman at the library had. Normally he did not go with people applying for jobs. I was a special case, he said, but he did not say what made me special.

We sat quietly while Carol read the résumé. She flipped over the page to see if there was anything on the other side. Then she put it down on the table.

"We don't have any available openings," Carol said. "And we have a waiting list for graduate students in library sciences. They usually get the internships."

Big Todd sat up. "On the phone they said—"

"I don't know what they told you," Carol said. She took her glasses off and put them back on. Big Todd was moving in his chair.

"I am a hard worker," I said to Carol.

"I'm sure you are. But we don't have any jobs. And being a patron is different from working here. More rules."

The word *patron* means people who come to libraries. That was something I wrote in my cover letter: that I was an "avid patron of libraries" and knew how they worked and where all the books were.

"Can she maybe do some volunteer work and then transition into some paid shifts?" Big Todd asked.

Carol said that she didn't expect to have any vacancies in the near future. I asked how did she know the future, and instead of getting angry, she laughed.

"Uh-huh. Tell me why you want to work here?"

"Everything is in the cover letter," Big Todd said. We had worked on the cover letter for two hours before the interview, changing words until I sounded very smart.

"I wasn't asking you. I was asking her."

The question was one Big Todd had made me answer a hundred times before the interview. It was a question that people asked in every job interview. Big Todd had made a list of reasons why I was perfect for the library. He wrote all of it while I talked about what I liked about being there and reading. I had forgotten it at home.

Carol was waiting. She was treating me very seriously, which made me nervous but also like I was an adult and not someone who needed everything done for them. Big Todd cleared his throat and asked if I was okay.

I closed my eyes and counted to ten, not out loud, inside my head.

Big Todd poked me with his foot under the table.

"I forgot the paper with my answers about why I would be perfect to work in the library," I said.

"Do you need to read the answers?" Carol asked.

"She just gets nervous," Big Todd said.

"Just tell the truth," Carol said. "The truth is what I want to hear."

I told her that my brother and I had moved out from a bad place to live together. "He is very smart but didn't do well in school. He got a scholarship to the college."

I told her that Gert always worked so hard to make me safe, and that I wanted to help him now because he had a debt he needed to pay. I said that I went to the library by my house all the time, and that reading is very important and that I wanted to help others find books they wanted.

Carol put down my résumé. "Once or twice a week," she said. "That's the best I can do. And it's probably not going to be permanent."

"Does that mean I have the job?" I asked.

Carol said I had a trial period. If I did good, I could keep working. "We'll get you the forms and figure out your schedule when you come in next time. How does that sound?"

We got up and shook hands. Big Todd told me to not go for a dab, since employers want employees to be professional. Dabs are not professional.

Outside, Big Todd went in for a dab. I didn't want a dab. I wanted a hug. Big Todd had proven himself to be a powerful member of the tribe.

"All right, all right," Big Todd said. When we stopped hugging he touched my shoulder and got a very serious look. "Hey, that thing you said, about debt? What did you mean?"

I told him the definition of *debt* that he had taught me: when someone owes someone, or a company, something.

"With banks and businesses and in modern times, it usually means money," Big Todd said.

We walked to his car.

"It's none of my business, not really, but you can talk to me about stuff. Okay?"

I told him I knew that, and that even though he was not in my tribe, he was in a neighboring tribe that was very close to my tribe and which my tribe respected very much.

⇗

When Big Todd dropped me off, Gert came out to meet me. AK47 high-fived me and said she was proud of me. Then Gert did something he had never done before: he waved to Big Todd, who was standing outside of his car parked in front of the building.

"Hey," Gert said. "What are you doing tonight?"

"Uh," Big Todd said.

"We're going to dinner. To celebrate. Why don't you and your guy come with us."

AK47 and I looked at Gert.

"Yeah?" Big Todd said.

"Sure."

Once Big Todd was gone, we asked Gert what the shit was going on.

"What?" Gert said. "Stop looking at me like that."

"You don't like gay people," I said.

Gert said that wasn't true. And AK47 said it's kind of true, and Gert shrugged and said that was the old Gert. Me and AK47 looked at each other again while Gert walked back to the apartment. He asked if we were coming.

"Well, fuck me," AK47 said. "Excuse my French."

⇗

The restaurant we went to was fancy and Gert dressed nicely and so did me and AK47. I had never seen Gert so happy. It made me feel like we were getting close as a tribe. They asked me to tell them about the interview, and when I did Big Todd said that I impressed the librarian, even though she said there weren't any jobs at first.

"She cleaned house," Big Todd said.

Noah, Big Todd's boyfriend, was funny and didn't talk very much, and I was worried that Gert would call them faggots or make fun of them for being gay. But Gert said he looked fit and asked if he played football ever, and Big Todd's boyfriend said he had.

"What position?"

"Corner," he said. "You?"

"Wide receiver."

"You got the build for it. What happened?"

"He hurt his knee," I said.

"ACL?"

Gert put down his lemon water. "Yeah. Tore it to shit."

They talked about football for a while, while Big Todd and AK47 talked about how the government was talking about not giving the Community Center as much money next year to help make programs for people they called disadvantaged.

During dinner Gert's phone buzzed. Gert looked down and shut it off, turning it upside down so he couldn't see the screen anymore. AK47 was looking at him but pretending not to. Then she looked at me and smiled, because even though being nice to Noah and Big Todd and talking about football and the government wasn't one of the RULES FOR GERT, it was like he had added a rule to the RULES, one that said he should be nice to people like Big Todd and Noah and not say fuck-dick things about gay people.

chapter fifteen

We had to reschedule our time with Dr. Laird, since I now had to work at the same time as our Thursday meeting. Dr. Laird's secretary, Hanna, was at first not very happy, since we had to give more than a day's notice before canceling the appointment, and her entire schedule for the next month had me and Gert coming in Thursdays. Then Dr. Laird came on the phone and said it was all right by him.

"This is huge," he said when I told him why I couldn't come in. "And at a library. How cool is that?"

"Very cool," I said.

Normally changing my schedule would make me nervous, but in order to perform in the world, as Dr. Laird said, I had to become okay with schedule changes, since not everything works according to the same schedules.

Gert and AK47 and Big Todd had warned me that the library might schedule me to work a different day every week, and that it might mean my schedule would be changing a lot. But I told them I was up to the challenge and would defeat it by counting to ten whenever I felt nervous about not knowing what was going to happen next.

Thursday morning, on my first day of work, I told Gert that I would go myself, by bus.

"What's the difference? My morning's free," Gert said. "And what about our rules? We need to make sure you know where you're going."

"I am going to take the bus there, and also take it back." I showed the bus schedule. "It will take less than one hour."

"A ride would take fifteen," Gert said.

"Dummy, she wants to go herself. To her first day of work." AK47 elbowed him. "Hint hint, nudge nudge."

"What about the rules?" Gert asked.

"I am making new rules," I said back.

I had also made my own lunch—a tuna fish sandwich with mustard and mayonnaise and tomato slices. I made sure to put the tomato slices between the tuna fish and the mayonnaise, so that the tomato slices wouldn't get the bread wet. I also packed a water bottle, which I could refill at work. AK47 made sure that I dressed properly. That was the only help I allowed.

She gave me a hug and said she knew I would do great. "Just listen to the instructions, and don't be afraid to write them down."

"Got it," I said.

"And if you need anything, just call," Gert said. "Okay? And call when you're done with work and heading home."

"She's fine," AK47 said.

"I'm fine," I said. "But I will call."

⩶

The library is a very heroic place to work because librarians help people get stronger brains. They also help people who are homeless by giving them food in cans that other people put into the cardboard box by the door.

Being a librarian is mostly about knowing where books go, so that you can answer questions for the people trying to find them. Also people leave books on the tables. If you know where to bring the books, you do not need to go to the computer, which is the hardest part of being a librarian, and was something that I did not get to do right away.

The first thing I learned to do was to go around and pick up books and put them on a cart. If people left garbage, I took that too. Carol was the most important person who worked there. The library had four other women, and two men. But Carol was the leader of their tribe.

Even though Carol acted partly like a fuck-dick during our interview, she was actually really nice when nobody was around and it was just the two of us. I knew that she had to be a fuck-dick in the interview because you have to prove yourself worthy of being a librarian.

You cannot just be a librarian without overcoming obstacles.

The person who was working in the library before me was a college student named Teddy who did a very good job. That was what Carol said.

"So the bar is pretty high," she said.

She showed me how to use the Dewey Decimal System, and how to figure out where books go by the numbers and letters on their stickers, and how to use the computer.

I came in twice a week, on Thursdays for four hours, and on Sundays for two hours, but sometimes more if someone was sick. At lunchtime I was allowed to go wherever I wanted in the library to read, as long as I didn't bug anybody. I could also eat in a room that nobody else was allowed to see, in the back.

One of the most important Rules of the Library is you are not allowed to eat near the books, or drink soda except when your bottle has a cap. All the drinks needed lids.

There were people who always went to the library. Two old men named Tyrone and Mac played chess together in the morning. A woman who smelled bad, with red legs that looked like they had cracking skin, slept in the chair by the window.

A group from the elementary school came in once a week to read books, and on Sundays parents brought their babies to Sunday Bunny Reading Hour. Famous writers also came to read to crowds of people.

The best part of the library was being paid and being able to put money into my bank account, which I had opened in the Bank of America. You can take out money and put the money back into the ATM bank machine as many times as you want.

⌇

Marxy came to visit me at the library on my second day of work, which was a Sunday. He put his arms around me and tried to kiss me on the lips.

"Not while I'm on duty," I told him.

"Oh," he said, stepping back. "Sorry."

"But I'm very happy to see you."

It is against the rules to kiss at the library. Carol said once she caught two high school kids, a boy and a girl, snogging in the Cooking section, 641.5, which is where International Cookbooks are.

Snogging is a British word for kissing.

She said that sometimes kids from the high school down the street came in and smoked pot in the washroom or snogged inside and that neither was allowed.

"Everyone is very proud of you," Marxy said. "That you have a job and your own money." He pulled on his fingers, one at a time. They went *pop pop pop*. "I miss kissing you."

Marxy asked me if I was still a Viking.

"Why wouldn't I be a Viking?" I asked.

He shrugged. "You are a librarian now. And I haven't heard you talking about Vikings in a long time."

"I'm both a Viking and a Librarian," I said. "Ask me where you can find a type of book."

And Marxy thought about it and said, "What about comic books?"

Many librarians will try to find comics. But actually the comics in a library are called Graphic Novels and so I knew where in the library to find them. I brought him to 741.5 and showed him all the different comics we had.

"There are also comics over there." Across the library there were stacks of magazines and newspapers and on spinning racks there were comic books, the newest ones that weren't made into books yet. They were covered in plastic to make sure they didn't get ruined.

Carol came over and asked how things were going.

"Good. I am helping this patron find comic books," I said. "His name is Marxy."

"I'm her boyfriend," Marxy said.

"Is that so?" Carol said.

"We will not be snogging while I am on duty," I told Carol.

She nodded. "I was just about to check on the Cooking section." She told Marxy it was nice to meet him, and then said there were books to put away by the Children's Books. "The middle school section," she added.

"I'm very proud of you," Marxy said. He reached over and held my hand and squeezed it. I squeezed back and told him I had to go back to work.

Pearl came to pick Marxy up a half an hour later. I was trying to show her that I was responsible and heroic and a good girlfriend for Marxy. She said that it was good to see me, and that she thought me working in the library was a good thing.

"Marxy wants to get a job now," she said while Marxy checked out books with Carol at the front desk. We watched him.

"I think he can do it," I said.

And then Pearl smiled at me. "I still need those Tupperware containers back," she said, putting her arm around Marxy, who checked out the comic books and waved to me on the way out.

chapter sixteen

For Vikings, a *hólmganga* is how people who have conflicts with each other solve problems. They fight according to serious rules and who-ever wins the *hólmganga* wins. It turned out Gert had lied to us and that he actually was kicked out of school. Since Gert couldn't duel with the school, he had to do a *Þing*, which is a group of people who decide whether you need to be punished for your crime. *Kepple's Guide to the Vikings* says that a group of wise elders would hear about the crime that was committed and would decide what happens.

The Dean would be the wise person who would decide Gert's fate.

There is also a Viking ritual called *járn-burðr* or *jernbyrd*, which means trial by fire. You walk holding something hot from across the room or field to the other side. That is how you prove you are brave and worthy of being forgiven. Inga from Varteig did it to show that her son Håkon Håkonsson should be the king of Norway.

Gert had to do it to prove he should be allowed back in school.

He said he probably wouldn't get to go back to school, so what was the point. AK47 wanted him to wear his suit to show that he was serious. Gert hated the suit and wouldn't put it on, so AK47 told him to stop being a baby.

"You think Zelda didn't have odds to beat when she got the job at the library?"

"That's totally different," Gert said.

"Yeah. Totally different as in she's got more balls than you. So put on the damn suit."

I said going in the suit and acting sorry, even though he hated doing that, was important.

"This is your trial by fire," I said. "Where you prove that you are worthy."

"All right, but don't expect me to be goddamn Beowulf in there," Gert said, picking a piece of fluff off his shirt.

≷

We went to the college, not to the building with the tower, but to an ugly building that looked like a shoebox. Inside the air-conditioning was very intense and too cold and made the hairs on my arms stand on end.

We were going to war. We walked up stairs, down a hallway, to a big room that reminded me of the bank, which had a maze of people standing to get to the front of the line.

"Holy crap," I said.

"Do we really have to wait in this line?" AK47 asked.

Gert nodded. "We could always not go."

The woman at the front called out a number and the line moved a little bit.

AK47 punched his arm. "No chance."

After a while AK47 walked past the line and told a person behind one of the desks that we had an appointment. They talked for a while and then she waved for us to come in.

As we walked by, the people in the line gave us dirty looks. Gert hung his head down and looked embarrassed and I patted him on the back and told him to be strong.

The woman who brought us to the back said that AK47 and I were supposed to wait outside, on chairs that did not feel great to sit on. Gert went inside with the Dean, a tall woman with short curly hair. I held out my hand to give him a dab but AK47 pushed my hand down.

"Not now," she whispered.

Gert looked back for a second before going inside. And then the door closed.

⧽

On either side of the door to the Dean's office was glass, not the kind you can see through but the kind that was cloudy. I could only kind of see Gert's shirt on the other side. It was almost like what things looked like when you opened your eyes underwater. I could also kind of hear them talking, not so much Gert but the Dean.

She had a very loud voice, the powerful kind.

"Why is he so afraid?" I asked AK47. "He is smart."

"Don't I know it. Your brother has a bit of a failure complex. He is so afraid of screwing up that he'd rather not try."

"That sounds like something Dr. Laird would say."

"Man, it probably *is* something he's said. My best friend was like that when I was a kid. She was pretty, Zee, and smart as hell."

"What happened to her?"

"Got pregnant when she was, like, fifteen. Started doing drugs."

I told her I didn't understand. Why would someone screw up on purpose?

"Well, I can't speak for her, but my thinking on Gert is he's gone through life with people thinking he's one way, dumb, a thug, whatever, and it's less scary to have people keep thinking that than to try to prove them wrong and fail and know that they were right all along."

But Gert was smart, I said, and the people who didn't believe in him were shit-heels. AK47 said that we might know that, but the problem was that Gert didn't know it.

"It's hard for him. I get it," she said.

I wasn't sure I got it. For me, my legend was about showing people that I was not dumb or a shit-heel, that I could help the tribe and also show the world that people like me and Marxy could become powerful. Gert not knowing that he was powerful and believing when people thought he was dumb and a thug was like the opposite of a legend.

It was like being given a suit of armor and a magical weapon, like the sword Lævateinn, and leaving it in its sheath, even when it's time to use it in battle.

AK47 slapped my leg and got up and said she had to go to the bathroom. "Don't move, okay?" she said.

And as soon as she was gone I did move. I went to the door and put my ear to the glass to see if I could understand anything people were saying. The glass was too powerful, though.

Since Gert wasn't talking very much, I thought he was losing the battle. Maybe she had even defeated him and told him he couldn't go back to school. That would be disastrous. I needed to go inside and provide backup for him, the way warriors support other warriors when they are losing.

I would be his reinforcements.

Turning the handle, I pushed open the door, making sure to stand very tall and to make myself look as big as possible.

The Dean was behind the desk. Gert had one leg crossed over the other and was sitting in a small chair, while the Dean's chair was gargantuan, like the throne Odin sits on in Valhalla.

"I think you should allow Gert back into school," I said.

"And you are?" the Dean said.

Gert stood up. "Sorry, this is my sister. Zelda, this is Dean Horowitz."

"Ah," the Dean said. "The one you wrote about in your scholarship essay. Do you want to sit down?" She pointed to the chair beside Gert.

"No. I want you to take Gert back. I think he is the smartest person going to this college, and he might be different from almost everyone but that is what makes him a powerful student."

AK47 came up behind me. "Shit, sorry. I had to go to the bathroom and she just went rogue." She waved at the Dean. "Hi. Sorry." AK47 tried to pull me out of the room.

"Not until she agrees to let Gert in."

The Dean laughed. She put up her hands. "Okay, okay. Gert, you just fill out these forms. Get them back to me. Pass summer school, and we're back in the saddle. Fair?"

"Fair," Gert said.

They shook hands and Gert took the forms.

Outside, Gert sighed. "She had already agreed to let me back in, you goon," he said. "And where were you?" he said to AK47.

"Bladder the size of a thimble. Remember?" AK47 took Gert's hand. "But you have to admit, she was willing to go to battle for you."

We started walking out of the Dean's office, down the hallway and past the line of people.

"I was," I said. "Part of being legendary is proving that you can pick up the sword and stand up for what is good and right."

Gert raised his eyebrow. "That's a little dramatic, isn't it?"

I stopped walking. "I'm talking about how you are not dumb or a thug and should start believing in yourself and your own legend, which involves kicking ass in your classes." Being legendary was about taking all of the power that the gods have given you and making the most out of them, I said.

Gert put his big arms around our shoulders as we left the ugly air-conditioned building. "My tribe," he said, practically pulling us along with him.

I stopped and said I had to go to the bathroom, and told AK47 and Gert I would meet them at the door of the building.

Instead of going to the bathroom, I ran back to the Dean's office and knocked on the door. The Dean opened it.

"Did you forget something?" she asked, and I said yes and she asked me to come inside.

I stood in front of her desk and took a deep breath while the Dean sat down. She looked up. "Can I help you?" she asked.

I held out my fist.

"What's that?" she asked.

"It's called a dab. It is a sign of respect within my tribe."

She waited for a second before standing up and straightening out her skirt.

"Your brother was right," she said, dabbing me back. "You are a brave girl."

"He said that?"

She said that I was her favorite part of Gert's scholarship letter. She shook her head. "What you two have been through. My God."

"Can I read it?"

"Pardon?"

"The letter. Gert won't let me read it because he says it's none of my business and—"

The Dean held up her hand. "Stop right there. That's something you'll need to sort out with him." She walked me to the door. "You are the first person I have ever dabbed," she said, opening it for me. "And I'm honored to have earned your respect."

chapter seventeen

Sundays were very serious days at the library because of the Sunday Bunny Reading Hour. Parents brought their young children to come listen to a woman with bunny ears play a small guitar and read from books. When I found out that the Sunday Bunny Reading Hour was why everyone at the library hated working on Sundays, I did not understand. Reading is good for making your brain stronger, and guitars and music are good to listen to.

For the Sunday Bunny Reading Hour we had to put pillows around the Rumpus Room for parents to sit on, and then the babies would sit on their laps.

I learned that the babies threw up a lot and yelled and cried, and after they left the library smelled like shit and dirty diapers. The babies who came with their parents to the library, for the programs there, were loud and smelled, but for some reason they did not bother me.

Carol did not like babies at all.

"You think the Vikings were savages? Wait until you see these kids."

"It is a common myth that the Vikings were savages," I said. "They actually had very well-developed agriculture."

Carol took off her glasses and cleaned them on the sleeve of her blouse.

"Either way. Get ready."

The parents and their children did not come in like other people of the library. They did not "trickle," like a stream that moves very slowly. They came all at once like a flood. I did not know where they all came from.

"See?" Carol said. She was smiling a big fake smile to all the people coming in.

The strollers were sometimes big and looked like they came from the future. Most of them were not very nice. This is because the people who came to our library didn't have a lot of money. Carol said that the other library had "higher-end clientele," but that rich parents were usually way more annoying.

"They want to protect their kids from everything. These parents just want to survive."

My job was to show the parents where to go during the Sunday Bunny Reading Hour, and also to clean up any messes. It was not very hard to do that. There was a sign at the front, and another sign once you got past the detectors that went off if you ever tried to steal a book without checking it out first. The parents were usually loud. The regulars who came to do their crossword puzzles and to play chess or read books shook their heads at the loud parents.

I also had to check to see that the right people were going in and that the wrong people were not allowed inside. People had to sign up for the Bunny Hour, but people were always coming without signing up.

Sometimes we had to tell them they couldn't come in, since too many people in the Rumpus Room, which was upstairs on the second floor, was a Fire Hazard. Carol said if one or two people and their children came in over the limit, then it was okay.

"But no more than that."

I stood at the front of the Rumpus Room and waved and pointed to the door. "Hello, have a nice day, hi there, howdy, *góðan dag*!" I said.

Most of the parents did not even act like I was there. They just walked by holding crying babies. All of the people looked very tired, and all of them were women and girls who I thought couldn't be parents because they were so young.

"The walking good-luck charm," a voice said, and it was a man and also someone I recognized. He held on to a baby with one arm so the baby looked like it was growing out of his shoulder. "You're Gert's sister, right? Zelda? Remember me?"

"I remember," I said. "We played poker together."

The baby spit up some yellow stuff. Hendo saw me looking at the baby.

"Shit. Easy, little man," he said, and wiped the yellow spit with a napkin.

I was surprised that I remembered his name, since names were something I was not very good at. Not as bad as Marxy, who had to write the names down on cards he kept with him, and when he couldn't remember the name of someone important he would pull the card out and then read it and get the name. Except when situations are special. When we first met, he remembered my name and I remembered his. That was how we knew we were in love the first time.

Hendo held up the baby and said his name was Artem.

"My grandfather was this old-school Russian dude. Doesn't Artem look old-school?"

I wasn't sure what that meant.

Artem and I had a standoff with our eyes. Then he smiled and spit again. He was wearing a small basketball jersey and didn't have very much hair, but the hair he did have was very light-colored brown, almost blond, and his eyes were blue.

"Almost a year old," Hendo said.

"Is he your baby?"

"I mean, I'm the dad, yeah."

We did not say anything for a while. People with strollers pushed past. Artem looked at me again and made a baby noise and then he stuck out his hand. It was a very small hand.

Hendo laughed. "I think he wants your finger."

"Why?" I asked.

"I don't know. He's into this phase where he just likes to hold things. Watch."

Hendo stuck out his finger and put it in front of Artem, who took his small fingers and wrapped them all around Hendo's one finger, which was gargantuan.

"See?"

I stuck my finger out and Artem held on to it. The feeling was weird. The baby did not have a tight grip, but it felt like Artem was holding on as tight as he could.

"Whoa," I said.

"Right?"

Artem pulled my finger and because I was way more powerful than him I didn't try to stop him, since I didn't know how to stop him with the right power. Out of nowhere he put my finger in his mouth.

His mouth was wet around my finger. Inside his mouth the tongue poked.

"Whoa," I said again.

"Think he likes you," Hendo said.

A woman came up to us. "You know where her finger's been?" she asked.

She was very skinny and had a lot of makeup on. She smelled like smoke and did not look happy that I was playing with Artem. She grabbed the baby away from Hendo. My finger left his mouth.

Artem clapped his hands together.

"Relax. You see the hand sanitizers everywhere? It's like a hospital in here."

"I don't want a stranger's finger in my baby's mouth." She turned and asked Hendo who I was.

"Zelda," Hendo said. "You work here, right?"

I nodded. "I am contributing to the tribe. Since Gert is not in school anymore."

The Rumpus Room was almost full. The woman with the bunny ears, who read to everyone and sang during Sunday Bunny Reading Hour, had taken out her little guitar.

"It's starting," I said.

"Cool," Hendo said. The woman took the baby past him inside the Rumpus Room. Hendo took a deep breath. "And away we go," he said.

⍦

While all the parents and children listened to the Bunny Lady playing guitar, I went around and started reshelving books. I could do that whenever I didn't have anything else to do.

I was surprised that Hendo had remembered me. I had almost forgotten about him, but now I remembered the way we played poker and how he made me feel like part of his tribe. I pushed the cart and thought about the woman who was Artem's mother and how she seemed like a fuck-dick, and how someone as cool as Hendo should have a girlfriend or a wife who was just as cool.

He and the woman and Artem were in the corner of the Rumpus Room. I could see them from the window in the door. Hendo bounced Artem on his knee while the woman chewed gum and did not act like she cared very much about the songs. All she did was look at her phone. But Hendo sang along and lifted Artem up when the Sunday Bunny woman raised her arms, and the other parents all raised their arms too.

After a while he handed Artem back to the woman. He came out.

Since I had parked my cart in front of the door I had to move it quickly and spilled some books.

Hendo bent over to help me. "Shit, sorry," he said. "Here." He picked up a bunch of the books and put them on the cart, stacking them not the perfect way, which was spines up so I could see the numbers.

"You have to make sure the numbers are up, like this," I said, and started moving the books.

Hendo laughed and fixed them. "How's that?"

"Good."

He put his hands in his pockets. "I can only take so much of that shit. I need a smoke like fucking crazy." He asked if there was a place he could have a cigarette.

I told him that you could only smoke outside of the building, "But not within fifteen feet." He gave me a military salute and held up a cigarette.

"You want one?"

It was almost time for my break. I nodded. I told Carol I was going on a break and as I went out with Hendo she said, "I didn't know you smoked," and I gave her THE LOOK so she'd be quiet.

⁊

I learned that Artem was Hendo's baby but he lived with the Baby Mama, which is what Hendo called the mother. They were not a couple.

"We never really were," Hendo said.

"You don't want to have the baby live with you?"

"Don't have much of a place yet. I'd like to get some more money, you know. Get a pretty nice place. Get him in a nice school."

We were sitting on the curb watching cars. A bright-red one went by and Hendo flicked ash off his cigarette and pointed. "Now, that's a fine car. You see it?"

I nodded.

"Mustang. Man."

Since I had never smoked before, except once when AK47 put her cigarette down and forgot to crush it all the way, I tried to copy every-thing Hendo was doing. He tapped his finger onto the end of the ciga-rette again, so I tapped, and then I sucked the smoke like I was slurping spaghetti. He laughed when I coughed.

"You don't really smoke, do you?"

"I've smoked before," I said.

"You look like you're having an aneurysm in slow motion," Hendo said.

"What's that?"

He stubbed the cigarette on the concrete. "Nevermind." He stood up and wiped his pants off. "I guess I should be getting back in there."

"Yes. Sunday Bunny Reading Hour is only an hour."

When the Sunday Bunny Reading Hour ended Hendo left with his Baby Mama and Artem. They were arguing loudly. He did not wave to me. His Baby Mama was giving him shit about money.

"You think he can live on macaroni and cheese?" she was saying.

She was so angry I did not want to have our eyes meet. When they walked by I turned and pretended to be looking at a book.

The Bunny Lady took her guitar and said she'd see us next week. Her name was really Martine, and when she wasn't a bunny, Carol said, she worked as a lawyer for some big company that was actually evil.

That was called being a hypocrite, Carol said, who smiled and said under her breath, "Bitch," when Martine walked by.

Once everyone left, Carol and I went into the Rumpus Room and started cleaning up.

We picked up crumpled paper, and candy bar wrappers, and small baby-food jars. I held the garbage bag for Carol and she put all the garbage inside it. "You want kids?" she asked.

"I think maybe. I don't know if it's okay."

"Why wouldn't it be?"

I told her about the articles that were about people who were like me having babies, and how nobody knew if we should be allowed to, because some people just aren't smart enough or powerful enough at being parents to have a baby.

Carol took the bag of diapers and garbage to the back door, opened it, and threw it in the big metal dumpster.

I held the door for her so she wouldn't get locked out.

"That's stupid," she said. "You're ten times more responsible than ninety percent of the men I've been with."

⇗

That night I had a dream about Hendo. The library was empty. We were talking about books and Vikings in the dream. And then he leaned over and kissed me. We were sitting beside each other and he put his hand on my cheek. I put my hands on his arms and felt the muscles there.

That was when I woke up, and felt bad. I looked around my room in the dark. In my dream, I was kissing Hendo, not Marxy.

I lay in bed, my heart beating, my head full of Hendo. I tried to go back to sleep and couldn't, because I was afraid of what would happen if I did—if I would dream-cheat on Marxy.

I decided to send Dr. Kepple another letter.

Dear Dr. Kepple,
It's Zelda.

Whenever Viking heroes win the love of their fair maidens, they end up marrying them and having children. I don't know if I want to have children, but I definitely want to have sex with Marxy, who is my boyfriend and fair maiden.

Something in your book confused me.

In the Friðþjófs saga hins frækna, Frithiof and Ingeborg got married and their love was eternal, even when Ingebord was married to an old king because Frithiof had been sent away by people who were jealous of him.

How did Frithiof know that he was in love with Ingeborg, and why didn't Ingeborg refuse to marry the old king?

Also, how do Vikings tell the difference between dreams that are serious and sent from the gods, and draumskrök, which are dreams that don't mean anything?

Skál,
Zelda

chapter eighteen

The most famous Viking love story in Viking sagas is about Gudrun and Kjartan. A beautiful woman named Gudrun falls in love with Kjartan, who is very "charismatic," meaning people like him and not just for his looks. But Gudrun is bad luck, since one of her husbands died and the other one divorced her when she was young. Kjartan likes Gudrun too. But her dad doesn't like Kjartan and he sends Kjartan away. Which is when Bolli, Kjartan's cousin, tries to convince Gudrun to marry him instead. Kjartan's gone a long time, so Gudrun agrees to marry Bolli, and then when Kjartan returns Gudrun realizes that she messed up.

It is a very complicated story, because love is very complicated.

I reviewed my THINGS LEGENDS NEED list, and while Marxy was my "fair maiden," I needed to win his love in the face of danger. Fair maidens are usually people who are not strong, who cannot protect themselves and need someone powerful to help them, and then they fall in love with the hero, who shows bravery and strength. I also believed that part of my legend was to show the world that people like Marxy and me can be powerful together, the way that Gert and AK47 are powerful, and that we can create a tribe of our own one day.

To make a tribe involved having sex, and many people do not like the idea of people like Marxy and me having sex. I told Marxy that it is not our problem that fuck-dicks do not want us to have sex. We are making our own legend.

The problem was Viking legends never talked about actual sex. They talked about love.

For a person who liked to have sex, Gert did not want to talk to me about how it worked. He would begin talking and then pick at his nail, which wasn't even really much of a nail, since he kept his nails short.

Whenever people in TV shows and movies talked about sex, they said "the birds and the bees." That was a way of talking about sex without actually talking about sex.

One night when AK47 and I were alone, I asked if she could tell me about sex.

"Gert hates talking about it," I said.

She laughed and said that's Gert for you. "Sometimes it's easier for someone not in the family to explain how these things work," she said. "I get it."

She asked if I knew what it was like to have an orgasm, which means you feel really good inside yourself. I told her that I did know what an orgasm was like. She asked me if I had ever had sex.

"I won't tell Gert," she said, her voice going quiet.

I shook my head. "Marxy and I haven't gone past kissing," I said.

I asked AK47 how she knew she was in love with Gert and how she knew Gert was in love with her. She put her hands in her pockets and said that the first part was easier to answer than the second part.

"Your brother isn't the most talkative person in the world."

She broke down the signs. She said that when guys want to talk a lot, that usually meant something.

"But most of the time they don't ever say what they mean."

I nodded, even though I didn't know how that worked. She meant that they will talk a lot about things without actually saying what is important to them: which is being in love with you. And that's because boys don't cry.

"Yes they do. I've seen Marxy cry. And Gert."

"Yeah, but think about how pissed Gert gets when you see him cry. Guys aren't supposed to cry, or show emotions like that, or be too sad. It's a gender thing."

I asked what she meant by "a gender thing." She said that people expect men and women to behave in certain ways. Guys are supposed to be serious all the time, not showing emotions, and women are supposed to be more emotional and like pink and flowers.

"What about Valkyries?" I asked.

"A noted exception. There just aren't a lot of Valkyries out there, Zee."

"So if a guy shows you a lot of attention, and you hang out all the time, and he tells you personal things, it usually means he likes you."

We sat by the computer in my room, AK47 in the spinning chair and me on the bed.

The Internet browser popped up. She did some clicking and turned down the volume on the computer. "In case it's loud right off the bat," she said. "The Internet, as you're aware, is a disgusting, perverted place, Zee. Which is part of what makes it so good."

She turned the computer monitor so we didn't have the light from the window shining right on it.

We went to a page with a black background and a woman in her underwear looking at the screen. She was sucking on her finger like it was a lollipop. AK47 took the mouse arrow on the screen and made it go right over the AT LEAST 18 box. She waited before clicking.

"Okay, so bottom line is that pornography isn't what real sex is like. At least, not completely."

"What's the difference?"

"Think of it as more of a fantasy. Or dream. Things that we imagine in our minds and aren't sure we want to do, or can't do."

"Fantasy," I said, and gave her my notebook and she wrote the word down for me to add to the Word of Today list, even though I was pretty sure I had heard the word before.

"People get aroused, like turned on," she started saying.

I knew what she was talking about. "Like lightbulbs," I said, "only on the inside."

"Right. And for men that involves the penis getting filled with blood and it makes it really hard. Here." She started clicking on the porno page, and then turned to me. "Actually, forget porn. Get me a carrot or a cucumber or something," she said to me. "Condom use should be lesson one."

She went into Gert's room and came back with a condom, and I went to the kitchen and brought a carrot.

"Okay," she said. "Let's do this."

AK47 started telling me about babies, and why it is important when having sex to make sure you are safe. When someone doesn't want a baby, they can have an abortion, which means stopping the baby from coming out.

"It's actually not a baby at that point," AK47 said. She chewed her gum.

"And Gert thinks it is and was angry when you got an abortion and that was part of why you broke up," I said.

AK47 laughed and shook her head. "You have a way with words, Zee."

I asked her why she didn't want the baby. "I think you would make powerful parents."

AK47 shook her head. "Why would I want a baby? We can barely get through life without the added stress of having a family. Neither of us makes a lot of money."

"You needed to wear more condoms, then," I said.

"Too true."

One of the things that AK47 told me was that sometimes accidents happen. Sometimes the condoms will rip accidentally and the woman will get pregnant that way.

She held up the condom package.

"So first, you need to make sure it's not expired. Look at the date." We checked the date on the wrapper, written down the side. "Make sure it hasn't been popped or is open. So give it a little squeeze. Now, really important—when you open the condom, do not, I repeat, do *not* use your teeth. *Comprende?*"

"Why not?"

"You don't want to tear the condom inside, or cut it open with your teeth. You tear it open in the corner—here." She held the golden condom package on the corner and pretended to open it. "Do you want to give it a try?"

I took the condom from her and held it the way she held it.

"Good. Now, if you actually want to open it, I can show you how to put it on."

I opened the condom and then she handed me the carrot. She showed me how to tell which way the condom was supposed to unroll, and how to pinch the tip of the condom so that it doesn't pop while inside. She got more condoms from Gert's room and together we put four condoms on the carrot.

One of the condoms she had was supposed to taste good, and when AK47 was talking I licked the condom and it did taste good, like strawberries.

"Dude," AK47 said. "So gross." She sorted through the condoms and found one she liked. "This one's my personal favorite." She ripped my strawberry condom off of the carrot and put on a condom that had weird shapes running along the side. "Ribbed for her pleasure. This is the king of condoms. Go on. See those ribs on the side? Those really make it feel good."

I took the carrot and felt up and down. "How does this feel good?"

"This one might be a case of you having to take my word for it." She laughed and peeled it off. "Jesus Christ, replacing these is going to cost a fortune."

Once we were done with the condoms, we watched many videos, with AK47 telling me when things were unrealistic. For example, when the man picked up a woman, who was much smaller, and held her upside down.

"Nobody does that," AK47 said.

"They're doing it."

"Yeah, but they're making a crazy movie on the Internet."

"And she has no hair underneath her underwear."

"That's a matter of personal preference. Some people like shaving down there. Some people go all natural."

"Got it. Does sex always start with the woman taking off his pants and underwear? Are those the rules?"

"No." AK47 clicked the mouse and paused the video. "This is very important. Sex is what you want it to be. Some people like different things. But you should only do what feels good for you. Not what some goddamn video says." She clicked the mouse again and the sex continued. "You make your own rules."

I blinked. That was not how rules worked, I thought. I asked AK47 what happened when there are no rules.

"Zelda, honey, I know you and Gert have rules, and I know why they're important. They help you feel safe. But one thing I know for sure is that the world is too complicated to have rules for everything. And when it comes to things like love and sex—you need to kind of figure them out on your own."

⇗

I decided to text Marxy and ask him when he wanted to have sex. We had been talking about sex for a while and now it was time to make our plans official.

I sent him a text that said, When do you want to have sex?

After three minutes he texted back: I will have to check my calendar and also with my mom. When do you want to have sex?

I told him that I had to check my calendar too. Do you have to check with her?

If it's on the calendar, I won't forget, he said. She's the one who puts things on the calendar so I don't forget.

He sent three smiling faces and also one that was upside down but still smiling.

⇗

I realized that there was a lot of planning to do. For example, where do people who live with their brothers and mothers have sex?

The next morning I asked AK47 if she could give me advice. Gert was in the shower so we didn't have to worry about him overhearing. We brought over our bowls of cereal to the table and she asked me what was up.

"I'd like to have sex with Marxy but I don't know where to do it."

She scooped up cereal into her spoon. "We should talk to Pearl first."

"Marxy is already asking her. We texted and he will put it on the calendar, once we have a date. But I realized we need a place to have sex."

"That isn't the backseat of a Camaro," she said. I asked what a Camaro was and she said nevermind. "Let me see what I can cook up. Maybe Pearl'll have an idea."

Gert came into the room, wearing a towel around his waist.

"An idea about what?" he asked.

"You're dripping all over the floor, you fool," AK47 said.

He wiped his face and told her to put on coffee, and before going to put on some clothes he said, "And who has a Camaro?"

AK47 got up to turn the coffeemaker on and on the way slapped Gert's butt. "Nobody has a Camaro. Now get out of here."

chapter nineteen

AK47 told me she had taken care of a place to have sex. She had talked to Pearl and they had a plan. The date was on Marxy's calendar and I put it on mine, with a star. All week I could not stop thinking about Marxy. I was nervous and excited at the same time, and they were very similar things to feel. Carol said that I was acting weird and when I told her why she smiled and put her hand on my shoulder and said it was amazing.

"I remember my first time," she said. "It was not ideal."

"Why not?" I asked.

"We just had no idea what we were doing, that's all. Fumbling around and all that." She sighed. "Johnny Tannenbaum. I still remember his name."

"Was he handsome?"

Carol laughed. "The bluest eyes you've ever seen. But he was a good half a foot shorter than me."

Since Marxy is taller than me, I wouldn't have to worry about that.

Whenever I had a chance, I studied pictures from a book in the library called *The Joy of Sex*, which people always looked at in secret. It was filled with naked drawings and a lot of the pages were ripped out.

Carol said that people liked to masturbate to the pictures. All the people in them looked happy and beautiful, and unlike the porno videos, they all had hair still around their penises and vaginas. And there was even armpit hair in the women's armpits.

I made sure that Carol did not see me reading *The Joy of Sex*.

One day that week I saw Hendo at the library and *really* did not want him to see me reading *The Joy of Sex*, so I hid it under a book on the cart and tried to push the cart past him. It was the first time I had seen him in the library without Artem and he saw me before I could push by.

"Hey, Lucky," he said. "What's happening?"

"I'm just working," I said. I asked him what he was doing in the library, since it was not Sunday.

He shrugged. "I had some time to kill, so I thought I'd do some reading." He held up the magazine he was looking at. It was about basketball and he did not have the newest issue.

I shook my head. "We have the new one in the back. I'll get it for you."

When I came back with the new basketball magazine, he was reading *The Joy of Sex*, which I had left on the cart. My face got red.

"Man, look at this," he said, laughing, turning the pages.

I looked and he was pointing at the armpit hair. "What's wrong with that?"

"Nothing," Hendo said. "I mean, if you're into that kind of thing." And he laughed again.

Most of the women in the porno movies shaved their armpit hair and the hair above their vaginas. Hendo turned the pages and laughed and I asked him if he was into armpit hair.

"Not really. I like women to be smooth, you know?"

I nodded. He handed the book back to me and took the new basketball magazine. "More respectable reading material," he said, and thanked me and started reading.

After I pushed the cart away, I texted Marxy and asked if he liked armpit hair or not.

BECAUSE I CAN SHAVE MY ARMPITS OR LEAVE THE HAIR.

And he responded:

I DO NOT CARE IF THERE IS HAIR IN YOUR ARMPITS!

⌁

After my shift I was waiting for the bus. It was rainy and the bus was late. There were so many people waiting in the bus shelter to hide from the rain that I only fit halfway in. One side of me was getting wet and the other side was staying dry.

I did not want to go all the way inside because I do not like being surrounded by so many strangers. I also did not want to wait outside because of the rain.

"There's plenty of room, honey," a woman said.

I took another step inside. That was as far as I could go.

And then the bus came and it was too full and did not even stop.

"Come on," the woman said, bumping into me.

Everyone went back into the bus stop and I went and stood with one foot inside and the other foot out again.

That was when a car pulled up and the window rolled down. It was Hendo. He asked if I wanted a lift. "I'll be going right by your neighborhood."

"Really?"

Someone from the bus shelter asked if she could get a lift too. "Nice try," he said, unlocking the door and pushing it open. "Hop in, Lucky."

The seats were warm when I got in. Hendo said the car was pretty new and the seat warmers were good in winter. "Or rainstorms."

"Do you need my address?"

"Naw, I've been there before."

He drove away and as he did the woman in the bus shelter, the one who asked if she could come, gave Hendo the finger. He laughed and turned on the music and the bass.

"When were you over at our house?"

"Huh?" He turned down the volume. "Oh. Once or twice."

"With Toucan?"

"Yeah. Do you mind?" He held up a cigarette. I said he could smoke if he wanted to, since it was his car. "Cool. Didn't want to be an asshole." He blew smoke out of the window. "Haven't seen Gert around very much. How's he been?"

"He got kicked out of school, but now he's going back."

"Didn't even know he was in school. Right on. What's he studying?"

"Economics, I think."

Hendo took another puff of his cigarette. "Seriously?"

"Yeah."

"Huh." We kept driving. "I guess that's why he's tight with Toucan. Good with money."

I told him that he was not tight with Toucan anymore, not since AK47 said he couldn't hang out with gangbangers. "She thinks Toucan is a gangbanger."

Hendo laughed. "Gangbanger. Sounds like a porno."

I did not laugh. "What do you mean?"

"Nothing. It was a dumb joke. Nevermind."

Hendo said he needed to make a stop. "Got to deliver this," he said, reaching to the backseat and bringing out a stuffed giraffe. "It's Artem's birthday in a few days and I'm probably not going to be at the party. Little guy loves giraffes. He's goddamn crazy about them." He gave me the giraffe to hold. "Pretty cool, huh?"

"Giraffes can clean their own ears with their tongue," I said.

"Really?"

"I read it in *National Geographic*."

We drove to his neighborhood, which wasn't far from our neighborhood. I tried to make a map in my brain of where it was.

He did not turn the engine off when he parked the car. The rain had stopped.

"If I leave it running, you're not going to steal my car, are you?"

"No," I said.

He got out and ran into one of the houses.

It was the first time I was alone in his car. I looked around it. His glove box wasn't locked and when I opened it a bunch of papers and garbage fell out. I started putting all of it back as fast as I could when I saw that Hendo was already coming out of the house.

He got into the car and I said, "Sorry, it just opened," meaning the glove box and the garbage, but Hendo was already trying to put the car in gear.

His Baby Mama came out of the house and started running toward the car.

"Shit," Hendo said. "Get down." He pushed my head down so I sank back into the seat. "Pretend you're not there."

I tried to hide myself like he said. He got out and shut the door, and I could hear them shouting on the other side of the window.

"I told you," he said. "I have to work."

"Work?" the Baby Mama said. Her voice was loud. "I can see her." She knocked on the door and said, "I can see you. Hello? I'm not blind."

Hendo opened the door and told me I could sit up. "I have to take care of this. Hold on."

I sat up again, since she had already seen me.

She pointed at me while they argued. Another woman came out of the house, carrying Artem. The second woman brought the baby to Hendo, who took the baby in his arms and kept holding him while all three of them continued fighting.

The second woman walked up to the car, toward my window. She looked villainous and I pushed down the lock, which was a smart thing to do, since she tried to open the door. She was shouting and calling me a "slut" and other names that AK47 would not like me to repeat.

"Go away!" I shouted at her. She punched the window and I punched the window, until it was like a drum being played on both sides.

Hendo handed the baby to the Baby Mama and ran and stood between her and the window. That was when she started punching him, on his chest, and he held her hands and then, out of nowhere, there was no punching, just hugging. He had his arms around her and her face was in his chest, her hair going all around his shoulders until her face was buried in him.

He went inside and came out. He started the car.

"Sorry about that. She thinks you're my new girlfriend. She always gets jealous whenever I'm seeing someone new. It's why I try to avoid her at all costs."

ᛦ

Nobody had ever thought I was anybody's girlfriend. Except Marxy. Some people could tell we were boyfriend and girlfriend, since we held hands. Neither of us was normal. It was like we were doing battle together. A lot of people, like AK47 and Dr. Laird and Pearl, wanted me to know that Marxy and I were still very different. He would never be as smart as me, and even if that wasn't a problem for me now it might be later.

Hendo was very beautiful. Men are not usually called beautiful. They are called handsome. Hendo had a kind of beautiful face that was like a movie star's. I looked at him and started to think about what it would be like if I was his girlfriend. We would go out places and talk about the books from the library, and we would kiss and nobody would say, "Look at those retards," the way they said that to me and Marxy.

He was very cool too, and was not embarrassed to be with me and have people see me.

"What?" Hendo said as we drove away from his angry Baby Mama. "What?"

"You're looking at me weird," he said, and one of his eyebrows went up. He asked what I was looking at and touched his face and asked if he had food on it or something.

I took all the spit in my mouth and swallowed it back down.

"Are you in love?" I asked.

"With Artem?"

"With your Baby Mama?"

Hendo laughed. "No. In fact, I can't stand her. The only reason I even bother is Artem."

We were coming close to my neighborhood. My body felt like it was two hands being rubbed together, getting warmer and warmer. My pulse was getting powerful and I could feel it in my neck, *thump thump thump.*

He turned on the music, to a song that I liked. He nodded his head and left his arm hanging out of the window. As we drove out of the neighborhood people waved to Hendo, and I realized that he was legendary with many people. While we were driving I thought about how Hendo said that his Baby Mama thought I was his girlfriend.

I had thought about having a family, but so many people said that two people like Marxy and me shouldn't be allowed to have babies. Hendo was normal, and if his Baby Mama thought I could be his girlfriend, maybe I could be someone who has a baby too.

Like Mom. If I was AK47, I don't know if I would have gotten an abortion.

"She has big boobs," I said.

He laughed. "Yeah, yeah, I guess they are big. But I'm an ass man. And legs. You got nice legs. Do you run?"

"Sometimes," I said.

"Anyway, Gert doesn't need to know about that compliment, right?"

Hendo pulled his car in front of our building. He shut the car off and we sat there for a second. My seat belt got sucked up by the car. In movies, people are always asking people they like to come upstairs. They also kiss in cars. I wasn't allowed to kiss Hendo, since I was Marxy's girlfriend and that was cheating, which I hate. Hendo's fingers made a drum on his leg.

I closed my eyes and made a movie in my mind about Hendo leaning over and putting his hands in my hair. I saw him move my face and hold my head and we kissed. And then I thought about the stand-up thing AK47 said never happened in real life and I laughed.

"Cool," Hendo said, reaching across my lap to open the door. "I guess I'll see you around. Good hanging."

There was exactly eleven seconds, which I counted in my brain, where we looked at each other in the car, not making moves, not saying anything. This was the time I should have kissed him. I did not realize this time was perfect until he was gone.

chapter twenty

was meeting with Dr. Laird, who must have had psychic powers. He always seemed to know where I was going with something, or what I was going to say, even before I said the thing. I guess that was why he had been to school for so long, to be able to do that. His walls were covered with proof that he had gone to a million schools.

One of our rules was that I could tell him anything, but that I wasn't allowed to ask him things about his life. Our meetings were about me, not him, he said. I could talk about Gert if I needed to, and he promised he wouldn't tell Gert what I said.

"Except in extreme circumstances," he said, like if I was in danger.

When I was younger and Gert was my legal guardian, he got to hear everything. Since I turned into an adult, I had a lot more that I could say without worrying about Dr. Laird telling him.

Dr. Laird had been talking a lot about Marxy and how I felt about him, since he was my first boyfriend and since sex was something that boyfriends and girlfriends did.

"All right, Ms. Zelda," Dr. Laird said. "Lay it on me."

I told him that there was a new person I found sexy. "Even though I'm still in love with Marxy," I said.

"This new person in your life." Dr. Laird wrote in his notebook. "Does Gert know?"

I picked up Dr. Laird's squeeze ball. "You are always saying I should stop asking permission from Gert."

"Of course. That's important. But I've never heard of this person before."

When I put the squeeze ball down, it took a long time for it to go back into the shape of a ball. We watched as the lumps my hand had made turned smooth until the ball was perfect again.

"So tell me about him."

I shrugged. "He's a normal person."

Dr. Laird moved his hands in a circle. "Normal as in . . . ?"

"He is not like Marxy," I said finally.

"Got it. Tall? Short? Fat? Skinny? Blond hair, brown?"

"He's taller than me but not as tall as Gert. And he has veins you can see on his arms. Where the muscles are. Which is sexy."

"Is he your age?"

"I think he is older, but not older like you. He is around Gert's age."

"Where did you meet?"

We had met at Toucan's, but I was not supposed to mention that. Since I knew Dr. Laird would want me to explain who Toucan was, I decided to tell a half-truth and told him that I met Hendo at the library. I said that Hendo hung out with me when he got bored of the Sunday Bunny Reading Hour, and that sometimes he just hung out to read about basketball. I told Dr. Laird that he treated me like I was normal too and that he was into Vikings.

"But not as much as ninjas, which is okay, because they are badass too."

Dr. Laird's pen went crazy writing notes. I tried to see, but it was too squiggly for me to read any of the words.

When I was done talking, he said, "How does all of this make you feel?"

"I feel good, and also I feel gross."

"Why?"

I closed my eyes and tried to ask my heart why it was telling me to feel bad, even though it was also telling me to feel good at the same time.

"I love Marxy," I said. "And we are going to have sex and it's dishonorable for me to be finding someone else sexy. That is one of the big rules about being in love."

"Okay. And how has that changed? Do you still find Marxy sexy?"

I nodded. "Very sexy, but not in the same way. With Marxy I find him sexy to look at, and also sexy as a person. He is very honorable."

Dr. Laird said that was good. "But it's not against the law to feel attracted to someone new, Zelda."

I asked him if he ever thought about having sex with people that aren't Mrs. Laird. He laughed and said, "Oh boy. You're not going to tell her, are you?"

"No, sir."

"Like I said, Zelda. *Everyone* has sexual fantasies. Which is not to say that you always act on those thoughts. But it's good they're there. Otherwise you'd just get bored. Right?"

"I don't know," I said. "I don't think Marxy is boring."

"Okay, fine. I've got a soft spot for Julia Roberts."

The movie *Pretty Woman* stars Julia Roberts who has sex with Richard Gere for money and in the end she stops being a hooker and they finally kiss on the lips.

"So this is the week," Dr. Laird said. "For you and Marxy."

Dr. Laird asked me if I was ready. I took a deep breath and told him I was.

"I know all about sex."

"And Marxy? Does he know all about sex?"

"He knows everything too."

He asked me to tell him everything I knew about sex. I told him how it happened, and I also told him what I had seen in the porno videos, and before he could say anything I told him what AK47 had told me: those are fantasies and real sex is different. That made Dr. Laird happy. I told him about putting condoms on the carrot, and that I would bring a bunch with me, and that Marxy would bring some too.

"AK47 will be there, in another room, and so will Marxy's mother."

We stared at each other.

"There will be no Gert," I said.

I expected Dr. Laird to tell me to tell Gert, but he didn't. He read over his notes and then asked me about what else was new. I told him about the library, all the different books, and how even though there were not many books about Vikings, I could order them, and that I had already ordered a book on Vikings that Carol said was brand-new.

"Nice work," Dr. Laird said. "How's Gert doing?"

"I don't know," I said. "Fine."

"You don't know?" Dr. Laird raised his eyebrow.

I did not know what to say, or what he was really asking me, because I had just told him I didn't know what Gert was doing.

"Is Annie still his girlfriend?"

"They got back together."

A big smile came across his face. I asked him why he was smiling.

"Because you are not talking about Gert anymore."

"Okay," I said.

"Do you know why that's important?"

I told him I did not. His smile stayed on his face and he leaned forward, like he was going to tell me a very important secret. I leaned forward so that our faces were having a meeting in the middle of his desk.

"Because you are living your own life," Dr. Laird said. And then he sat back in his squeaky chair. "You have a job, you have your own bank account and your own money. You could have your own apartment one day. And you have a boyfriend."

My face started smiling too. I did not ask it to start smiling. But I could feel it smiling and then I started smiling inside of my body when I understood what Dr. Laird was saying.

"In other words," he said, "you are finally living your own legend."

⚡

When I got home from Dr. Laird's I took out my list and looked at it:

THINGS LEGENDS NEED

- ☑ A hero who is skilled in hand-to-hand combat
- ☑ A powerful weapon for the hero to use
- ☑ The hero must win the love of a fair maiden in danger
- ☑ Every hero needs a wise man
- ☑ Pillaging rival villages for treasure
- ☐ The hero must defeat a villain who threatens the tribe

Dr. Laird was right. I had accomplished almost everything on the list. I still did not have a villain to defeat, but maybe sometimes legends don't have villains. Maybe mine would be the kind of legend where the hero is good and just, like Knud the Great, a Viking king who brought his people many years of peace, so that they could trade goods with other tribes. And I was the hero of my legend, where the next step was to have sex with Marxy.

⚡

However, I wanted to talk to Marxy in secret. The secret to secret meetings is to make sure that nobody finds out about them, so you need to make sure it is in a place that is secret, and also make it so that nobody asks questions. I did not want to lie, so AK47 said that the best way to do something secret and to not lie is to make sure nobody asks questions that make you need to lie.

I texted Marxy and told him to call me, but only when he was sure he was alone and his mother or father was not around.

He called that night.

"I am calling because I'm alone and nobody is around," Marxy said, almost whispering.

"Why are you whispering if nobody is around?"

"Oh." His voice got normal. "Okay. I am home alone, so I guess nobody can hear me." He made a noise that was like a smaller sneeze. "Sorry," he said.

"Did your mom talk to you about our secret meeting?"

"She did."

He said that she had told him everything about sex, including how to use condoms. "I've been practicing," he said.

That made me smile.

I told him I wanted to meet him in secret, before we had sex. "Without anyone knowing. Just us two."

"Without AK47 or my mom?"

"Yes."

He got quiet. It was not a good quiet.

"Hello?"

"I don't like this," he said. "I don't like hiding things from her."

I sighed. "But when we have sex, she won't be there, in the room."

"I know."

"It will just be me and you."

He got quiet again. "Yeah."

I told him that having a secret meeting would be like practice, being alone without his mother or AK47 or Gert. I said that for Vikings, you are a man when you are able to ride horses and drink with other men, and when fifteen winters have passed.

"I don't know how to ride a horse," he said. "My dad lets me have beer sometimes."

"You have passed fifteen winters," I said. "And nobody rides horses anymore."

We agreed to meet alone, without telling anyone where we were meeting, or what time. It was not a very special meeting spot, the way secret places are always special and dark and scary in movies. This meeting place was a McDonald's by the Community Center.

I got there first and ordered fries for us to share.

We always spent time together with other people around, watching us. We had not been alone very much since we first met at the Community Center exactly eleven months and fourteen days ago. All of the things I read on the Internet say that boyfriends and girlfriends that do not spend a lot of time alone with each other often break up. And Marxy's mother did not let him be free. I believed Marxy could do more than she thought he could. It was like when I started working at the library, after people thinking I was too retarded. I proved them wrong.

I ate the fries and made sure to have lots of ketchup in the little paper cups for Marxy. I put two of the paper cups in front of the chair for him, and a small packet of salt and pepper, which I knew he would like. Two old people, a man and a woman, were sitting across from me and the man ate his fries with his mouth open. The old woman wiped his face with a napkin. He kept his mouth open while she wiped around his lips.

I reached out to take the longest fry, and a hand reached for it first.

The hand was not Marxy's. It had tattoos of eyeballs on the knuckles.

"These are my favorite," Toucan said, dipping it into the ketchup.

"Mine too."

"Oh. Shit, sorry." He held out the half he had not put in his mouth. When I did not take it, he said, "What, you think I have germs?"

"You do have germs. Everyone has germs."

He shrugged and put it into his mouth. Then he sat down. "Relax," he said when I started to tell him he couldn't sit there. "I'm just waiting for Jumbo over there to order the food."

The Fat Man was waiting in line.

"How are things?" Toucan asked.

"Things are fine. Can you go?"

The door to McDonald's opened and Marxy came in. A stranger was with him, and he patted Marxy on the shoulder and I waved to Marxy and Toucan turned around to see who I was waving at.

Toucan took another fry and watched Marxy come over. "What the fuck is this now?"

"Hey," Marxy said, out of breath. His shirt came up just above his stomach, showing little black hairs, and he pulled it down.

"Who was that man you were with?" I said.

"Oh. I got lost and he helped me." Marxy turned to Toucan and stuck out his hand. "Hi. I'm Marxy. Who are you?"

Toucan finished chewing and wiped his hand on a napkin. "Toucan. I'm a friend of Zelda's."

"Of Gert's," I said.

"Oh. I'm Zelda's boyfriend."

Toucan stared at him. "No kidding."

"You can go now," I said to Toucan, who kept staring at Marxy.

The Fat Man brought over the McDonald's bags and Toucan got up. "Good seeing you," he said, and as he left he patted Marxy on the shoulder, and Marxy flinched, because he does not like being touched.

"I didn't like him," Marxy said as Toucan left.

"Yeah," I said. "He's a real shit-heel."

⪡

We ate our fries and then Marxy was still hungry, so we got hamburgers too. He told me about how his mother hadn't told his father about us having sex, and I told him that Gert did not know either. He ate his hamburger very quickly and asked if I was going to eat the rest of mine.

Marxy started telling me everything about sex that he had learned, about spermicide and condoms, and all the different ways to do it.

"I wrote it all down," he said, and took out a piece of paper that had been folded a lot. There were words by the pictures of naked people.

"Wow," I said.

"This one is my favorite," he said, and pointed to one where the woman and the man faced each other. "Because you can kiss while having sex."

He was getting "riled up," which is what AK47 said whenever Marxy got too excited. He took out his asthma puffer and inhaled.

Some of the people in the McDonald's were looking over but I didn't care. I thought it was very sexy how excited Marxy was getting about us having sex. I thought that this was my boyfriend, and he loved me so much that he couldn't breathe.

chapter twenty-one

On the day of sex, AK47 didn't pick me up in the school bus. She came in her car and told me to be ready to go before she got there.

"In and out," she said on the phone, and I made sure before she came over I had my shower and shaved my armpits and legs. Even though Marxy didn't care, I wanted to be smooth.

I did the perfume like AK47 told me, putting some on my neck and the insides of my wrists, not too much, since some people didn't like loud smells. Especially spies. Being quiet and hidden about things is not a very Viking thing to do. You should be brave and stand up to your enemies face-to-face.

"Except there are no enemies here," AK47 said. "Unless you count Gert."

People are always telling women and girls what to do, AK47 said. And people were always telling me what to do too.

"I'll be back in a few hours," I told Gert. "AK47 and I are having girl time."

He was lying on the couch, not listening. He put up his hand and gave me a thumbs-up.

"Sounds awful. Tell her I say hello."

I said I would and he did not ask any more questions. He had been working on an e-mail he was going to send to Dean Horowitz, who said that he was allowed back to school, but would need to take summer school classes to make up for the ones he stopped going to.

When I got in the car AK47 looked at me and smiled and said, "You did good on the lipstick, Zee," and then licked her finger and rubbed my face where some of the lipstick had gotten smudged.

※

We drove to the hotel. It was not very fancy, but it was also not like the hotel near our apartment, which AK47 said is where men bring women to have sex with them for money. The hotel was a Holiday Inn and when we were going in we walked by people holding briefcases and talking about banks.

Marxy and Pearl were waiting in the lobby of the hotel. Marxy was wearing a shirt and tie with Batman on it. He waved at me and I waved at him. Pearl was already talking to the woman at the front desk and AK47 went there to talk too.

"Are you all going to be staying in the room?" the woman at the front desk said.

AK47 handed over her credit card and said, "What's it to you?"

The woman was looking at me and Marxy. I wondered if she knew what we were going to do. I went over to Marxy and gave him a kiss on the cheek. I got on tiptoes until I was off the ground, since he was taller than me. My lipstick left a picture of my mouth on his cheek.

"I love you, Zelda," he said. "Go then dang."

"I love you, Marxy," I said, and held on to his hand.

"It's extra for double occupancy," the desk woman said.

AK47 gave her THE LOOK and the woman at the desk swiped the

credit card in the machine. AK47 put her hands on her hips. The credit card machine beeped.

"Here are some keys," the desk woman said, handing over plastic cards.

When AK47 got the keys, she gave the woman one last mean look before we all walked down the hallway.

The carpet was brown and orange and had shapes that were like arrows, with other shapes that were colored green and looked like cactuses. The arrows were a good omen because they looked like *Tiwaz*, the rune for Tyr, who is a god that lives in the sky.

"You look very beautiful," Marxy said.

He put his big hand around my hand and we held them together like that, like they were praying together, just like the Bon Jovi song where he sang about living on a prayer. We held hands and lived on the prayer of our hands all the way up to the fourth floor. AK47 and Pearl had also gotten a room, across the hall.

They would stay there in case we needed them.

"Let's take a look-see," Pearl said, putting one of the plastic cards into the door. A green light beeped and we went inside.

There was one bed and curtains that were white and you could see through, and an alarm clock on a table next to the bed. Pearl took a bottle of water from her bag and put it on the table beside the bed. She also took out a few other things, containers and also a package of napkins that were wet, in case we needed to clean up "any messes."

"What messes?" I said. The hotel room was very clean and we would not be eating in it.

AK47 and Pearl looked at each other and then Pearl said, "Just in case."

"We'll be right across the hall," AK47 said. "Okay?"

"Okay," I said.

"I am trusting you with my son, Zelda," Pearl said, giving me a hug.

"You can trust me."

"Do you know about safe sex?"

"Everything and then some," AK47 said. "Condoms. The moves. Everything. Boom."

Pearl nodded. "Marxy also knows everything there is to know. And you know things will have to go step by step?" Pearl asked me. "He has been going through the steps today."

"I don't even need the paper with them written down," Marxy said, pulling on his Batman tie.

"I think we don't need the paper either," I said. "I think we will know what to do."

"He might need to take his time, so don't get frustrated. Things might not go as fast for him as you'd like."

For other people it is not very romantic, having a list of things to do. People are supposed to have sex "naturally," meaning without having to think. But because Marxy isn't good at not-thinking, he needs to be really sure about what he is doing before he does it.

This was one of the deal-breakers for the sex: that Marxy would need to go slow and I wasn't allowed to get mad if he needed to stop and go back to steps that made him comfortable. That was fine because I liked to use steps when I did new things too, and I had my own steps. For example, I wanted to kiss a lot before having sex, and before having sex he had to put on the condom.

AK47 hugged me. "Are you ready for this? You can always not do it. It's no pressure."

"I want to do this," I said. "I want to have sex like an adult and be legendary."

Marxy's mother came over and held my face in her hand. Then she kissed the top of my head and told me I was a good egg.

I was going to achieve another part of my legend. We were finally going to have sex, like normal people who are in love do.

≷

When the door closed we stood across from each other. We were each holding a condom. The condom in my hand was blue. His condom was red.

"Hi," he said.

I said, "Are you ready to have sex?"

"I think we should kiss," he said. "That always comes first."

The hotel room smelled like the little cardboard tree that Gert hung from the mirror inside his car. The bed had a white sheet that was like a trampoline when I sat down on it.

"Do you want the lights off?" I asked.

In porno videos people are always having sex with the lights on, but one of the things that I knew from being home when Gert had sex with people was that he liked to have sex with the lights off.

"How will we see what's happening?" Marxy asked, and I told him maybe for the first part we should only keep one of the smaller lights on, to make things more romantic.

I had looked at Marxy's list of ORDER OF THINGS TO DO WHEN HAVING SEX before coming into the hotel room. Marxy had it on the bedside table and kept looking at it.

"We take off our clothes," Marxy said. "That's what comes next."

"Okay," I said. "Can we stop saying what we're going to do before we do it?"

Marxy tried to unbutton his shirt. His fingers were having trouble with the buttons, which were small. My shirt was easy to take off, and I did it myself, even though in the movies the man takes off the woman's shirt almost every time.

Marxy's breathing was getting faster. He was stuck on one button.

I started to take off my pants. "No," Marxy said. "My shirt still has to come off."

"Do you want me to help you?"

He shook his head and held out his hand for me to stop. "The man takes off his shirt and then his own pants. Okay?"

It was taking a long time for him to get the buttons undone. I remembered what Pearl said and to have patience. I sat down on the bed and bounced a few times. The wallpaper had flowers on it, and someone had stuck chewing gum to the bottom of the bedside table.

"Gross," I said.

Marxy looked at me and I told him it was the gum, not him, that was gross. "You're very sexy, Marxy," I told him. "Are you sure you don't need help?"

"I said I can do it," he shouted. "Stop asking."

Finally he undid the buttons and put his shirt over the chair by the window. Marxy had lines where his arms stopped being tanned. He had small brown birthmarks on his stomach and tiny brown hairs around his nipples.

Next he started taking off his pants, which he had even more trouble with than his shirt. He got one leg out and had to put his hand on the wall to stop himself from falling over. It was very unsexy, because he forgot to take off his shoes first and the pant leg got stuck.

"You have to take off your shoes first," I said.

"I know that," he said. "You can start taking off your pants now too."

I tried to take off my pants slowly, so that our pants could be off at the same time, but ended up taking them off faster. I sat down and waited. I wanted to continue looking sexy, but it takes a lot of effort to hold sexy poses, so I decided I would wait until he had his pants off before getting into the sexy pose again.

Finally Marxy had to sit down on the ground so that he could get his one leg out of his pants. Then he stood up and I could smell that his deodorant wasn't working very well.

I was wearing the fancy underwear that I had bought. Then I stood and stepped with one leg and turned and showed him the pose I had been practicing in my room, after my push-ups, in front of the mirror. The porno women did this in pictures to look sexy, and so did models who wore underwear.

"Hello, stud," I said.

Marxy raised his eyebrows. "We already said hello. And why are you standing like that?"

"Do you like what you see?"

"I like you, Zelda."

"What about these?"

Trying to keep the sexy pose, I pulled the underwear and they made a snapping sound.

Marxy's eyebrows wiggled. "They are okay."

"Just okay?"

"Can we kiss? We should kiss. We should kiss before we do anything else."

I felt crappy that he did not like the underwear so much, and that the sexy pose made his eyebrows go up. But this was one of the things about Marxy that AK47 told me would happen: he would not be like the men in the movies. I would have to accept that about Marxy. I started to wonder about Hendo, and then felt bad thinking about someone who was not Marxy, while kissing Marxy.

"Okay," I said, taking his hand.

We kissed again. Marxy put his tongue in my mouth and moved it around. I told him to not be so angry with it and to move it around less.

"Go slower," I said.

He kept doing things that made it hard for us to move in the same way. When I went to put my arms around his neck, he moved his head away from me, and when he moved forward toward me so I could put my arms around his neck, he moved too much and we hit our teeth.

"Ouch," he said, putting his hand to his mouth.

"I think I bit my lip," I said. Marxy did not look very happy. I told him to not panic. "Let's try to kiss again," I said, and this time the kiss went much better.

The bed bounced underneath us. He put his hand on my leg and I touched his cheek, very gently. His cheek was smooth and warm. His hand on my leg made me shiver, even though it was hot instead of cold.

"Okay," he said. "I think it's time to have sex. We need to take off our underwear now."

He was wearing loose boxer shorts and pulled them off his legs and put them beside the bed. I took off my underwear in a slow sexy way until we were naked on the bed.

It was the first time I had seen Marxy naked. He had some hair on his stomach, near his belly button, and his ribs poked out and moved up and down when he breathed.

"You are very handsome," I said, since I knew that people liked to be complimented when they have sex. I told him I could help him put the condom on.

"No. Let me do it," he said.

"Make sure you don't break it," I said.

I thought of practicing with AK47 and saw that Marxy wasn't holding it correctly. He did not pinch the condom on the edge and was trying to rip it right down the middle. Then he went to use his teeth.

"Stop!" I said. "You don't use your teeth. Ever." I asked him to give me the condom to open, since I didn't want him to open it the wrong way.

He didn't want to.

"I know how to do it," he said.

Finally he got the wrapper off and then he tried to put it on. It was a

Trojan condom, with a warrior's helmet on the front. He started trying to put it on and had it upside down, and then did not pinch it properly. He had said he practiced with condoms, so I didn't know why he was so bad at it.

"Did you use a carrot to practice?" I said. "Because you have to hold it up and see where the ring part is before putting it on."

"Can you please stop talking, Zelda?" Marxy yelled.

"A cucumber works too, for practice," I said. "But a cucumber is bigger than a penis usually is, and bigger than your penis too."

I sat on the bed and watched him. The condom wasn't going on at first, and I wasn't feeling like I wanted to have sex anymore. I didn't like being yelled at.

"Okay," he said, putting the condom on. "I'm ready."

"I didn't like when you yelled at me," I said, "and got angry about the condom. And I don't like that we are saying what we do and going through steps. Sex is where we make our own rules."

He shook his head and held it in his hands and said, "This is going bad," and when I tried to tell him it was okay, he said it wasn't okay.

I tried to kiss his face but he was turning to the side, so that his ear was by my eyes and his hair was in my face.

"Okay," he said, and we went onto the bed and he put himself on top of me.

I couldn't breathe easily, because his stomach was on my stomach pushing the air out. Marxy sat on me once when we were wrestling and I forgot how heavy he was.

I asked if he could get up off of me, so that he wasn't so heavy. "I can't breathe very well."

"This is the way that we do it first," he said. His face turned to me and I could smell his mouth, which was hot and made me feel like I was being trapped in a room.

He put his hands next to me and looked down. His face became red.

"What?" I asked him.

"Nothing."

I tried to hold his face. "Marxy, what's going on?"

He got off me and I saw the condom was falling off. "It's not work-ing like it should."

"We can just kiss," I said. "And start from the beginning."

He balled up his fists and pressed them together until the knuckles cracked. "I don't want to have to start from the beginning."

I sat up. "Stop yelling."

He took out another condom from his bag. "This isn't working," he said again, turning so that he was not facing me. "This isn't working."

"Is it on?"

He was trying to rip open the condom package.

"Marxy? Is it ribbed? Because mine is ribbed and it feels better."

"Stop talking."

It was getting cold from the air-conditioning in the room so I put my shirt back on. I waited for him to get the condom on. I was watching him hold his penis. When he turned around the condom wasn't prop-erly stretched out. It looked like a silly thing hanging from his penis, and even though I didn't mean to I laughed.

"Are you laughing at me?" he said.

"Sorry," I said. "You just said you practiced a lot but then did every-thing wrong. We could get carrots from room service. I can show you how to do it."

He took the condom off with a loud snap and threw it on the ground and said we weren't going to have sex anymore. "I don't like the way you're being mean," he said.

"I'm not being mean. But you said you practiced and then didn't know what to do and didn't want me to help. If you didn't know, you should have told me."

He crossed his arms and said he wasn't turned on anymore and that nothing was sexy. "I want to leave," he said. "I want to go home." Then he went to pick up his phone and I got to it first. "Give it. I'm supposed to call when I want to leave."

I held the phone away from him and jumped on the other side of the bed. "Grown adults don't call their mothers during sex," I said.

"We're not having sex," he said. "We're finished and you're being a shit-heel villain, Zelda."

"And you're being a baby. Fine. Take it." And I threw the phone onto the bed between us and told him I had to go pee and to do whatever he wanted.

〉

I went into the bathroom and looked at myself in the mirror. My makeup had smeared. I wiped my face and heard some of the Grendels, coming from the other side of the shower curtain, where they liked to hide.

"Shut up," I told them, taking a deep breath.

The Grendels like when things screw up and people get hurt, and I knew I had hurt Marxy. There was a knock at the bathroom door and AK47's voice asked if I was okay.

When I came out, Marxy's mother was in the room and helping him get dressed. She held his shirt up for his arms to slip through.

"It's okay," Pearl said. "Just put this on."

"Are you leaving?" I said.

AK47 took my arm. "You probably want to put on some pants," she said, and I realized I was still naked and didn't feel sexy anymore, just stupid. She handed me my underwear and I put them on. "What happened?"

"He was getting angry and was having trouble with the condoms and I wanted to help. He didn't want help and couldn't get it on properly. And it looked silly and so I laughed and—"

Pearl told me to be quiet, holding Marxy's pants for him to step into and pulling them up to Marxy's stomach. "You can button it yourself," she said. Then she took some Kleenex and picked up the condoms and stretched them out. "Not broken," she said. "So there's that."

Crumpling the condoms up, she threw them in the trash.

"I didn't mean to laugh at him," I said. "Marxy, I didn't mean to laugh at you."

AK47 picked up Marxy's socks and handed them to Pearl. "Here. I think these are his."

It felt like the world was happening around me and I was not a part of it anymore. Pearl and AK47 said quiet things to each other, while Marxy stood behind them. When I tried to go around to talk to him, AK47 held me back and said, "Just a second, okay?"

Pearl and AK47 talked, and every so often they got even quieter and tried to look at me without making it look like they were. I wanted to apologize to Marxy and tell him I was sorry for laughing about the condom not staying on. He stood in the corner and stared out the window and then started walking in place. I tried to get his attention and wave to him, but he kept walking and walking, like in cartoons how someone who thinks a lot goes back and forth and ends up walking themselves into a deep hole.

And then Pearl said they had to go and she led Marxy out of the room.

"I'm sorry," I said to Marxy as he walked by. They went out and shut the door. "I didn't say anything that bad," I told AK47 when we were alone. "I just thought it looked silly. Why is he so mad?"

"Men are weird about their private parts. It's not your fault." She sighed. "We knew this might happen."

"He kept talking and it was nothing like how it was supposed to go. But having sex and making love is like water, not stone," I said, which is what one of the magazine articles I had read on the Internet said about being a good lover.

"It never goes the way it's supposed to, Zee. It's something you learn." She put her arm around me and put her head on my head. "Tomorrow's another day."

chapter twenty-two

We went from the hotel to AK47's apartment. AK47 wanted to take some time to figure out what to do next, and also to get me into fresh clothes. Because we had told Gert we were going to a movie, she sent a text telling him we would be a bit late coming home, that we were going out for some dinner after.

While she texted Gert I tried calling Marxy from my own phone. Pearl had told me not to, but she wasn't in charge of me or my legend. I wanted to tell Marxy that even though our first try having sex didn't work, that I wanted to try again. AK47 told me that everyone's first time is weird, to not feel so bad.

"I feel like a fuck-dick villain," I told her. "I have let my fair maiden down."

And she put her hand on my shoulder and told me it wasn't my fault. "It'll be okay," she said.

Nobody answered the phone the first time I tried calling, so I kept pressing the button for redial and let it ring. The answering machine came on and I told it that I was Zelda and that I was in love with Marxy and I was sorry for whatever happened.

On the third call someone answered the phone. I said, really fast, that I loved him, and that I was sorry for making him upset and saying that he didn't know how to use a condom. But it wasn't Marxy.

"He needs time," Pearl said. "Stop calling, Zelda." Then she hung up.

The next time I called, the phone kept ringing.

More memories started coming, and when they did I started to feel ashamed.

For example, one rule is that you are not supposed to make fun of how people look when they are naked. And I accidentally did that to Marxy. He had also worn his Batman tie, which was not very sexy, and I had worn my underwear. When I thought about it, I was angry that he did not try harder to be sexy, and then I felt bad again for laughing at how his penis looked.

AK47 brought me coffee with chocolate powder in it and told me to breathe.

I asked when we were going to tell Gert. "I have no idea." We sipped our chocolate coffees. "Not yet, anyway. I need a game plan."

᛫

AK47 told me to let her handle Gert, and when we got home they got into a fight, though not as big as when Alf came into the apartment and Gert went Berserker. There was not much yelling this time. Instead of yelling, Gert got quiet and seemed more sad than angry.

Gert was mostly sad because we didn't tell him that Marxy and I were having sex.

"It's like you cut me out," he said.

AK47 plopped next to him on the couch. "Well, we sort of did. You don't exactly have the best track record for calm under fire."

I said, "It was my decision to have sex. I am not a car you drive. You do not control me."

Gert got quiet.

Neither of us told him how it went badly. He did not need to know everything, AK47 said.

Gert calmed down and then apologized to AK47 and apologized to me.

"I just . . ." he started saying, "I don't like not being able to help. You know?" He was picking at a string on his jeans.

AK47 nodded and said she knew that. "It's okay. We know you just want to do what's best for Zelda."

"But sometimes I have to decide what's best for me," I said. "Even if it's wrong."

Gert sighed and sat up. "So how did it go?"

AK47 and I exchanged glances. "Well, nobody's first time is all that great," she said.

Gert nodded and said, "You can say that again."

〃

All that week Marxy did not call or come to the Community Center, which made me sad. None of the things I liked to do were fun anymore, including basketball.

On the court I decided that I wouldn't play any basketball games, any real games, until Marxy came, since I didn't want to be playing when he walked in and my heart kept hurting. I wanted to be able to run toward him, like in movies.

I had a present for Marxy, a printed paper from the Internet of his favorite basketball player, Larry Bird, making a shot to win a game. In *Kepple's Guide to the Vikings* I learned about people called *þræll*, who were basically slaves who owed people debts. They worked for the person until they didn't owe anything anymore. I wanted to show Marxy that I was willing to work as a *þræll* until he was ready to forgive me. Slavery is evil, which is something I learned in school. But when someone owes something, they should pay the person they owe back. I wanted to pay Marxy back.

I wanted to be moving really slowly, running toward Marxy, holding the Larry Bird photo in my hand. His face would light up and he would say, in Viking, that he loves me and isn't mad and that we are two Vikings, just like always, in battle together.

Instead, I sat on the side of the gym, on the bench, while everyone played. There weren't enough spots on the teams for everyone, so people subbed in and out. I was the only one who didn't want to get subbed into the game. I just held on to a ball and squeezed it, moving my fingers all along it, along the skin, which felt like an old crusty orange.

Hamsa subbed out of the game and sat down next to me.

"You aren't playing," Hamsa said.

"I'm watching the game."

Then he got serious and punched my shoulder. "Marxy's not coming back because of you. That's why Marxy isn't here. He's my best friend and you fucking fuck-dicked him."

There was a ball near the bench we were sitting on, so I got up and threw it at Hamsa so hard it hit him in the arm. His hands didn't go up fast enough to catch the ball. The ball bounced off of him and hit the ground and he said something not in English.

"Fuck-dick," Hamsa said, and pushed me.

Before anyone knew anything, we were fighting. Not like Vikings, not honorably. We were grabbing onto each other and pushing and pulling. When Hamsa's arm came close to me I bit it as hard as I could. Hamsa screamed and pulled his arm back.

I don't know if Vikings bit others in battle or not, since they had swords and didn't need to. It did not seem like the honorable thing to do in battle, since animals bite, not warriors. Berserkers would do anything to win, though, so in the end biting Hamsa to win the fight was okay. Gert says that in a fight there are no rules.

"Break it up," Big Todd said.

One of the volunteer adults took Hamsa to get his arm fixed and to stop the bleeding. People have germs in their mouths, just like animals, and Hamsa's arm needed to be cleaned so that he wouldn't get the germs from my mouth and get sick and die.

"Come on, now," the volunteer said. He was the father of one of the retards who I didn't know. He put his arm around Hamsa and told Hamsa to hold his hand over where I had bit him. "I know it hurts," he told Hamsa.

Yoda and the others were watching Hamsa cry. Then they watched me. Their mouths were open, like they had questions to ask and couldn't remember how to ask them.

"Stop looking at me," I said, since their staring made me feel like I did whenever Gert and I would go somewhere new and people would look at me and think, *What is wrong with her?*

Big Todd ran a hand through his hair. No fighting was one of the Rules of the Community Center that was near the top.

"He called me a fuck-dick," I said.

"Zelda. The office. Okay?"

I sat in the office until the end of the hour, in the same chair with Larry Bird. In that time Big Todd came in and told me that I had wounded Hamsa, and I had hurt his feelings too.

"You acted like a villain," he said. "Right?"

He was correct. But it was actually worse than being a villain: I had acted like a Berserker, like Gert when he attacked Alf, who is smaller and not able to defend himself. I had acted like Uncle Richard when he smashed the bottle on Gert. My list of THINGS LEGENDS NEED was becoming a list of THINGS THAT VILLAINS DO.

Before Hamsa left, I wanted to make sure that I apologized. Hamsa was waiting by the Community Center door with his uncle. He had a Band-Aid on his arm.

"I'm sorry, Hamsa," I said. "I shouldn't have done that."

Hamsa's uncle gave him a push. Hamsa looked at his uncle and then said, "I accept your apology."

Hamsa's family knows what it's like to be different, according to AK47. People have even bigger problems with Muslims than they do with gay people like Big Todd or people who dress like thugs, the way Gert dresses. Hamsa has two problems: he is retarded, and he is Muslim. Ever since villains flew the planes into the towers, everyone has started hating Muslims.

Even though Marxy was still not talking to me, I felt like I had done the right thing for once, even if it was only after doing a bad thing first.

⟩

I got onto the bus and Yoda did not want to sit with me. AK47 said for him to stop being a goon and he said that I was a villain for hurting Marxy.

"And she bit Hamsa," Yoda said.

"Is that true?" AK47 asked.

"It's true," I said. The first part of becoming legendary and a hero is to overcome your mistakes.

"Did you apologize?"

"I apologized."

"She's still a jerk," Yoda said, and when the bus stopped in front of Yoda's house he did not give me a fist pound.

The doors closed and AK47 turned around in her seat. "Don't worry. He'll come around." She held up a cigarette. "Sorry. I'll explode if I don't have one."

⟩

She parked the bus in front of a playground. We were not allowed to smoke on the bus, so we sat on a swing set and smoked together. Our feet went up and down and the cigarette smoke went up in the air. We were laughing after a few swings, especially when the cigarette flew out of her mouth and went in the air and almost landed in her hair.

For a little while I forgot all about Marxy. Then I got sick and we had to stop swinging.

We sat on the sand cross-legged. AK47 said that she felt partly to blame for how the sex went, and for fighting Gert in front of me. And not just fighting. Yelling and slapping and hitting. "That's a goddamn bad example to set. Fighting isn't how you solve problems, even if you are a Viking like us." She leaned back and stared at the sky.

"You can't change the past," she said. "But going forward. What does your legend need?"

I thought about it. She told me to think about all the heroes in all the legends I had read about, in *Kepple's* and on TV and in movies and books. What did all the heroes do?

"They fight," I said.

"Well, symbolically, sure. But sometimes fighting isn't actual fighting fighting. Sometimes it's not giving up."

I looked up. AK47 folded her arms.

"I want to symbolically fight," I said. "I want to win back Marxy."

She sat up and slapped all of the sand off her legs. "Good. Then let's go get you some Marxy."

⇗

AK47 knew the way to Marxy's since she had picked him up a hundred times in the bus. It was a good day for battle. The sky was very cloudy. You cannot do battle when the sky is too nice and blue, with the sun shining, since you would just want to sit and relax, instead of fighting.

We drove into Marxy's neighborhood, where tall houses faced each other with big windows like eyes and doors that were bright red and green. It was enemy territory, meaning it was not a place where I went, and I was prepared to do battle with Marxy's mother, and with Marxy too, in a way, since I wanted to defeat his bad feelings toward me.

AK47 parked the bus. I took a deep breath. We did a dab, and then I went off to battle.

I went to the door and turned around. AK47 waved then made a fist, which was to show that she was with me in spirit. The doorbell did a bunch of different rings, like a song. Across the street a woman was pushing a baby carriage. She waved at me and I waved at her.

The door opened, and it wasn't Marxy or Pearl. It was Sarah-Beth.

"Hello," she said. "How can I help you?"

"What are you doing here?"

"What are *you* doing here?" she asked me back.

"I asked you first."

She frowned and called out behind her. Pearl came to the door. "Zelda," she said, putting her hands on her hips, "what are you doing here?"

I said that I had come to win back Marxy's heart. "Is he home?"

Pearl told Sarah-Beth that she should go back inside. "I'll be back in a minute."

Sarah-Beth nodded and did as she was told. Once she was inside Pearl stepped out onto the front porch and closed the door behind her.

"Marxy doesn't want to see you," she said. Then she saw AK47. "Is that Annie?"

"I want to see him," I said.

She waved to AK47, who put down her phone and waved back. I told Pearl that I wanted to see Marxy, even if he didn't want to see me. I said we were in love.

Pearl did not respond. She walked to AK47. I followed after.

"What are we doing here?" Pearl asked AK47.

AK47 got out of the bus and crossed her arms. "The star-crossed nature of love," she said.

"Marxy doesn't want to see you now, Zelda," Pearl said.

With a shrug, AK47 said that it was between me, Zelda, and Marxy. "Can't they talk?"

"That's what I want," I said. "Just to talk."

Pearl shook her head. "We have company over."

"It'll only take a few minutes. Right, Zelda?"

I had a speech written down that AK47 had helped me write. It took me less than two minutes to read when I practiced it. "Two minutes," I said.

Sighing, Pearl said to wait on the porch. "We'll see if Marxy wants to."

⇗

AK47 and I waited as Pearl went back inside. I told AK47 about Sarah-Beth being over. AK47 said she was probably the company that Pearl was talking about. AK47 watched the house for a minute, not saying anything. She had THE LOOK, which meant that her brain was working on something very hard, so hard that she couldn't use her mouth to say words at the same time. I asked her what she was thinking.

"Why won't he see me? And why is he hanging out with Sarah-Beth?"

"Nothing." She took my hand. "There's a chance that Marxy's not going to want to be your boyfriend again, Zelda."

That was not possible. Or it was possible, but I would win his heart back. That was one of my strongest skills: not giving up in battle, no matter how much I was losing. Finally Pearl opened the door and waved me over.

"You have ten minutes. He's up in his room."

I went in and passed Sarah-Beth, who was sitting in the living room, watching TV. She didn't say anything when I walked back. Pearl walked behind me, up the stairs, which had cushiony steps with carpet. The house smelled like a mall at Christmas, like flowers.

We got to Marxy's room. The door was open. Marxy was sitting at his computer. He spun his chair around and did not smile back at me when I smiled at him.

"If you need me," Pearl said to Marxy, "just holler."

"Okay," Marxy said.

Pearl closed the door, but not all the way. I could hear her walking down the stairs. When she got to the bottom I took out the piece of paper from my pocket, where I had written what I wanted to say to Marxy.

"'Dear Marxy,'" I read.

"What is that?"

"It's my speech," I said. "Just listen."

Marxy wasn't good at sitting still. I knew that, so I made sure that the speech I had written was short. While I read he twirled in the chair and played with his fingers.

"'I know I have messed things up, but I am in love with you and I would like to be girlfriend and boyfriend.'"

He started patting his hand on his legs. It got louder the more I read. I tried to ignore it. Marxy wasn't saying anything. Sarah-Beth knocked and said Marxy was going to miss the basketball on TV.

"Okay," Marxy said. "I'll be there in a minute."

She closed the door. Marxy kept patting his knees until he finally stopped. "Okay, I think the time is up and you should go."

"Why is Sarah-Beth here?"

He started patting his knees again. I tried to make him stop the patting and his knees just got crazier and moved more and his hands got louder. I told him to stop it and he made a noise that was very different from any noise I'd ever heard him make before. That was when Pearl opened the door and said I had to go. Marxy got up and took a deep breath.

"Sarah-Beth is my new girlfriend," he said, so fast that I did not even have time to understand what he was saying properly.

"What do you mean?"

"We are boyfriend and girlfriend," Marxy said. "You and I are broken up and now I am Sarah-Beth's boyfriend. You were a shit-heel to me in the hotel, and I feel good enough about myself to say no, Zelda. I don't want to have mean people in my life."

⊱

Fuck Marxy. I have never said that before in my life, but that was what I thought. I was a Berserker when I got home. AK47 wanted to stay but I told her that I wanted to be alone. My head-veins pumped blood and my heart shouted. Inside I wanted to break something, so I punched the lamp standing in the corner. The lamp fell over very slow and boring. I thought it would break but it didn't. It just fell in a stupid way.

I went to the bathroom and when I came back I stood it back up, since the lamp hadn't done anything to me, and because it was in the way how it was sitting on the ground.

In Viking legends when people died they were put on boats and pushed off into the middle of a lake, or to the sea or ocean. The boat would be set on fire and the dead person's body burned until it was ashes and the boat would burn and sink too.

I thought that the best way to forget him would be to do what Vikings do: I would burn him.

When dead Vikings got put on their boats, the things that they used in life were put with them, like swords or armor or magical charms or toys. Sometimes their wives and girlfriends were burned alive too.

I had drawings Marxy had made me. Plus the love letters he wrote. I decided I would make my own boat for them.

Vikings burn things in order to show that they are dead. Since Marxy and I were broken up for good, I wanted to make a funeral fire for him.

"You are dead to me" is one of the things AK47 said to Gert when they got into the big fight that broke them up the first time.

"You are dead to me," I told the drawing Marxy had made for my birthday.

Since I didn't have a real boat, I had to make one. I ran the bathtub, filling it with water. Then I found a plastic bowl that we made salad in. I put all of the things that were going to be made into ashes into the bowl. Gert had a lighter in one of the drawers for candles, in case the power went out in the building and we didn't have electricity.

"Good-bye," I said to Marxy. And then I read the words in Viking: *Góða nótt*, which means "good night."

The bowl floated in the bathtub. The fire inside of it didn't go crazy. It wasn't very big. When enough of Marxy had burned, I tipped the bowl over and all the paper floated on the water for a while, until it got wet. Then it fell apart and made the water gray.

chapter twenty-three

Before my appointment with Dr. Laird, I wrote Dr. Kepple a letter. I was still so angry that I made lots of spelling mistakes and had to type the letter out twice.

Dear Dr. Kepple,

My boyfriend Marxy is now in love with another person named Sarah-Beth, who chews on her hair. I believe that this makes them both villains, because he has betrayed our true love, and she has stolen him. I have burned a picture of him to show the gods how angry I am with him.

Are there any other ways to make it clear to the gods that we are no longer together anymore? Also, are there any special Viking ways to curse their union?

Zelda

I clicked SEND and waited until Gert knocked on the door to tell me it was time to go to see Dr. Laird.

I clicked REFRESH one more time before turning off my computer.

During the drive to the meeting, Gert tried to get me to talk, but I was too angry, and at our meeting, Dr. Laird wanted to talk to me alone, not with Gert there.

"For now, I want to understand how you feel," said Dr. Laird.

"Marxy is dead to me," I said.

Dr. Laird put down his notebook. He said, "Just start with the hotel. And go from there."

I went over all the things that happened in the hotel room, including how Marxy was not good with the condom, and how I had accidentally laughed at him.

"I didn't mean to laugh at him. He just looked so funny." I grabbed the stress ball and started squeezing it. "But I was wearing sexy underwear, and he didn't notice. And I did sexy poses, and he didn't find them sexy."

"I can see how that would be frustrating," Dr. Laird said.

"And he got angry with me and his mother came in." I squeezed the ball until it almost popped. "Why does she have to do everything for him all the time?"

"What kind of future did you imagine with him?"

I asked what he meant by asking that question.

"You know," he said, moving his hands around. "In five years, what does your life with Marxy look like? Are you married?" He told me it might help to close my eyes and imagine a picture of it. "Just take a picture of the future and tell me what it looks like."

I closed my eyes and tried to do what he said. In my mind we had a big house, kind of like the one Marxy lived in with his mother. "But not with his mother," I said to Dr. Laird.

"So you live together independently. Not with her."

"Correct."

"Is Gert there?"

I went back to the house I was imagining. He was washing his car in the driveway, using a plastic bucket and a yellow sponge.

"He's there."

"So you and Marxy and Gert would live together."

I opened my eyes. "I don't know. Maybe. Why?"

Dr. Laird spun his ballpoint pen around in his fingers. "Do you think Marxy and Gert would get along?"

"Well. Maybe we don't live with Gert. But for sure no Pearl."

"Earlier you mentioned that you think she bosses him around too much."

"All the time," I said, and then I went over all the different ways she controlled his life.

"You use the word *control*," Dr. Laird said. "I'm interested in that, because there's another possibility."

"Okay," I said.

"Which is that he actually needs someone like her to help him. That he's not as independent as you are."

"He can do more than people think," I said, and found myself getting angry.

Dr. Laird put his pen down gently on the notebook in front of him. "I guess what I'm trying to relay to you is that, while I know it sucks that you guys broke up, it might actually be for the best."

It was one of the only times I got very mad at Dr. Laird. I threw the stress ball at him. It hit him in the stomach and rolled onto the floor. We watched the ball roll down his stomach and onto the ground.

"Okay," Dr. Laird said. "Can we talk about that?"

I decided I would give him a powerful Silent Treatment to show how angry I was. We sat quietly for another two minutes until the buzzer rang.

I stood up and did not shake Dr. Laird's hand.

"He is who he is, Zelda," he said. "And that's okay. But that means he might not be right for you, either."

"Screw you," I said, opening the door and walking out.

⋰

I did not do well at working in the library that day because I was upset about Marxy. I was not excited to help people find books or to take books out. I made mistakes twice. Once I put a book that a patron had returned back in the shelves before telling the computer that it was back, and once Carol found me putting books about war in the section for Sports.

Carol knew that I was upset and I told her I didn't want to talk about it.

"Well, tough. Because if you keep moping around all the time, you're going to start making more mistakes and this whole freaking place will start crumbling to the ground. So spill." When I did not spill, she said, "Is it guy trouble?"

"Nevermind," I said.

We were standing at the front desk of the library, where I worked a lot, since I had gotten so good with the computers. Carol made her fingernails tap on the desk. I pretended I did not notice her head right by my head. She did that whenever she wanted to get my attention without making noise.

"Hmmmmm?" she said and poked me in the shoulder with her finger.

"Stop it," I said.

Someone came to take their books out. I scanned the books and Carol took the receipt and slipped it into the top book.

"Is it that boy who came around? Mark? Marco? What was his name?"

"Marxy," I said.

"Ah."

She was not going away, not even when I gave her THE LOOK. All she said was, "Please, that's not going to work, so you might as well tell me."

I took a deep breath. "We broke up. Marxy and me."

"That's a shame." She stopped floating her head near me and passed over a book to put into the system. "Breakups are rough."

After scanning the book into the system I put it on the cart behind me. "And he's got a new girlfriend."

"Already?" Carol whistled.

Carol did not have a husband or a boyfriend, but she had a daughter that hated her guts. Carol did not want to talk about why her daughter hated her. She did like to talk about how good her daughter was doing in school.

"She is a wizard when it comes to calculus. Math, all that stuff. She doesn't even have to try. I'm terrible at it, but she can tell you all the digits of pi to the fifteenth number."

"Whoa. I know it has three."

Carol laughed. "Right about my level." She sighed. "She's a wild one, like I was when I was her age. Her father was out of the picture before the pin dropped."

"My dad too."

Carol was actually like my mother and didn't get married and had to raise her daughter by herself. But she did not drink alcohol while she was pregnant with Nancy, who she called Nance for short.

"Speaking of man-whores," Carol said quietly, and when I looked I saw who she was talking about. "Brace for impact," she said.

Before I could tell her to shut up, Hendo was standing in front of me.

"Hey, Lucky," he said.

Carol went to put some other books into the library catalog, but I could tell she kept watching, even though she acted like she wasn't.

"It's not Sunday," I said. "I thought you came on Sundays."

"I have a reading emergency that can't wait," Hendo said. "I was wondering if you could help me find a book, since you're an expert and everything." He said he wanted a book for Artem about trains. "He's crazy about them. This weird cartoon has them, and I don't even think he's old enough to even know what I'm talking about. But it's good to read to kids that age, they say."

"Picture books, we got a new one that's a doozy," Carol said, beeping another book under the scanner. "Zelda can show you." She wrote down the call number and gave it to me.

I said to Hendo, "I can show you."

We went to the section of the library on Picture Books. While we walked I could smell him, and he smelled nice and once his hand touched mine and I didn't know if it was on purpose or not. My brain exploded a bit but I made sure inside I counted to ten, not on the outside, because I didn't want Hendo to think I was being weird.

"Here are our best books on trains," I said, and showed him my three favorites.

The one Carol was talking about made train noises while you read. You pressed a button and the book said "CHOO CHOO" and made the sound of screeching on metal train tracks. He pressed one of the buttons and rubbed his chin.

"This is perfect," Hendo said. "Nice work."

We dabbed. Instead of taking the book to the front desk, he sat down at one of the tables. While he flipped the pages he said I could sit down, if I wanted.

"I mean, I don't want to keep you from doing work."

Carol was scanning books and the library wasn't busy, so I told him I could sit and talk for a bit. Hendo asked me what was new with me.

"Fine," I said. "He's in night classes and will be back next semester."

"Do you always think about him first?"

"What do you mean?"

"Instead of saying what was up with you, you started talking about Gert." He pressed a button on the train book to make the conductor go "ALL ABOARD."

"Oh." I looked at my hands and wondered how much I should tell Hendo. "My boyfriend broke up with me," I said.

Hendo closed the book. "Seriously? Fuck that."

Carol heard him swear and made a noise with her throat. He waved and said sorry.

"Man. It's his loss, though. A girl like you?" He made a spitting noise with his mouth and shook his head again. "He doesn't know what he's missing."

I did not know what to say. He held up the train book. "I guess we should check this out."

We walked to the front desk and I went around behind it, to the computer. Carol turned and kept watching us.

"Card?" I asked.

He patted his pockets. "Shit. Forgot my wallet in the car. Can you hold on while I get it?"

"I can search for your account by phone number," I said.

He smiled and told me his phone number. I put it into the computer and his name came up with his phone number and address. Once I gave him the receipt he thanked me, and when he left Carol came beside me and said, "He looks like a goddamn swan in a cemetery."

When I asked her what she meant, Carol said that it was something her mother had told her about boys who were trouble. "Beautiful creatures to look at, but in an ugly, ugly place."

chapter twenty-four

Hendo came to the library more after that, which helped me forget about Marxy, who hung out with Sarah-Beth at the Community Center and held her hand and sometimes kissed her.

Every time I saw them I acted like I did not care. He was not my boyfriend anymore. Sarah-Beth ate her hair and her jokes were dumb and she could not figure out how to cash a check at the bank. Hendo was smarter than Marxy, and I thought about kissing him instead.

Hendo liked to read books about war and even *Kepple's Guide to the Vikings*. He asked me what my favorite book was and I told him it was *Kepple's*.

He knew all the Viking words right away, unlike Marxy, who was always getting things like *góðan dag* wrong. He even liked my Words of Today, and whenever we talked at the library he would use them. For example, one day we were talking about Bruce Lee, a famous kung fu fighter, and Hendo said, "He was pretty indefatigable in battle," and *indefatigable* was my Word of Today and even though I had only mentioned it to Hendo once, he remembered the word and how to use it and also put it in a sentence.

Carol had started calling Hendo "the Swan," even though I hated when she called him that.

In legends this is the most boring part, where everyone is happy. Sometimes when I forgot about Marxy I was so happy, especially being around Hendo, though alone in my bedroom I would cry and think about Marxy.

When Hendo and I hung out we did not go to his house or my house. We mostly were at the library, or McDonald's, or the coffee shop across the street from the library. He asked me about Vikings a lot, and about Gert and Mom and AK47. He reminded me of Dr. Laird, who was not very good-looking like Hendo but always asked lots of questions.

Gert and AK47 noticed I wasn't so sad. Gert said I wasn't moping around. AK47 asked me if there was someone new in my life. I told them I was just happy that they were together, and that we were a tribe and I had a job and Gert was going to go back to school.

One day Hendo told me that he and Gert did not get along. "We're both alpha dogs." That meant that both Hendo and Gert thought they were the most impressive warriors. "But we can still be friends," he said. "Right?"

I told him we could.

᠈

Hendo was my secret who belonged to nobody else, and he made me happy. When you are too happy the villains strike because your guard is down. In the *Saga of Beowulf*, for example, which is the most famous legend, Hrothgar and his wife, Wealhtheow, and all of the Vikings are happy and singing, which makes Grendel, the villain of the legend, very angry, because he is not happy and is jealous. Hrothgar and the other Vikings forget that even when everything is peaceful, a Viking must be "vigilant" (Word of Today) and constantly on the lookout for villains, who like to attack during peacetime, especially when people are sleeping and cannot defend themselves. The worst part about Grendel is that he actually eats people while they are asleep.

The villains came while I slept, just like when Grendel came for Hrothgar and the other Vikings.

I woke up because they were using loud swearwords and smoking, something that was not allowed in the apartment. The voices did not belong to Gert or AK47, which meant that we were being invaded, just like Grendel invaded the hall where Hrothgar and his wife and Vikings were celebrating. A shameful thing is being a coward. When the voices woke me up, I felt very afraid and pretended to sleep, which is something a coward does.

Then I understood that I had to protect my tribe from whoever was in the apartment.

"You can do this," I heard the voice of Odin saying in my brain, and then I heard my mother's voice agreeing with Odin. "Protect the hearth," her voice said to me. In my brain I told them I would not let them down.

I took my alarm clock from beside my bed and prepared to throw it. Normally a Viking would take out his sword when it came time to protect the home, but my sword was under my bed and I did not want to risk alerting the enemy by getting it out.

I opened my bedroom door carefully and stuck my head around the corner. The voices continued talking. The hallway floor was louder than the floor in my bedroom to step on, so I had to move very slowly, one toe at a time, in order to stay quiet and sneaky. I also pressed my back against the wall in the hallway as I moved to be invisible, combining my Viking skills with the skills of a ninja, since I wanted to have the element of surprise.

I moved closer to the living room until I could see light from the lamp shining on the carpet. My heart thumped and in my brain I counted to ten, closing my eyes only a little bit so that I would not have my eyes closed and could defend myself if someone decided to attack.

One . . . two . . . three . . .

When I got to four, the toilet flushed, and I realized that one of the villains was in the bathroom. This is called a "tactical error" because I did not check to make sure nobody was behind me before moving forward. Hendo taught me the expression and said that Hitler invading Russia during winter was a tactical error too.

I realized that I was stuck between two villains and it was too late for me to get back into my bedroom.

I froze and did not know whether to run forward into the living room to defeat the villains there, or to face the villain in the bathroom.

The bathroom door opened and the villain who came out was doing up the zipper of his pants. It was the Fat Man. He stared at me and froze too. He made the same "tactical error" I had made, and since I had made it first I was more ready.

It was time to act.

I yelled the traditional Viking battle cry, *"Tyr!,"* which is the name of the god of war, and charged forward, and threw the alarm clock.

He said, "WHAT THE FUCK," and put up his hands. The alarm clock hit him in the stomach and bounced on the ground, and before I could defeat him with a crushing blow he grabbed my wrist and said, "Calm the hell down." Then the Fat Man grabbed my other arm.

I tried to squirm free and then he brought me to the living room with one arm around my stomach, picking up the alarm clock on the way with his other arm.

"Fuck-dick!" I shouted.

Gert was standing in the living room. Toucan was also there, and they were standing over a gym bag and lots of papers and baggies. There was also money on the table, and beers.

"I found her in the hallway," the Fat Man said.

"Come here, Zelda," Gert said, and at first the Fat Man wouldn't let me go. Then Gert said, "If you don't let her go, I'll break your arm," and the Fat Man looked at Toucan, who nodded and said, "She's cool. You're cool, right?"

So the Fat Man let me go.

"Sorry," the Fat Man said. "I didn't mean to hurt her, but she went apeshit and threw this at me." He held up the alarm clock.

Everyone laughed, even Gert, who isn't supposed to laugh at me, no matter what. I gave him THE LOOK and he stopped laughing, then I rubbed my arm where the Fat Man had been holding me.

"Fuck-dick." I asked Gert what was going on. "Why is there all this stuff? And why is Toucan here? Does AK47 know?"

"Nothing is going on," Gert said. "Go back to bed, okay?" He told Toucan that everything was fine. "She probably just had bad dreams. Right?"

"What is AK47?" Toucan asked. "Like the gun?"

"They shouldn't be here," I said. I pointed at Toucan. "Especially him. You said you weren't going to be part of his tribe anymore."

"Is that true?" Toucan said to Gert. "I'm hurt."

"Zelda," Gert said. "Bed. Now."

Toucan sat on the couch and patted it next to him. "You." He pointed at me. "Come. Sit. We need to have a conversation."

I didn't want to sit down next to Toucan. A lot of Gert's friends were scary, but I never worried that they were scarier than Gert, who could be the scariest person on the planet. Gert acted like he was scared of Toucan.

Gert said I should go to bed, but Toucan said not yet.

Gert nodded at me, so I sat down on the couch. Gert also sat down, and on the other side of me was Toucan. The Fat Man didn't sit down. He leaned against the counter and lit a cigarette.

"You didn't see the house rules?" Toucan said to him, pointing at the sign near the door. "Take it out on the balcony if you're going to smoke."

The Fat Man tipped his head with the cigarette still in his mouth. "Seriously?"

"Very seriously. You don't like smoke, do you, Zelda?"

"No," I said. "Not even Gert is allowed to smoke in the house."

Toucan pointed at the balcony window. "You heard her."

The Fat Man took himself and his cigarette out to the balcony and shut the door. Toucan put his arm around me, which I hated, since he was not a member of our tribe.

"So, you know that everything that has to do with me has to do with your brother, which means it has to do with you. I have your brother help me out with some things. In exchange, I pay him. That's what capitalism is."

"Capitalism," I said.

"I give you money, you give me goods and services." He watched the Fat Man on the balcony with his cigarette. He was leaning over the edge and letting ash fall down. "So this is very important. I need to know I can trust Gert, and part of that is knowing I can trust you. Can I trust you?"

His arm was squeezing my shoulders so hard that it was starting to hurt. It reminded me of Uncle Richard on the couch, except Toucan's grip was stronger. When I tried to wriggle free, he didn't let go.

"Gert," I said. "He's hurting me."

"Can I trust you?" Toucan repeated.

"You can trust her," Gert said. "Can you relax?"

"I want her to say it," Toucan said.

Now Toucan's squeezing made me feel tiny. I felt like I was about to pop, like a balloon. "You can trust me," I said, and Toucan let me go. He stood up and smiled, and Gert stood up too.

"All right," he said. "It was nice to see you again, Zelda."

The Fat Man knocked on the glass of the sliding balcony window. Toucan nodded and the Fat Man came back inside, throwing the cigarette on the balcony before stepping on it.

"Time to go," Toucan said. "Gert, walk us down."

He turned and walked out with the Fat Man behind him. Gert said, "I'll be right back, just sit right there," before following them.

Gert was gone for ten minutes. My shoulders hurt and when I pulled my sleeve up I could see the skin was red, like a bruise that was waiting to happen.

Then I saw that I had peed myself. I didn't notice at first. But between my legs, and the couch under my butt, was wet and getting cold.

Gert came back with a new Reebok gym bag and shut the door. He saw me sitting on the couch, and my wet pants. And I was crying, which made me feel even worse.

I hadn't wanted to cry in front of Toucan. Now I could cry, so I did. I had peed myself and was crying. Gert put the bag down. He ran over and lifted me up.

"I'm sorry I peed on the couch," I said, and Gert put me over his shoulder, the way parents hold their kids.

He brought me to the bathroom and put me down. "Get out of those clothes. I'll bring you some new stuff, okay? They'll be outside the bathroom door. Get changed."

In the shower, I thought about how stupid I was, peeing myself in front of Gert, in front of Toucan, who was a shit-heel that I didn't want to be afraid of. But I was afraid of him. When I came out, Gert was in the living room, with a spray bottle of soap and a bucket of water. The couch cushions that I'd accidentally peed on were by the door.

⌐⌐

That night I couldn't sleep. The person I wanted to talk to, whose voice I wanted to hear, was Hendo. I had taken his phone number from the library computer and had it in my phone. Going under the covers, I called him.

"Who is this?" Hendo said.

"It's me."

"Me who? Oh." He coughed into the phone. "Man, what time is it?"

I looked at the clock and told him the time, which was 1:32 a.m. He asked me what was going on. I first made him promise he would not tell anyone.

"Yeah, fine. Just let me get back to bed."

I told him everything that happened—Toucan, the Fat Man, and Gert. The only thing I left out was peeing myself. It was gross and very unsexy. Hendo listened for a while and when I was finished he asked if there was anybody else there.

I said no. "Unless they were hiding."

"What were they talking about?"

"I don't know. Toucan just said 'capitalism.'"

Hendo said he had no idea what that meant. "Did Toucan give Gert anything?"

"There was his gym bag and beer and cigarettes, which are not allowed."

"Did Toucan take the bag or leave it with Gert?"

I rubbed my eyes. I did not know why he was asking. Hendo said to think, that it was important, and then I asked him why it was important and he said nevermind, which I did not like.

"Sorry," Hendo said. "I know you don't like it when people say that to you. Accept my apology?"

"Okay," I said. "I think he left the gym bag."

Hendo asked if I was working the next day, and I said I was. Hendo told me he would pick me up and we could talk it over in the car. "Okay? Right now I need to get some sleep."

"Can you talk a little longer? I like hearing your voice."

"Tomorrow," Hendo said.

I hung up and threw the phone at the bed. It bounced up and onto the ground.

chapter twenty-five

n the morning Gert had cleaned everything. The cushions were not wet anymore. When I came out of my bedroom he was waiting for me. He said he was sorry for last night and for Toucan.

"I know you don't like being in the dark about what's going on."

I crossed my arms and said, "Or lying to AK47," because he had asked me not to tell her that Toucan had come over.

"I don't like it either," Gert said.

I asked him why he was still being around Toucan, when he promised he was finished.

"This is the last thing I'm doing for him. Then we're all done."

He would not talk any more about Toucan or what he had to do for him. "Capitalism," I said, and Gert sighed and said, "Something like that."

He asked if we were cool. I said we were, and he told me he would do some laundry, to clean the clothes I was wearing the night before.

While he was doing laundry in the basement of the apartment building, I got ready very fast so that he would not have a chance to come back and ask more questions. I left him a note saying I was going to work and I would see him later. Since I was going to see Hendo, I wanted to look nice and actually wore my fancy underwear, even though Hendo could not see them, and also very nice jeans that AK47 said make my ass look good. I put on my lipstick quickly.

I met Hendo by the bus stop, where he had told me to meet him. He pulled up only a second after I got there.

"Hey," he said.

"Hey," I said, getting into the car.

He drove with his arm on the wheel. "Sorry about last night. I was tired. You okay?"

I shrugged. "I'm okay. Gert is being a fuck-dick and a liar. He's not supposed to be friends with Toucan anymore, and I am not supposed to tell anyone."

"You're telling me," he said.

"You will not tell anyone, though."

He said that was true. We drove a little while and I saw that he wasn't turning to the library. I asked him why he wasn't going to the library. He said he thought maybe I could skip work and we could hang out for the day.

"Call in sick. Have you ever missed a day?"

"No. Never. Vikings don't break their pacts, especially when it comes to work that is important to the tribe."

Hendo said that was true, but didn't Vikings also take breaks for themselves to get rest? Besides, he said, he was looking forward to getting some alone time.

"Right?" he said.

I blinked and looked down, where he was holding my hand and putting his thumb over my knuckles. His thumb jumped over each one.

≷

I called the library and asked to speak to Carol and told her that I could not come in. Hendo turned down the music and rolled up the windows so she wouldn't know I was in a car.

"I'm sorry," I said, coughing. "I am not feeling well."

I expected Carol to be mad at me for calling at the last minute. Instead of yelling at me for breaking my promise to work, she said it was cool.

"You aren't mad?"

"Zelda, honey, you'd walk uphill barefoot in the snow both ways before you missed work. Get some rest. I'll get someone to fill in." She told me to feel better before I hung up.

"See?" Hendo asked. "That wasn't so hard."

It wasn't hard. But I still felt bad.

Hendo asked me what I wanted to do with our day together. Then he asked if I had ever had sushi.

"Isn't that raw fish?"

"Yeah," he said. "And other stuff too. But if you haven't had it before, you have to try it."

I made a face and said it sounded gross. "Okay." He tapped his fingers on the steering wheel. "What about a movie? Nobody will be at the theater now."

That sounded better than going to eat raw fish. Hendo let me pick the movie I wanted, so I picked a movie about Spider-Man.

All during the movie we ate popcorn and once Hendo put his hand on my leg and rubbed it. I put my hand on his leg and rubbed it too, to show him that I found him sexy. And then it happened: we kissed.

It was the most legendary kiss I had ever had. Marxy kissed a weird way, and Hendo kissed perfectly.

"Holy crap," I said.

Hendo said, "*Shhhh*," and laughed, because we were still in the theater and the movie was playing and I had said HOLY CRAP very loud.

Then he kissed my ear and my body became water. Hendo took my hand and squeezed it. My neck felt hot. On the screen, Spider-Man hung upside down and swung from one building to another building before saving the day.

❧

The movie ended at 2 p.m. I did not feel bad about missing work anymore. Hendo kissed me again and put his arm around me while he walked.

"What do you say about going back to your place?" Hendo asked, finishing the soda from the movie and throwing it into the garbage can outside the movie theater.

"For what?"

"I don't know. We never really hang out alone." Then he turned to me and got serious. "Gert's not home, right? Or his girlfriend? Can you call?"

And he kissed me and his tongue touched my tongue and I said okay, I would call Gert.

My heart was beating very quickly. Hendo's hand touched my knee, and I put my hand on top of his hand and our fingers did a romantic thing where they pretended they were also kissing.

AK47 was driving the bus all day and would not be finished until 6 p.m.

Gert answered the phone and said he would be home by 4 p.m. He was going out to buy textbooks for his summer courses, which meant the apartment would be empty for two hours. "Why?" he said. "Is everything okay at the library?"

I told him I wanted to maybe hang out, after work, and he said that sounded nice.

"Well?" Hendo asked when I hung up, taking my hand.

"He won't be home until four p.m."

Hendo smiled, showing me his very white teeth.

In the car ride Hendo kissed me at every stoplight. Once someone crossing the street whistled at us and we both laughed.

Kissing Hendo was more legendary than kissing Marxy. He did perfect things with his tongue. He did not push it too much in, and he tasted good, like gum or toothpaste. He also smelled amazing.

When we got to the apartment and went inside, Hendo took off his shoes. "See? I remembered," he said, and tapped the RULES OF THE HOUSE sign with his finger. While we kissed his hand touched my neck, behind where my hair started, and his fingers pulled the hair a little bit. That was so good I felt my kneecaps wiggle.

When he stopped kissing me it was like he took all of the air I had been breathing out of me.

"I want you to do something for me," Hendo said. "Can you do something for me?"

He held on to my hands and stared into my eyes. I felt like I was about to fly away if he let me go.

"What is the thing?" I asked.

"I want you to wait in the bathroom for me."

"Why?"

His hands squeezed my hands and then he put his hand onto my cheek, making it a pancake that warmed my face.

"It's a surprise," he said. "I am going to get ready and when you come out, you'll be really happy. Trust me. You'll like it."

I took a deep breath. He touched the back of my neck so I said, "Okay. I do not normally like surprises."

"But you'll like this," he said. After kissing me again he said, "Just count to a hundred and when you come out you'll see."

I caught my breath. "Just one hundred?"

"Just one hundred. After that, we'll be all ready."

※

I shut the door, sat on the edge of the bathtub, and started counting. My brain was swimming when I thought of Hendo's muscles and what he would look like naked, and his penis and also what having sex with him would be like.

"Are you counting?" he asked through the door.

"I'm at eleven," I said.

"Good. Keep going."

I kept counting and went and looked in the mirror. The person I saw looked very sexy, and this person was me. I went close to the mirror and kissed it and even touched it with my tongue. When I stopped and stood back there was a picture of my mouth and lips stuck to the glass.

"Louder," Hendo said from the hallway. "I want to be able to hear you."

"Is this loud enough?" I said, and shouted the number twenty-five.

"Perfect," Hendo said. "But count slower. I need time to get your surprise ready."

I continued counting, loud the way he asked me to. He said I was doing well, and that I should keep going, but also to slow down even more.

"Do the Mississippi thing, where every number is a Mississippi," he said.

I got to one hundred and said I was coming out. I turned the door-knob, but when I pushed to open the door it would not move.

"I think something is wrong with the door," I said. There was a loud noise on the other side. Something heavy had hit another thing, it sounded like. "Open the door," I said, pulling on the doorknob and turning it back and forth. Then I pushed on the wood as hard as I could. If I was strong enough, I could crash through it.

I called out for help again, this time as loud as I could, in case Hendo had not heard me.

There was no answer.

chapter twenty-six

do not like being in a place and not being able to get out, and while I
was in the bathroom I thought I could hear Grendels so I made sure
the bathroom closet and cupboards were open, and the shower curtain was pulled back. That way nothing could sneak up on me. I started
counting the seconds, but the number got so high that I stopped being
able to count, and it felt like I had been trapped forever. Also I had to
go to the bathroom but didn't want to sit on the toilet, in case Hendo
came back, or the Grendels came out of their hiding place, and so I held
it inside until the place below my stomach got sore.

Then I heard someone come in the front door, which was not far
from the bathroom, and Gert said my name. I shouted, "HELP," again
and punched on the door so that he would hear me.

The doorknob jiggled.

"Zelda?" Gert said. He opened the door very slowly.

Then I pulled it open quickly and ran into him and put my face
in his shirt, which smelled safe and like my brother who had saved me
again.

"Okay," he said, stepping back and pulling me off of him. "What's
going on? Why were you stuck in the bathroom?"

That was when Gert saw that the door to his room was open. And not just open. The door had been broken. Pieces of wood were on the carpet in front of his door.

"Fuck," he said, letting go of me and going to his room. He told me to keep back.

"He's gone," I said. "He already left."

He turned back to me.

"Who?"

I looked down, at my feet and the carpet, which was covered with shoe dirt. And then at the door, which was actually empty on the inside—you could see that where the wood had broken off. A little bit of wood covered the door and made it look like the door was all wood, when actually it was some wood and the rest, on the inside, was air.

Gert's room had been turned upside down. The dresser beside his bed was turned over. His clothes were all over the floor.

Everything exploded inside my skull and I felt sick and pressed myself against the wall.

"Fuck me," Gert said.

I did not go into his room and watched from far away. When Gert came out of the closet he sat down and put his head in his hands.

"Fuck," he said.

He got up and held me tight by putting his hands on my arms by my shoulders and I couldn't move. "You need to tell me, right now, what happened."

"I don't know," I said, and he asked me who I was talking about before when I said someone had left.

I didn't know if I should tell him who had come in and robbed us. He would get mad at me if he knew that I had let Hendo come into the apartment.

"You're hurting me," I said, because his hands were crushing my arms.

He let go and kicked a pile of his clothes. A T-shirt went into the air like a bird, hanging and then falling like it was dive-bombing to eat a mouse.

I sat down on his bed.

"I'm sorry," I said.

"Do you remember anything at all about who it was? What they were wearing, how tall they were—anything?"

He stood over me and I looked at my hands. He bent down and said, "This is important, Zelda. Come on."

I looked at my hands and felt myself being pulled in a million directions.

"Zelda," Gert repeated.

I told him it was Hendo. "But he was not supposed to rob us."

Gert got up and stormed out of the room, but not before stopping to say, "And what the hell was he supposed to be doing?"

He did not wait for me to answer.

As he walked out, he swore and pushed the door so it slammed against the wall.

᛭

Gert made a call on the balcony and I wanted to be with him, but he told me to stay in my room. I tried to tell him that I was sorry. He just pointed to my room and shut the glass door of the balcony. I went to my room and sat on my bed and felt like throwing up.

In my room I looked at myself in my mirror and how my makeup was all over my face, from crying and from rubbing my eyes.

Gert came into the room and told me that AK47 was on her way.

"I told her there was a break-in and she's going to stay with you until I get back."

"You're going?" I asked.

Instead of answering, he turned to leave the room.

"You need to stay," I said, getting up off the bed and going after him. I grabbed his arm from behind. "Okay?"

He did not look at me. "AK47 will be here in twenty minutes."

"Can't you stay twenty minutes?"

He didn't answer my question. "Just stay in your room and lock the front door after I go. Put the chain up."

"Please," I said. "Don't leave."

He turned and put his hands on my shoulders and looked me in the eyes.

"Do not open that fucking door for anyone besides AK47," he said, and stepped out the door. "And when I come back, we're going to talk about what the fuck you've been doing hanging out with that scumbag."

⇗

When he was gone I took my Viking sword from under my bed. I promised myself that if anyone got into that door, I would become a hero again, instead of a victim. I put the phone on the coffee table.

I watched it and waited for the phone to buzz.

He had left so fast that I did not have time to ask why he was leaving, or where he was going. I got on my knees on my bed, by the window in my room. I watched and Gert came out of the building. There was a nice car waiting out front, a red one that I knew I had seen before. Toucan was standing outside of it, smoking.

He had two other people with him. One opened the door for Gert and got in beside him. The other person went around and got in the driver's seat. It was the Fat Man.

Then the car turned and drove away.

Protecting the home is the most important thing a Viking could do, even more important than conquering lands with villains in them, so I sat by the door, holding my Viking sword, and went from there to the window to watch if the car came back. I had failed to protect the home once already, and I wouldn't do it again.

I also watched for AK47's car. It was red, but a lighter color and older and a Dodge Spirit, which is not a fancy car like Toucan's.

Finally I saw AK47's car pull into the parking lot. She parked in the visitor spaces and was wearing her rock-and-roll hoodie with the hood up.

I ran to the door and waited for her special knock on the door and when the special knock came on the door I took off the chain that you can only open from the inside of the apartment.

"Easy, Zee, easy," AK47 said, coming in. We hugged and she closed the door and then I went and put the chain on. She took down the hood of her sweatshirt and ran her hands through her messy hair, which looked like cartoons where a person gets shocked by electricity and their hair sticks out in every direction.

"You said he left on his own?" she said. "Like, nobody physically forced him to?"

"Nobody physically forced him," I said. "But it was Toucan."

AK47 rubbed her face in her hands. "Fuck me right in the face. That asshole." She breathed out some air and flopped down on the couch.

I came and sat down next to her and put my head in her armpit, which smelled a little but not in a way that made me feel bad. I closed my eyes and pretended that I was hidden and could not be seen by the world.

"When this is all over," AK47 whispered, "I am going to tear Gert a new asshole."

ᛦ

I had fallen asleep on the couch and there was a blanket over me. I was in the middle of a dream about Grendels again, and in the dream they had taken Gert from the village we lived in and burned everything down, except for me. I hid and did not save Gert, because I am a coward, and the Grendels laughed at me and Gert screamed for me to help him but I could not do anything.

When I woke up from the dream I did not know where I was and thought that I was still in the village, still being a coward, and that the Grendels were still calling me names as they drove their boats into the sea.

AK47 touched my arm.

"Easy," she said. "It's me. It's AK47."

"Gert?" I said.

"He's back."

I sat up and rubbed my eyes and asked what time it was.

"Five." He had been gone for many hours, but at least the Grendels were not eating him.

"I want to see him," I said.

"He's not in good shape. Okay? You need to stay calm. Can you do your counting to ten?"

I did not want to do my counting to ten. I wanted to see Gert. AK47 would not let me see him, so together we took our deep breaths and did the numbers.

"Okay? The heart has slowed down?" AK47 asked.

I gave her my wrist and she touched where the big vein is and smiled.

"Atta girl."

We walked to Gert's bedroom, where he was lying down on the bed with his back to us.

"Hi," I said, very quietly so I did not hurt his head. I made a scared noise when I saw the way he looked. He had a black eye, which was actually purple, and his lip was fat.

"I'm fine," Gert said. "Relax."

"If by 'fine' you mean you look like a frigging pumpkin that's been beaten with a baseball bat," AK47 said.

Gert looked at me. "How are you doing?"

"How am I doing?"

AK47 put her hand on my shoulder. "Get me a towel from the bathroom, okay? Can you wet it a bit with warm water under the tap?"

I ran out of the room and did what she told me.

I brought it over and she used it on Gert's face. He was turned away from me. AK47 pressed the towel against his face. When she took it away from it, there was blood on it.

AK47 told Gert to hold it to his face until she came back.

We went to the kitchen and she shut the door behind her.

"Is he going to be okay?" I asked.

"He'll be fine. He might need some ice, but that's it." She opened the fridge and took out some frozen vegetables that we never eat. She put the bag on the kitchen counter and hit it with her elbow until it was flat and not clumpy.

I asked AK47 what we were going to do about the villains who did that to him. "We need revenge."

Váli, the Viking god of Revenge, is one of the only people who will survive Ragnarok, or the end of the world. He is the son of Odin and a giant woman named Rindr.

Now I was angry. Not at Gert, but at Toucan and the villains who had hurt my brother, who was a warrior and did not deserve to look like a pumpkin.

"One thing at a time," AK47 said, taking the vegetables to Gert's room. I followed her and she stopped me in the door.

"Jesus," she said, and handed me the vegetables. She ran into the bedroom and went to Gert.

He was on his hands and knees and was throwing up onto the carpet. The sound was loud and made me feel sick too.

When AK47 came out of the room she said that Gert needed to be alone, and that he needed to be in the dark for a while.

"I think he's got a concussion," she said. "So for now we need to keep him in the dark and away from noise and light."

I went to my bedroom and took all my blankets and pillows and brought them outside Gert's room, in the long hallway, so that if Toucan or any Grendels were going to come for Gert they would need to go through me first.

I would not be the coward in real life that I was in the dream.

AK47 said it was not going to be a good idea, sleeping in the hallway. "You're going to be in the way," she said.

Without saying anything, I gave her THE LOOK to show her that I was going to stand guard. "Nobody is going to take Gert away again," I said. "He is not going to get any more concussions."

I was so mad with Toucan that all I could think about was killing him. I had never thought about actually killing people before. I thought of defeating monsters and villains, but actually the killing part was always not my favorite part of the Viking sagas.

I thought of Toucan dying in front of me. I cut off his head and held it up and showed the world what happens to people who fucked with Gert and my tribe.

I went to my list of THINGS LEGENDS NEED and crossed out all of the villains except Toucan.

chapter twenty-seven

A day later Gert called Dr. Laird to schedule an emergency appointment after the robbery. At first Gert didn't want to. He said I was going to be okay, and I told him I was too, but AK47 said that it was necessary.

"Trauma lingers, Gert," she said. "Don't forget that."

Lingering means to hang around, and *trauma* is when something really bad happens, so *trauma lingering* means that the bad thing hangs around.

Dr. Laird told us to come in earlier than usual, first thing in the morning, which is the worst time of the day for Gert. He likes sleeping in, and hated going to morning classes, back when he was going to school and not part of Toucan's tribe.

Gert was still upset over what had happened. He wouldn't tell me what was missing from his room, and he did not call the police, which made me glad, since I didn't want to have to lie more about Hendo.

I was feeling ashamed about Hendo. All night I kept trying to call him. The phone kept ringing until the voice of the recording said, "THIS NUMBER IS NOT IN SERVICE." Google said that the recording meant that Hendo had shut off his phone and that he turned the number off, so it couldn't have been an accident, or that he just didn't notice that his phone was ringing.

I felt stupid for kissing him and ashamed and like I had betrayed Marxy and Gert at the same time.

I punched my leg a few times, really hard, and told myself how stupid I was, thinking that someone normal and beautiful like Hendo could actually fall in love with me. He had defeated me by making me think I am a normal person.

He was a villain.

On the way to Dr. Laird's office, we did not talk about the break-in. Gert's brain was not really working. He was like a robot. We drove in quiet. Gert didn't put on the radio or his music.

Gert held the bottom of the steering wheel with one of his fingers. His other arm hung out of the car window and swung on the outside while he drove.

He sipped his coffee. I sipped my coffee and tried to forget that something bad had happened, and that more bad things would happen in the future because of the first bad thing, and that all of those bad things came from the fact that I had tried to have sex with someone who wasn't Marxy, and was a slut, a word that Gert sometimes used with his friends, and that men call women sometimes in porno films.

It means you try to have sex with too many people. It was too much of a fuck-dick word to be one of my Words of Today.

When we parked he turned to me.

"I don't want to lie," I said.

"It's not lying."

"Telling part-truths is lying when someone wants to know the whole truth."

"Look. Just say what I told you to say—that you were asleep, someone came in, and we're going to be talking to the police."

"Are we going to be talking to the police?"

He crumpled up his coffee cup and threw it on the ground of the backseat. "We'll talk after."

He got out. I was supposed to follow him out but didn't want to.

"Gert," I said.

"What? We're going to be late."

"I don't like this."

"What's the rule you're always saying? Tribe comes first? Well, this is all about the fucking tribe."

He slammed the door shut.

It was so early that the security guard at the front had to call up and get permission before opening the door for us and letting us get into the elevator. We got off and went to Dr. Laird's door, the one to his waiting room, which was locked. Gert knocked twice.

Dr. Laird opened the door. Hanna the Secretary wasn't even there.

"Jesus, Gert," Dr. Laird said, seeing Gert's face. "Have you seen a doctor?"

"I'm fine," Gert said.

Dr. Laird practically pushed us into the room.

He had a lot of energy. I wondered how he could have energy when Gert and I didn't. The air-conditioning robot wasn't on. The office was in between being hot and cold. Usually it was very cool. Now it felt like neither, and I felt my armpits getting wet.

Dr. Laird walked around his desk and picked up a cup of tea on his desk. His fingers picked up the little dangling string and made the bag inside the cup bob up and down. It was Earl Gray and had been sitting so long it had started to smell like wet feet.

"So," he said.

"So everyone is okay," Gert said. "Let's just get that out of the way."

"Okay," he said. He took out his notebook and asked for the story of what had happened. Gert told it, even though he wasn't there. Dr. Laird listened and then asked if Gert was home during any of this.

"Zelda was at home," Gert said.

"Alone?" Dr. Laird asked.

"Since she's an adult, and you're always saying she should have more responsibility."

Dr. Laird put his tea down and held his hands up. "Nobody is saying anything different. I'm just trying to get the facts of things straight. So someone broke in by pretending to be someone else. Is that right, Zelda?"

I nodded. My mouth felt sewn shut. I dug my fingernail of my thumb into one of the other fingers.

"So if Zelda was home alone, and you weren't there, why is your face bruised?" Dr. Laird asked Gert.

"Unrelated."

Dr. Laird looked at me and I nodded a second time. "Gert was not there."

He wrote something in his notebook. Then Dr. Laird asked me for my version of the story, which I had been practicing at home since I knew Dr. Laird would ask me. I took a deep breath and remembered where to start.

I said that one of the neighbors had knocked on the door, or I thought it was one of the neighbors. "It wasn't. And it was dark in the hallway outside the door so when I looked through the hole thing I couldn't really tell who it was."

Gert was frowning, his eyes staring at me.

I continued telling the story. "When I opened the door he came in and took me to the bathroom and locked me in there."

"He had a gun," Gert said.

"Gert," Dr. Laird said. "Please let her talk."

"Stop shouting," I said, and they looked at me and I realized nobody had been shouting.

Dr. Laird wrote something in his notebook. When I tried to look at the words he cleared his throat.

"Zelda," Dr. Laird said. "What's our deal?"

"I don't care about our deal," I shouted. "I care about the world being filled with shit-heels and fuck-dicks who hurt people."

Taking a breath, Dr. Laird looked serious, more serious than I had ever seen him. "Did you call the police?"

"I did," Gert said.

There were so many lies flying around that even I was confused about what had happened. I was lying about Hendo, and Gert was lying about calling the police.

"And what did they say?" Dr. Laird asked. "Do they have any clues?"

"I think it's important we focus less on playing detective and more about how Zelda is feeling. It must have been scary."

Gert sounded like Dr. Laird, who always talks about feelings.

"Sure," Dr. Laird said. "Of course."

I was having trouble figuring out what to say. I felt bad about what had happened, and I felt bad about having lied to both Gert and to Dr. Laird. I picked up the stress ball and started squeezing it, trying to make all of the explosions in my brain go from my hands and into the ball.

"I did not know he was going to be a robber," I said. "He said I was pretty and we kissed and—"

Gert looked at me.

"I thought we were hearing the truth," Dr. Laird said.

"Zelda," Gert said.

"Let her talk, Gert," Dr. Laird said. "You kissed a person at the door?" He looked at his notes. "I'm not sure I understand."

I remembered a video I had seen on the Internet. It was supposed to make you into a better person. The man on it said that lying is cancer. I know that Mom died of cancer, and the last thing I want is to get cancer and die like her, so I didn't want to lie to Dr. Laird. Cancer isn't contagious, meaning it doesn't get passed from one person to another person, but the video on the Internet says lying is contagious. The more you lie to people, the more people will lie to you.

"Honesty is like a sword you can use to cut through all that," the bald man on the video said, and since I am a Viking and I know how to use swords, I saw that he was saying that the truth can make you powerful and strong if you use it right.

"Zelda?" Dr. Laird said. "When you said you kissed the person who robbed you, what did you mean?"

My face was getting hot. The rule Gert had said about lying to protect the tribe was the opposite of the rule about telling the truth to the people you trust or care about, and I trusted Dr. Laird.

My hand was hurting from squeezing the stress ball so hard. I pressed it onto the desk and asked to go to the bathroom.

"Now?" Gert said.

"I have to go to the bathroom now, please," I said.

"Zelda, if something's the matter—" Dr. Laird started to say, and I said if I didn't get to go to the bathroom now that I would go to the bathroom where I was sitting.

"OKAY?" I shouted, and before they could say anything else I was standing up and going out of the room, past the desk where Hanna usually sat and out of the office, not looking back to see if Gert or Dr. Laird was following me.

I ran down the hallway to the elevator, where I pressed the button a hundred times. The number at the top of the elevator didn't change fast enough so I kept hitting it and hitting it until Gert caught up to me and took my hand, which was now pink and sore.

"Hey," he said. "What the hell is going on?"

"I can't be here anymore," I said. "Can we go, please?"

The elevator opened.

Gert put his hand in front of the elevator door so I couldn't get by. "Dr. Laird says he still wants to talk to you."

"I am done talking," I said, trying to get into the elevator, but Gert's arm held me back.

Finally the elevator closed and I felt my legs get noodly. Gert was there to hold me up.

"Okay," he said. "We're going. We just need to tell Dr. Laird first. Okay?"

I was crying, snot was running down my face, and Gert let me wipe it on his shirt while he walked.

When we got back into Dr. Laird's office, Gert explained that I'd had enough questions. Dr. Laird said that was okay, and he smiled at me in a very gentle way and said that he was glad I was okay, and that I didn't do anything wrong.

"Okay? Can we say that out loud?"

"I didn't do anything wrong," I said, even though I didn't believe it.

Dr. Laird said he would not call the police.

"But I want to see you, just you and me, when you're ready," he said to me. "And I want the truth."

When we got home I didn't want to talk to anyone. AK47 asked if I was okay and I walked right by her and into my room, where I shut the door and decided I would never come out.

She knocked and asked to come in and I said no, and sat with my back against the door to stop it from opening. Finally she gave up and I was left alone.

I had been looking for a villain to defeat, and actually I had become the villain. By letting Hendo into the house, I had threatened the tribe.

I did not want to talk to AK47 or Gert, since I had let them down very much. The only person who I thought could listen was Dr. Kepple. He had not responded to any of my other letters yet, but maybe he would understand how urgent my letter was and he would respond immediately.

> *Dear Dr. Kepple,*
>
> *I am a terrible Viking and I need wisdom. I know that for Vikings, protecting the home and your family is one of the most important things they can do, and I have failed to protect mine. I was fooled by a villain and he did something very bad that I am not allowed to talk about, not even with you. But it is all my fault.*
>
> *Reading many of the legends in your book, I think that sometimes heroes do bad things and end up being the villains.*
>
> *For example, Starkad ends up killing his best friend, King Víkar of Agder, even though he is the hero of many sagas. He becomes a villain.*
>
> *My very important question is: when a hero makes a mistake and acts villainously, how can they become a hero again?*
>
> *Zelda*
>
> *P.S. Please respond as soon as you get this.*

I pressed REFRESH on the Internet box over and over, waiting to see if he would respond, but there were no new e-mails, just the message that explains that Dr. Kepple will reply to the e-mail whenever possible. I fell asleep with my laptop on my lap.

ᚦ

The next morning AK47 woke me up. She was standing over me, putting a finger over her lips. She had grocery bags in her hands.

"What's going on?" I asked.

"Not so loud," she said. "You're coming to stay with me for the next little bit."

"I'm sorry I didn't want to talk last night," I said, sitting up and pulling my knees to my chest.

"Forget about it. You have nothing to apologize for. But come on. Get up." She told me that until Gert sorted his shit out, it wasn't safe for me in the apartment.

"Does he know?" I asked, rolling out of bed.

AK47 pulled open my closet and started taking out clothes.

"Not yet, he doesn't. Here. I have some shopping bags. Figure out what you need to tide you over for a few days."

"I'm not going to abandon Gert," I said.

"Honey, nobody is abandoning anyone. Underwear?" She pointed at a drawer. "In here?"

I wrapped my blankets around myself and told her even more powerfully that I was not going to leave Gert. AK47 opened the drawer and grabbed some socks and threw them at me.

"Zelda. Come on. Get dressed." When I didn't move, she sighed. "Listen. I don't know what happened exactly, but I know it's bad, and that it has to do with that Toucan scumbag. These shit-dicks don't play around."

I picked up the pair of socks that she had thrown at me and held them in my hands. They were black and had Vikings on them. Gert had got them for me when he saw them at the sports store.

"Aren't tribes supposed to stick together? What if they attack and we aren't here to protect him?"

"Protect who?" Gert asked. He was standing at the door in his underwear, his face still bruised.

AK47 kept putting clothes in the grocery bags. "Zelda's going to stay with me," she said. "This place isn't safe and you know it."

"I'm not going anywhere, Gert," I said, throwing the socks on the ground. "I am going to help defend the tribe."

AK47 stood up and told Gert this was nonnegotiable. "Either this, or I call the police. You decide."

They left the room to argue and I started taking the clothes out of the grocery bags and putting them back in the drawers. But not the Viking socks. I put them on. They were long and rolled up almost to my knees.

Then Gert came back in and told me that AK47 was right. "At least for the time being."

I crossed my hands across my chest. "You want to get rid of me?"

He sat on the bed next to me. "Never. But this isn't about you. It's about me. You're always talking about legends, right? How you have to prove yourself to the world?"

I nodded.

"Well," he said, "this is important for my legend. I have to do this alone."

〟

That first night at AK47's I couldn't sleep. All of the loud-thoughts worked their way around, flapping against the inside of my head. Hendo had stolen something very important that belonged to Toucan, part of his hoard. The tribe was not safe because Toucan was mad at Gert and was a villain. But why did Gert have Toucan's things in the first place?

I knew why we couldn't call the police. The part of the hoard Hendo stole was something that was against the law to have. So the police could not help, and I did not know how to make things right.

AK47's house was hot. Her house was a desert and made it hard to breathe, even though she had an air conditioner that sounded like it was whispering to me all night. My thoughts were saying: *I am very bad, I have ruined everything because I am bad, I've done only bad things, I loved Marxy and was terrible because I tried to have sex with someone else who took something that got Gert in trouble.*

I thought about the Viking woman in the grave, who was powerful and had armor and other things that showed she lived an honorable, legendary life. She probably completed everything on her list of THINGS LEGENDS NEED without screwing up and putting her tribe in danger. The gods smiled down on her and they were angry with me. Those thoughts were shouting at me and my heart, which was beating faster and faster the more I sat in the quiet of the night.

Shhh, I told my thoughts. *Stop flying around. Stop trying to smash yourselves against the inside of my head.* They kept flying, since I had to think to say to stop, and thinking more just made the thoughts flying around louder and louder. They were gunshots and exploding bombs. The words went KABOOM until sitting still and quiet in bed was too hard to do. I got up and walked around the room, back and forth, back and forth, until I was so tired I fell back into bed and stared at the ceiling.

chapter twenty-eight

n the morning I woke up to the sound of a text message. At first I did not even answer it, since I did not want to be awake. Being awake made me feel bad about being a terrible Viking.

Another message came. I sighed and took my phone and read the message.

Hello Zelda are you coming to the party?

I sat up and rubbed my eyes and read it again. The message was from Yoda.

I texted back: **What party?**

I waited.

Another message came in. **We are throwing Marxy a party at the Community Center and you should come because we miss you!**

The words sat on the phone's screen.

I stared at them. It had been a very long time since I had heard from my tribe at the Community Center. I was still ashamed for hurting Hamsa.

Yoda texted back: **Hello?**

I texted: **You are not mad at me anymore?**

Yoda texted: **Nobody is mad at you anymore. Are you coming?**

I texted: **What is the party for?**

Yoda texted: Just come!

I decided that it was time to go see my people, and after getting dressed I told AK47 that I needed a ride. I packed my backpack and made sure my Viking sword was in it, in case Toucan decided to attack again.

"Maybe it's best you just stick around here," AK47 said. She was getting ready to pick up the bus for the day's work and I knew from her schedule, which was on the fridge, just like Gert's school schedule back home, that she would be going to the Community Center.

"I have to see my people," I said. "And that's that."

⇗

At the Community Center, people weren't in the gym. I followed the loud voices down a hallway and passed a sign with an arrow on the wall that said MARXY'S PARTY and another arrow pointing to one of the meeting rooms. I opened the door.

Big Todd was there, Yoda and Hamsa, other people I did not know, and also Marxy wearing a funny hat. He was laughing in front of a big cake with candles on it. Sarah-Beth sat beside him, clapping her hands.

Big Todd saw me and came over. I asked him what was going on. "It's not his birthday," I said. All of a sudden everyone cheered. Marxy was clapping and singing.

"Marxy's got his first job," Big Todd said.

"Oh."

"We're throwing him a little party. You know, to celebrate."

I remembered that nobody had thrown me a party when I got a job and started to feel depressed again. Big Todd put his arm around me. "Nobody thought Marxy would ever be working," he said. "He's not very independent. Not like you. Or at least, he wasn't. But now he wants to change because he saw you do it."

"Really?"

"Yeah," Big Todd said. "You inspired him. That's huge."

"Does that make me an icon?" I asked.

He raised his eyebrow, thought for a second, then said, "Yeah, I guess you did make it fashionable to try your best."

He did not explain what he meant by that.

Marxy was so happy, and that made me happy. Then I felt bad when I remembered I was not Marxy's girlfriend anymore, and what had happened with Hendo.

"I'll go practice my free throws," I said. "Tell Marxy I am proud of him."

Big Todd said I should tell him myself. I said I might, and that was when something very unexpected happened.

As I was leaving, Sarah-Beth saw me and asked, "Would you like some cake?"

She was smiling and had some cake in her hair.

"I don't know," I said.

"Please? Marxy has missed being friends with you," she said. And Big Todd gave me THE LOOK.

"You are his best friend, and he still loves the shit out of you," Big Todd said. "Pardon my French."

Sarah-Beth said please a second time.

I did not know why she was being nice to me. She took my hand and pulled me into the room. Marxy saw me and waved and said, "I got a job!"

While having cake with Marxy, I got to see all the people I had missed. There were new people there, and also other people who I had not seen in a very long time. Everyone had hats from McDonald's, the paper ones, because that was where Marxy had gotten his job. At first I felt bad seeing Marxy and did not talk to him much. But it was hard to be sad when everyone else was happy, and wearing the hat made me laugh.

Marxy sat next to me and put his hand on my shoulder and said that it was because of me that he got the job.

"You were so good at being at the library," he said. "And doing things on your own, without any help." I tried to tell him I had help. He said that everyone needs help once in a while and that I had helped him. "If it wasn't for you thinking I was smart, I would not have tried."

He told me I was a legend in his eyes, and that Yoda was looking to get a job too.

When it was time for me to go to work, Marxy got up and gave me a big bear hug.

"We should shoot baskets sometime," he said.

I thought I wanted to kiss him and then remembered that he and Sarah-Beth were together. I held out my hand to shake, and Marxy shook it. He was not my fair maiden anymore, but Sarah-Beth's.

"You are a legendary person, and a hero to me," Marxy said.

I felt like I was going to cry, because I had been feeling very bad for a long time, and this was the first time I did not feel like a villain, and it was the first time in a long time that I felt like a legend again.

chapter twenty-nine

During part of my shift at the library I worked at the front desk, checking out books. I felt good. Not like a hero, but also not as bad as before. I could imagine Marxy working at McDonald's, making hamburgers and having friends who were more normal, and that made me happy.

Then I thought about my list of THINGS LEGENDS NEED and that I had failed at many of them. I did not have a fair maiden anymore, and I had hurt Gert and the tribe.

"Why the long face?" Carol asked.

"Nothing."

"If it's guy troubles with what's-his-name who used to come here, I think you're better off without him."

I did not know what to say, so I went to get the cart to roll around the library, looking to shelve books.

There were many books around the library, which means the person who worked the previous shift did not do a very good job. I looked and it was a new person named Olga who I had not met. I decided I would make the library perfect to show her how to do it properly.

I went around, collecting the books and putting them on my cart according to the numbers on the spines. When I looked up near the Sports section my heart jumped because there was someone sitting where Hendo usually sat.

"Holy crap," I said out loud, and realized that it was not Hendo sitting in the spot, but another villain.

"You're not going to piss yourself again, are you?" Toucan asked.

He was reading a *National Geographic* with his feet on one of the chairs. My knees felt noodly again and I held on to the cart to make sure I didn't fall down.

I felt my pocket for my Viking sword, but since it was in my backpack, I was defenseless.

"Why are you here?" I asked, trying to stand straight and powerful.

"I'm just reading." He held up the magazine. "Isn't this what your boyfriend used to do?"

At first I did not know who he was talking about. Marxy did not like *National Geographic* magazines at all. Then I realized he was talking about Hendo. I took a deep breath and squeezed the handles of the cart.

"He's not my boyfriend."

Toucan turned the page of the magazine. "I love these things. Mantis shrimps?" He showed me a picture of an animal from the sea that looked like a shrimp and crab covered in a rainbow. "They can attack so fast, like a bullet." Toucan punched the air really quickly. "And their eyes. They can see what we can't see. Like me. I see things other people can't."

One of the things Carol taught me is that when dealing with angry library patrons, or people who are being disruptive, you must always remain calm as a librarian and repeat the rules very clearly.

"Okay," I said. "Please take your feet off the chair."

He laughed and then turned until his feet were back on the ground and showed me his hands like he was surrendering. Then he closed the magazine and smiled in a way I did not like. "You know, Zelda, I think that you act stupid, because you like having people do things for you.

I've seen it a million times before. Right? Making people feel sorry for you, so you don't have to do shit. Correct me if I'm wrong here."

My mouth opened and I wanted to shout, only nothing came out, not even air. Toucan waited and then shook his head again and laughed into his magazine. He put it down, got up, and started walking toward me. I stepped back and went behind the cart, using it like a shield in case he planned to attack. From there I repeated a very important library rule.

"If you are done reading that magazine," I said, pointing to the *National Geographic*, "then I will reshelve it."

Toucan came even closer and said that he knew that I was having sex with Hendo, and that I might have fooled Gert, but I did not fool him. He called me a whore and made a noise with his mouth I did not like.

"Stop making that noise," I said, not as loud as I wanted.

"What? Excuse me?" Toucan put his hand to his ear. "Does Gert know all the disgusting things you've done, Zelda?"

Now some other people in the library started looking at us. I looked down at the cart and the book about cooking that was on the top. I closed my eyes and tried not to look at him.

He laughed again, like a Grendel laughs, and did not shut up.

"That's what I thought," Toucan said. "I'd like it a lot if you could tell your boyfriend to give me a call. You may have your brother and whoever else fooled, but not me."

That was when I shouted that he was a fuck-dick, which made people in the library look up from their books. I looked around for Carol, but she was on her break.

The security guard for the day, Larry, came over and asked if there was a problem. Toucan suddenly became happy and held up the magazine. "I was just reading. But I think we're done chatting. Say hi to your other friend for me," he told me.

"Come on, now," Larry said, pulling up the waist of his pants. "Let's lower our voices."

"The one at the Community Center," Toucan said. "What's his name? Max?" He snapped his fingers. "Marxy. That's it. The retarded kid."

I froze and could not think of anything to say.

He tossed the magazine on my cart and walked away, and Larry asked me to keep my voice down in the future.

"You know the rules," he said.

I watched Toucan as he walked out of the library, my stomach twisting. He stood by the book return for a second, and then his red car pulled up and the Fat Man got out of the driver's seat and went into the passenger side, so that Toucan could get in and drive away.

I got my phone and texted Marxy. My hands shook.

Are you okay?

A few seconds later my phone buzzed and he replied.

Yes! We still have cake where are you?

My heart stopped pounding.

⇗

I went back to the computer to calm down. I opened my e-mail and clicked REFRESH to see if Dr. Kepple had responded. Normally we were not allowed to use our personal e-mail accounts on the work computers unless it was very important, but I decided something very important had just happened.

Because I needed his voice, I took a lunch break and listened to the excerpts from *Kepple's Guide to the Vikings* on audiobook that were on his website. Dr. Kepple was talking about Beowulf, the hero who defeats Grendel, and about how after slaying Grendel's mother, who is even more powerful than Grendel, Beowulf becomes King of his tribe. Fifty years later, one of his people steals something from a dragon, who gets angry and starts destroying Beowulf's tribe.

Beowulf, who is now very old and not as mighty, decides to save his people and confront the dragon alone. Even though he was not the person to steal the dragon's gold, he takes responsibility for the people in his tribe who did.

His warriors want to help him, but Beowulf is the hero and in order to complete his legend fights the dragon alone. I shut off the audiobook.

Hendo had stolen the gold and Toucan was the dragon who had hurt Gert. I thought about what the Viking warrior from the grave would do. I would have to find Hendo to make him give Toucan back whatever he stole.

I decided to write Dr. Kepple one final letter.

Dear Dr. Kepple,
This might be the final letter I can send you, because I have come up with a plan that will help me become a hero again. I am going on a journey to defeat the villain of my legend. I believe I have honed my combat skills and am ready to face him.

I have not told anyone about this final battle because, even though Vikings have wise men who tell them what to do, sometimes heroes need to follow their own hearts and believe in themselves.

Wish me skál!

Skál,
Zelda

I clicked SEND and took a deep breath. It was time.

Even though it is against the rules to use patron information for personal purposes, sometimes Vikings need to break rules in order to save the tribe.

I went to the computer and searched until I found Hendo's library account, then I put his address into Google Maps and pressed PRINT.

chapter thirty

did not go home after my shift at the library. Instead of getting on my usual bus, I crossed the street, walked two blocks, and got on another one.

Hendo's house was not very hard to get to by bus, and when I got off the bus I recognized the neighborhood and took a picture of the bus stop so I could remember what it looked like.

Google Maps showed me where to go until I found the address I was looking for. It was not an apartment building but a brown box attached to another brown box and another one. The windows had boards over them instead of glass, which had been broken and still stuck out pointy like teeth.

I took a deep breath and knocked on his door.

There was no answer. I noticed the door had yellow gunk and eggshells on it.

"He's not here," someone said. I turned. A man without a shirt was standing on the other side of the fence. He had a very large dog on a leash that stared at me.

"Where is he?" I asked.

"Fucked if I know," he said. "One minute they were there, the next they were gone. Didn't even lock the door. You can probably go in if you want, but there's a good chance there's some squatters living in there and some busted glass."

He walked his dog away. This was an important warning that any Viking would heed.

I removed my Viking sword from my backpack, in case any of the squatters inside were villains.

Like the man said, the door was not locked. The house smelled like a toilet and also cigarette smoke.

I called Hendo's name. Nobody answered. I also called Artem's name, then remembered that if Artem was there, he was a baby and would not answer.

None of the lights were on. I held my Viking sword in front of me and used the light from my cell phone to shine inside. Empty plastic Oreo containers, baby food jars, and pizza boxes were piled on the floor. When I walked it was through an ocean of wrappers and other gross things.

Someone had spray-painted NIGGER on the wall and drawn a picture of a man having sex with a woman. The woman had a face with pain in it, the eyes closed in Xs and the mouth open with the tongue sticking out. It was not the way sex was supposed to be. I shivered.

In one of the rooms I found a bed that smelled like pee and puke. I did not stay in the room very long. None of the lights worked when I tried to turn them on.

I was very afraid but I knew that was part of being a legend. Without fear there can be no bravery.

The house did not have anyone in it, not even squatters. I checked all the rooms. As I was leaving I saw some books in the corner. They were library books. Since I was a Viking and a librarian, I put them in a pile and took them with me. Hendo still had the train book I had found him for Artem, and the train book was not there, which meant Hendo took the train book with him and would have to pay for late fines after he paid for all the other villainous things he had done.

When I came outside I had the books under my arms. There were so many that I had trouble carrying them, and almost dropped some on the dirty ground. I was even madder at Hendo now, because all of those books would have late fees, and people might have wanted to read them and now couldn't, since they were missing. I wondered if Carol had already entered them into the system as lost and had already ordered replacement copies. Some of the books were older, so they would not be able to get reordered.

I was thinking about which of the books were too old to be replaced, like the one with the picture of Elvis Presley on the cover, and almost walked right into a police officer on the sidewalk. Behind her was a police car.

"Crap," I said, bending over to pick the books up, and the police officer helped too.

"Didn't mean to frighten you," she said, handing me two of the books, which I put on top of the other books I was holding.

"That's okay," I said. "I have to go now."

She walked with me and said she was wondering if we could have a little chat. "It's technically trespassing, going into a place that isn't yours," she said.

I pretended I didn't hear and started walking faster toward the bus stop. I said to my legs, which felt heavy, *stay strong*.

The policewoman followed me up the sidewalk. "Where are you headed?"

"Nowhere."

"For someone going nowhere, you're sure going there fast."

I started walking even faster and the policewoman said for me to wait up. I did not want to wait up, and also inside of me I had so much going on that if I stopped to talk I might accidentally let out all the things I had been holding in—about Gert and Hendo and Toucan.

So I started running. I dropped the library books to run faster, which was a very cowardly thing to do as a librarian, and tried to run behind some of the houses.

But the policewoman was faster than me and caught up and grabbed my arm.

"Hey, easy," the policewoman said. "Slow down. We just want to talk."

She did not hold my arm very tight and I pulled it away and said she would need to take me by force, even though I wasn't sure that fighting the police was something a legend would do. The policewoman did not get angry and attack like I thought she would. Instead she said she wanted to talk to me about a friend of mine.

"The one whose house you were in," she said. "I thought maybe we could work together to find him, that's all."

"I don't have a friend who lives in any house," I said.

"So you were breaking and entering? Because that's a crime."

I swallowed and tried not to look at her eyes, since I am not very good at staring contests.

"Relax. I just want to talk. Okay?" That was when she held up the Viking sword. "And you dropped this. Which I think qualifies as a weapon. So we could arrest you if we wanted to."

⇗

They said they would give me a ride wherever I had to go, so I didn't need to take the bus. Since I had the library books with me, I said to take me to the library. I made sure not to say anything about Gert or Hendo or Toucan. I held the books tight to my chest and tried to decide what I would do if they asked me serious questions while shining a bright light on me, the way they did in movies, and what I would do if I got so thirsty from the hot light that I asked for a drink of water and they wouldn't give me one unless I confessed everything.

"Everything okay back there?" the policewoman said.

"I will say nothing," I said.

"Sure. You're just shaking a little bit."

"So you wanted to get the library books back," the other police officer said. He was driving.

"The patron's address was in the computer system," I said.

"You're the most dedicated librarian I've ever met," the woman said. "Do you have any siblings?"

I stared straight ahead.

"Zelda?" the other officer said. "Because I think we might know your brother. Gert?"

I did not say anything. My throat was already getting like a desert and they weren't even shining a bright light on me.

They pulled up in front of the library. The woman police officer got out and came around and opened the door for me. I got out of the car.

"If you do ever want to talk . . ." She handed me a card, and my Viking sword, which she had taken.

I said thank you, taking Hendo's library books and putting them into the return bin on the way inside.

chapter thirty-one

did not tell anyone about the police, not even AK47, or Dr. Laird. I hid the card that the police officer had given me in my Word of Today book, with an old word for August 14, *proliferate*, which means to make a lot of things and expand and reproduce.

I felt like inside of me the things I had to keep inside of me were proliferating. I did not like having to keep secrets from people, especially not AK47, and those secrets were expanding and reproducing.

After one of my shifts at the library, AK47 and I went grocery shopping for Gert and brought the groceries to the apartment as a surprise. AK47 was parking the car and I went to open the door.

Alf was in front of the apartment building, smoking. We had not seen each other for a long time. He waved and I waved and started to go in. That was when he said he wanted to talk.

"I know you don't like me," he said. "And I know Annie doesn't like me either."

He sucked the last bit of smoke out of his cigarette before putting it out on the sidewalk, under his foot.

"You want to steal her from Gert," I said. "You are his enemy and also my enemy."

"Yeah," Alf said. "I'm such a stupid asshole that I got a black eye from trying to stop him from beating her."

"He wasn't going to beat her. Shut up."

That was when AK47 arrived, holding bags of groceries, and Alf tried to help her. She did not want his help and pulled the bags away from him when he tried to grab them.

"I got it," she said.

"Well, let me get the door at least," he said.

He jogged in front of AK47 and opened the door for her, into the part of the apartment building with the mailboxes and the intercom. "I was just telling Zelda here that even though you don't like me, I'm always looking out for her."

AK47 put the wrong key into the door and swore to herself, not listening to Alf. He had his key ready and when she took the wrong key out of the lock, he stuck his in and opened it.

"Because that doesn't sound creepy at all," AK47 said, and walked quickly inside while Alf held the door.

Alf held the door for me and I walked by and shrugged. I knew that Alf wanted her to stop and we both knew that if AK47 did not want to stop, there was going to be no stopping her.

She was already pressing the button on the elevator.

"Can I just say something?" Alf asked.

"Not now," AK47 said. "Let's go, Zee."

The doors of the elevator opened. All three of us got in. Alf stood on one side of the elevator and AK47 stood on the other. I was in between them and it felt weird, since usually it is Gert on one side and AK47 on the other. The elevator shook and started going up.

But Alf held the button of the elevator.

"I'll mace the shit out of you," AK47 said, and pressed the button for the elevator to start up again. The walls made a groan and it started moving again.

Alf put his hands up. "Relax. No need for that. I just wanted to say I've heard *things*."

"You're always saying things," I said. "You talk a lot."

AK47 laughed and held out her hand for a dab. "Amen, sister."

But Alf kept talking. "I mean I've heard bad things. About Gert. And the police."

AK47 pressed the button to stop the elevator again. "What are you talking about?"

"The word going around is that he was picked up yesterday." Alf took another cigarette out and put it behind his ear. "And I know it's none of my business, but some of the people he hangs around with aren't big on that kind of thing."

AK47 hit the button again and we started going up. "Stop talking," she said to Alf.

"I just thought you should know. Since I don't give two shits about that asswipe, but I do have what we might call a soft spot in my heart for you two."

The elevator stopped on the second floor and a woman with laundry got on. Alf stopped talking. On the fourth floor the woman stayed on and Alf, AK47, and I got off.

"Mind your own business," AK47 said to Alf, pushing him with one of the hands holding the grocery bags, and turned toward our apartment.

AK47 closed the door and was normal until she leaned against the wall and went down, like the elevator. I locked the door and put on the chain before sliding down the wall next to her.

She called Gert and shook her head at the phone. "Motherfucker," she said. "Can you give him a call? He's not answering."

I tried my phone and then sent texts. Gert did not respond. I started to worry that Gert would know that I had been with the police and hadn't told him.

⤳

Gert came home an hour later and when AK47 started asking him questions he said he did not want to talk about it.

"What's 'it'?" AK47 asked.

"The police?" I said.

Gert sighed. "So now she knows. Yes, the police." He sat down and started taking off his boots. "Dr. Laird put in a call after your last meeting." Gert gave me THE LOOK.

"That's not my fault," I said. But I felt happy he did not know I had talked to the police and almost made a noise and covered my mouth.

"Nobody said it was, honey," AK47 said. AK47 folded her arms across her chest. "She's right, you know. If you hadn't been fucking around with these people—"

"We'd still be living with Uncle Fuckface Richard. That's what we'd still be doing. We'd still be living with that abusive cocksucker."

AK47 stopped talking. Everything got quiet for a minute, until AK47 cleared her throat. "I made dinner," she said. "I have to do some bus runs tonight, and some early in the morning, so I'll be crashing at my place tonight. Is she going to crash here tonight, or are we going to have a Tony Montana cocaine shootout?"

"A what?" I asked.

Gert had his head in his hands. "Cute. Tony Montana." He said something none of us could hear, and when AK47 asked what he said, he told us that he wasn't in the mood for *Scarface* jokes.

"Aren't you always in the mood for *Scarface* jokes?" AK47 said.

"I'm doing the best I can," he said.

"What does that have to do with *Scarface*?"

"Easy there," AK47 said.

She went to Gert and kissed him and then gave him a slap on the cheek—not a bad one, one that was meant to show love. "We'll talk later, okay? And if you can, don't forget she has the Community Center tomorrow."

"Fine," he said. "Got it."

"Fine," she said, the way he said it, and then put her arms around his shoulders and kissed him, in a more sexy way, and told him to not get arrested or shot before she got back.

She left, and Gert and I ate our dinner together, which was pasta. I tried to pretend that things were back to normal and asked him how his school was going.

"Fine," he said, his fork clinking against the plate.

"Do you have any tests coming up?"

He wiped his mouth and crumpled up the napkin, slamming it onto the table. My glass of water shook and I felt like I had to hold it to stop the glass from falling over.

"Whoa," I said.

He looked at me. "Did you tell him anything else?" he asked.

"Who?"

"The fucking Pope."

"What does the Pope—"

"Dr. Laird. Jesus Christ." He shook his head. "Did you tell him about the other night? When Toucan came over?"

I shook my head. "I promised you I wouldn't and so I did not tell him anything."

"Are you sure you didn't, I don't know, forget?"

"Gert, I didn't forget. I know when I tell people things."

He picked up his plate and brought it to the sink. I asked him what the police said to him, and if he was going to help them defeat Toucan.

"We don't help the police," he said, running water in the sink. Then he loudly put the plate in the rack beside the sink.

"Even if they're on our side?"

"They're not." He came back to the table. "Did they talk to you?" He put his hands on the chair and made his face right in my face. I closed my eyes, because I knew that if I looked at his eyes I would not be able to lie.

And after a while there was nothing to do but look at him and take out the card that the police officer gave me and show it to Gert.

He took one look at it, then turned and punched the wall so hard it made the world shake.

"Shit," he said, holding his hand.

"Okay," I said, getting up. I went to the fridge to get the bag of frozen peas. "Here."

"I don't need that shit," he said, but he took the bag anyway and put it on his hand.

Even though he was taller than me, I put my hand up and touched his shoulder and gave it a squeeze.

"I will put away the dishes and clean up," I said. "Okay?"

He did not say anything. He just nodded and looked at his hand, which was already turning red.

chapter thirty-two

Before AK47 came to take me to the Community Center, I ripped up the card that the police officer gave me and threw it in the garbage to show Gert that I trusted him.

It was Friday, and the gym was open at the Community Center, which meant you could go into the equipment room and play with whatever you wanted, as long as you put it back. People were playing hockey instead of basketball, though, and I hated hockey. I took a hockey stick and went to say hello to Hamsa and Yoda, who were talking about a very powerful battle.

"I heard it was ninjas," Hamsa was saying.

"Ninja Turtles," Yoda said.

"They don't attack nice people, stupid," Hamsa said. "Only crooks and robbers and the Foot Patrol."

I asked what they were talking about.

"It's not the Foot Patrol, it's the Foot Clan," Yoda said, hitting his hockey stick against Hamsa's. Hamsa hit it back.

I put my hockey stick on top of their sticks and asked them what they were talking about.

They looked at each other. "Nothing," Hamsa said.

"Come on," I said. "Who was in the battle?"

"Marxy," Yoda said.

"Oh." I tried to pretend that I did not care what they were saying, since it was Marxy and I was not his girlfriend anymore. I lifted up my hockey stick off of theirs.

Hamsa and Yoda looked at each other again. "He got into a fight," Yoda said.

"A big fight," Hamsa said. "Maybe with ninjas."

"We don't know if it was ninjas," Yoda said.

They were quiet. Then Yoda looked me right in the eyes. "He's messed up bad."

⧢

Marxy's gate was locked so I reached over it and opened it and walked up to the steps. I rang the doorbell. I was not sure what I was going to say to Pearl if she answered.

Nobody answered the doorbell so I rang it again.

That was when the door opened and a man answered it.

"Can I help you?" he asked me.

"Who are you?" I asked.

He stared at me. He was tall and skinny except for the belly he had. He was wearing glasses and shorts.

We had a standoff.

"Pearl?" he called over his shoulder.

"I want to see Marxy. Is he here?"

Pearl came up behind him. She saw me and said, "Oh, Zelda. Come on in."

When the man didn't move she said it was okay, that I was Marxy's friend.

"Now, quit being alpha dog. She's not going to hurt him." Pearl bumped him out of the way and took my arm and pulled me inside the house.

The man was Marxy's father. We shook hands and he said his name was Mark. The more I saw his face the more I saw that they had a lot of the same parts. The same nose, which was straight and got big at the end. And the same eyes, which were green. They were also both tall.

"Wait, he's got another girlfriend?" Mark said. "What about what's-her-name? Sarah-Beth?"

"Oh, she's not his *real* girlfriend." Pearl told him that if he was around more, he would know things like that. She asked if I wanted something to drink. "Marxy says you like grape soda. Is that right? Mark, can you—?"

Pearl pointed at the kitchen, and Mark shook his head and went to get me grape soda. We watched him and she shook her head.

"What is it you and Marxy are always saying? Fuck-dick?"

"Yeah," I said. "And shit-heel."

"That man is both. Always late to the party."

⇌

She took me upstairs to see Marxy and told Mark to wait in the kitchen. "He doesn't want to see you right now," Pearl said.

Mark threw up his hands and asked why he was called in the first place, if all he was going to do was sit around and get people grape juice.

"Grape soda, there's a difference. And stop being a baby."

Pearl and I walked up the steps. She told me that Marxy had gotten into some kind of fight. "Well, I don't think 'fight' is right. Someone just hit him. I know he can be a bit much sometimes, but who would do that kind of thing?"

"Shit-heels," I said.

Pearl rubbed her face with her hands. "Goddamn it, sometimes I am just so sick of this world and the people in it." She looked like she was ready to cry, so I put my hand on her arm. She looked down at the hand, then at me. "I'm sorry," she said. "It's just hard to keep it together all the time."

"I know the feeling," I said, because I did know.

We got to the top of the steps. Marxy's room was closed. We stood in front of the door. She put her hand on the doorknob at Marxy's room.

"It's not as bad as it looks," Pearl said. "Well, actually, it probably is. We called the police and filed a report."

Marxy did not look good. His face was purple in places. It made me very sad, seeing him hurt, but I was also very happy that Pearl had called me Marxy's *real* girlfriend.

Marxy was sitting in bed and when he saw me he pulled himself up. Pearl went to move the pillow behind him.

"Mom," Marxy said. "I can do it myself."

"Okay, okay," she said, and kissed him on his pumpkin face, very fast, before leaving. She did not close the door, so I went and closed it behind her.

I asked Marxy what happened.

He said, "I was playing basketball by myself, at the park down the street, and someone came up to me and punched me." His nose made the squiggly sound. "I don't know why. He just punched me."

"Villain," I said.

"My head hurts," Marxy said. "Can you come here and sit near me?"

I went onto the bed and put my arms around him until he stopped breathing so hard. The door handle jiggled and I could hear Pearl on the other side, asking if everything was okay.

"I am okay," Marxy shouted, and he took a Kleenex from the box beside his bed and blew his nose. It came out red. He put the Kleenex into the garbage can very gently.

"Did he steal anything?" I asked. "In our neighborhood people do that when they want to steal from them."

"He took my Larry Bird ball." He turned his head to me and asked if we could kiss for a bit but when we tried his mouth hurt too much, so I just sat in the bed until he fell asleep. He started snoring and so I had to get up slowly. I did not want to wake him up.

While I was leaving, Pearl walked me out. On the way I said good-bye to Mark, who was watching football on the television set in the living room. He did not say anything and only lifted his hand and shook it a little bit.

When we got to the door Pearl asked me if I could come by tomorrow. I was surprised.

"You want me to come back again?" I asked.

She picked a string off of her shirt. For the first time I really looked into her face, into her eyes, and she did the same.

"You make him happy," she said. "And right now, I just want that for him."

Before I left the house, she did something she had never done before: she hugged me.

⁊

It was a villainous world and I was angry that it had hurt Marxy, who was so innocent and pure, even if he wasn't my fair maiden anymore. I put on my angry face so that nobody would try to talk to me until I got off the bus at the library. My shift was starting in less than an hour and Carol had scheduled me at the computer, where patrons went to check out books. This is the most powerful position in the library and Carol was counting on me.

When I got there, I went inside the library and said hello to Larry the security guard and went back to the staff room, where Carol was eating a salad from a plastic container.

"I am technically not late," I said, pointing at the clock.

"Never said you were." She put a fork of vegetable leafs into her mouth.

I went to get ready for my workday and saw Marxy's Larry Bird basketball. It was sitting in the Lost and Found box.

"Where did this come from?" I asked, holding the basketball in my hands.

Carol swiveled in her chair. "I found it on a table with some *National Geographic*s. Why?"

Why was a question I was also asking myself. It did not belong there. If I had found it on a basketball court, that would have made sense. But then Carol showed me the spot where she found it and I realized it was the same place Toucan had sat in. Then I remembered that Toucan had threatened me. At first I did not combine these two facts. Then I started to understand that Toucan had left the basketball for me.

Which meant that he had been the one to hurt Marxy.

Which meant that I was the one who was responsible for getting Marxy hurt.

༄

When I got home from the library, I looked at myself in the mirror and felt very small and stupid.

"You are not a legend," I said to my reflection and decided I would stay in bed forever.

But when I walked by my computer I saw a message that I thought would never come. "Praise Odin," I whispered, and clicked the e-mail that said, "From the desk of Dr. Joseph Kepple" and started reading.

Dear Zelda,
My apologies for not answering your messages earlier—I was out
of the country for some time, and my assistant had neglected to

inform me of your adventures. However, your letters are unlike any I've received, and so I feel almost like I know you.

Going through your messages, I see that you've found yourself the hero of your own legend. I remember being your age and finding myself just as lost as you seem to be.

I hope you find what you're looking for. What I can say is that sometimes life finds us, and when it does we have to rise to the occasion and have courage. And we make lists, rules, and try to order things, trying to control them, when actually the most important parts of life, the parts really worth cherishing, are the things that we don't expect.

Please do keep in touch.
Best,
Joseph Kepple, PhD
Professor Emeritus, Stanford

I read over Dr. Kepple's letter many times. Dr. Kepple had been lost, but had become a powerful writer who knew everything about Vikings.

The last line he wrote was very powerful, too. It said that sometimes the parts of life that are the best, which is what "worth cherishing" means, are the things that we cannot put on a list, because we don't know that they are coming, or are possible.

That was when I finally understood.

In many legends, where heroes had to defeat powerful villains, the villains always hurt innocent people who the hero loved. And once a hero is pushed too far by the villain, the hero goes to battle.

The hero in a Viking legend is always smaller than the villain. That is what makes it a legend. Toucan was bigger than me. That did not matter. What matters is the size of your heart. Like the Karate Kid, who in the movie got beaten up by a bigger fighter until he uses his special

technique, the crane kick, to defeat his opponent. Courage makes a
hero. I am not big, except when it comes to courage and protecting
people that I love, like Marxy and Gert.

I took many deep breaths before I realized that my legend was coming to its end. There was one villain left to defeat, according to my list.

In Viking legends, the hero goes to the monster in its cave. I did not
have Toucan's address. It was not in the library system like Hendo's. But
I did know that there was a place where Toucan could be found, where
he and his tribe spent time smoking and being villains.

I got my Viking sword. I took a Kleenex and made the blade shine
very nicely, then I put it in my bag. It poked out, so I wrapped it in one
of my old shirts and prepared my heart for battle.

chapter thirty-three

The place Toucan hung out a lot was in front of a store that sold cigarettes and smelled gross. He liked to sit on a plastic lawn chair and smoke and sometimes people came to see him. Gert had gone to see him a bunch of times, and sometimes I saw him sitting there when I rode the bus to the library.

Toucan was not in his plastic lawn chair, but there was another man sitting in it. It was the Fat Man. He was looking at his phone and yawning.

He got up off the lawn chair when he saw me. He asked me what I was doing on the wrong side of the tracks. I told him that he did not know what he was talking about, since the railroad tracks that go through the city go nowhere near where we live.

"We both live on the same side of the tracks," I said.

"Whatever." He had an apple with him and started eating it.

"I want to see Toucan," I said.

He kept chewing on the apple. Once he swallowed a big bite he told me to get in line. I looked around and there was no line.

He asked if I was really that retarded. "It's a metaphor, stupid," he said, throwing the rest of the apple away.

"You are fat and fucking ugly," I said, which I had been thinking and not saying, since making fun of someone for being overweight and for things they can't control, like the way their face looks, is as bad as making fun of someone for being retarded. But I could not help myself.

He did not move. "Go fuck yourself," he said, and started looking at his phone again.

"I don't want to fuck myself. I want Toucan. I know where to find Hendo."

He stopped playing with his phone. "What did you just say?"

"I know where to find Hendo and the gym bag that Toucan is seeking in his quest," I said.

He told me to tell him, and he would pass on the information to Toucan. I shook my head and said it was my legend. "I am the one who will tell him, and I want you to take me to him."

"No," the Fat Man said, "I don't think you do."

"Either take me to him or I will find him myself, without your help."

The Fat Man sighed and said, "Okay, have it your way." He told me to wait. He turned away from me and made a call on his cell phone.

"Zelda, right?" he asked me. I nodded.

He said that into the phone. I crossed my arms. He put his phone in his pocket and told me to come with him.

"Why can't he come to me?"

There was one thing I knew about battle, and that was it's better to fight in neutral territory. *Neutral* means that nobody has the advantage. Going to Toucan would mean he had the advantage. In sports the home team has the advantage. Going to play in another team's gym is going into enemy territory.

The Fat Man pointed to a car parked on the street.

"You either come or you stay. I got better things to do than this bullshit."

I had my Viking sword and knew that in legends the heroes don't always win, but that more than winning the Viking hero must stand up when the time comes.

I took a deep breath and walked to the car.

⇗

The Fat Man did not talk to me while he drove me there. Gert had said never to get into cars with people I don't know. The Fat Man turned on his rap music on the stereo and smoked. As he drove I started to wonder what I was doing, if I was actually going to be getting myself into more trouble that Gert would have to save me from.

This was the wrong thing to think. You cannot be afraid. A Viking who goes into battle thinking he will be defeated will be defeated. I put my hand into my backpack and made sure to hold my Viking sword inside the bag, in case I had to pull it out to defend myself. The Fat Man asked if I needed to turn on the air-conditioning.

"No," I said.

"Do you mind if I do?" he asked.

"No, go ahead."

"Cool," the Fat Man said, turning on the air-conditioning. He drove for a while then turned down the music.

"So what's going on with Gert?" he asked.

"What do you mean?"

The Fat Man moved his head from side to side. "I don't know. He's talking to police."

He slowed the car down at a stop sign but did not come to a full stop, which is called a rolling stop. I remembered when the police car pulled over Gert for going through stop signs and he threw up.

"If you do not like police, you should actually stop at stop signs. Gert got pulled over once by a policeman for not stopping all the way."

The Fat Man laughed a small laugh. "Yeah. Not in this neighbor-hood." He stepped on the gas pedal hard and the car went so fast it threw me against my seat. He turned the music back on.

He did not have to drive that far until I recognized where we were going, and then he pulled next to a house. It was Toucan's house, the one that Gert had taken me to before, with the hedges and the lawn and Toucan's nice red car in the front.

"Here we go," the Fat Man said, turning off the gas. I took off my seat belt and opened the door. He wasn't wearing a seat belt, which was stupid, and got out too.

The Fat Man spun his keys in his fingers. They jangled as they went round and round and then he dropped the keys on the steps leading to the front door. He stopped to pick them up.

When we got to the door he opened the door for me. I wanted to thank him, except you do not thank villains, so I just nodded and went inside. I made sure if I needed to I could take out my Viking sword to attack.

⇗

The house was dark. There was one light on in the corner of the house. All the other light was yellow from coming through the curtains. Music played quietly from somewhere. The Fat Man said to wait and he pointed to the couch.

"He says to sit down right there," the Fat Man said.

"Okay," I said.

The Fat Man went back out the door. Before he closed the door behind him he asked if I could tell Gert that Big Mike says hi.

"I'll tell him," I said.

"Cool," the Fat Man said, and then he walked out the door, moving slowly because he was so big that he almost hit the sides on his way out.

When he left I decided that the battle was almost at hand. I hadn't thought about what to tell Toucan. I just knew I had to defeat him. I wondered if he would come and try to attack, like in the legends from *Kepple's Guide to the Vikings*, or if we would have a conversation, like Luke Skywalker and Darth Vader, before pulling out our weapons and doing battle. I took out the Viking sword and put it on my belt, so that if I needed to I could wield it to defeat evil.

᛫

"Zelda," Toucan said, walking into the room. He was smoking and scratched his chin when he saw me. "Glad to see you. *Mi casa es su casa*, remember?"

"I am here to stop you," I said. "That is what I am here to tell you."

The cigarette Toucan was smoking got bright orange at the end. Smoke came out of his nose, just like smoke comes out of the noses of monsters. He laughed and then more smoke came out of his mouth.

When Beowulf defeated Grendel, he had to not be scared, even though Grendel was the biggest villain he had seen. Toucan was scary. I felt like there was a bird inside me, hitting against the insides of my body and trying to get out. To calm myself down I looked down at my shoes and began counting to ten.

"Are you having a stroke or something?" Toucan said.

"You declared war when you hurt Marxy. You stole his basketball and hurt him, just like you hurt Gert." I stood up straighter than I had ever stood up before. "I am going to stop you."

I expected Toucan to get into his battle stance. Instead he did not move, or even change his expression.

"I have no idea what you're talking about." He pointed back to the couch. "Why don't we sit down and talk about this like grown-ups?"

I told him I did not want to sit down. I wanted him to leave Gert alone, to leave Marxy alone, and also to stop selling drugs.

Toucan did not act like he wanted to fight. While he listened his head nodded, and he said, "Okay," over and over again.

This was not how battles were supposed to happen. He did not have a weapon, and he was not getting into a fighting position. I told him that him leaving us alone was a deal-breaker, and that we were not negotiating.

At the end of talking I said, "These are deal-breakers."

Toucan licked his fingers and put out the end of his cigarette by pinching it. Then he put what was left of the cigarette into an ashtray on the table. He asked if I was done.

"There is one more thing." I reached into my belt and pulled out my Viking sword. I held it out in front of me and got into a fighting position.

Toucan whistled.

"Well, look at that," he said. "That looks dangerous. You sure you know how to use it?"

I told him I was serious, that if he did not promise to leave me and Gert and Marxy alone, I would have to use it. He crossed his arms in front of him and took a step toward me.

It was a slow step.

I held the Viking sword out, to show that if he came any closer I would strike.

"Stay where you are," I said.

Toucan took another step. "What if I do this?" he asked. And then took another step, until he was close enough for me to attack.

"I said—"

His hands became unfolded and then one of them grabbed my wrist. He twisted my arm until it hurt to hold on to the Viking sword and I had to drop it. Then he grabbed me by the hair with the other hand.

"Stop!" I said. He did not stop. He pulled my hair so hard that I fell onto my hands and knees in front of him.

My hair felt like it was pulling my brain outside of my head. My eyes started watering from how it sent lightning bolts all throughout my body.

"What?" He pulled my head up so that I was facing his face. "What were you saying?"

I tried to bite but he pulled my head back by my hair so that I could not bite him. Then he threw me down. My sword was on the ground by my feet, but I did get my phone out of my pocket.

Number Two on speed-dial was AK47.

The phone rang once and she picked it up. I was crying so much that my tears and snot from my nose were getting on the screen.

"Where the shit are you?" she asked. "I've been fucking worried sick."

"Help," I said.

"What? Where are you?"

Toucan took my phone away and grabbed me by my hair again and called me a cunt and other words that were ugly.

I tried to pull back and he slapped me across the cheek, which made my eyes water even more. He slapped me over and over, on the same part of my face, and I thought that my mouth was going to fall off of my face.

I had peed myself again. It was warm and itchy on my skin.

While hitting me Toucan said I smelled like piss and called me disgusting and a cunt for making a mess on his floor. He hit me again and told me to shut up.

Then he picked me up and bent me over the couch, so that my stomach was on top of the place where you put your arms.

"You think your boyfriend fucks you good?" he said into my ear. "It's about time you were introduced to how a pro does it."

He pulled down my pants until they went to my ankles. I felt him squeezing my legs and scratching them.

"Please," I said, but he was so heavy I could not move.

Toucan put his leg between my legs and pushed them apart.

Somewhere I couldn't see, I could hear the Grendel laughing and making its growl and it sounded like wolves. My body inside was yelling but he was pushing me down so hard that all of that yelling was stuck inside.

That was when the Fat Man came into the room. He opened the door quickly and then saw us. I could not see him, except a little bit out of the corner of my eye. I could still feel Toucan's hand on my back, but he was not as heavy on me anymore.

"What?" Toucan asked.

I heard the Fat Man say, "I just—"

"You just what?"

Toucan pulled up his pants. I heard his zipper go up. Even though I was no longer trapped, I could not move.

The Fat Man held up his phone. "I don't know how she got my number, but it's Gert's girlfriend. She's on the phone."

"Watch her," Toucan said, pointing at me. He took the phone from the Fat Man and went to another room.

⪦

My stomach hurt from being pushed into the arm of the couch. The Fat Man waited until Toucan was outside before he asked me if I was okay.

I felt myself go onto the ground and closed my eyes and said I wanted to go home, please take me home, please anywhere, please.

"Here," the Fat Man said. "Take this." He handed me a blanket. I started crying. "Fuck," the Fat Man said. "This is fucked up," he said.

Toucan came back into the room. "What are you doing?"

"Man, she's all fucked up," the Fat Man said.

"So?"

"So," the Fat Man said. "Man."

Toucan told the Fat Man to take me to the basement. "Now she's got piss all over my fucking blanket. You think I want that?"

The Fat Man shook his head and started to swear more to himself. Toucan walked right up to the Fat Man, until their faces were almost touching. The Fat Man turned to look away.

Toucan grabbed his face with his hand and said, "What?"

"Nothing," the Fat Man said.

"You were saying something."

"Naw," the Fat Man said. "I wasn't saying anything."

"Good," Toucan said. He told me to pull up my pants, that he was tired of looking at me.

⇗

The Fat Man touched my arm. I tried to pull up my pants but they were wet and did not come up all the way. The Fat Man tried to help me and Toucan told him to just pick me up.

"She weighs like two pounds," Toucan said.

The Fat Man picked me up around the waist. I did not feel like I could move or say anything. The Fat Man said, "There, let's just take it easy," and he brought me to the basement, going slowly down every step. My body did not move.

There was a mattress down there and he put me down on it. The mattress smelled bad, like pee, but I also smelled like pee. The cold air of the basement made my wet legs prickle, and I started to shiver.

"You all right?" the Fat Man asked, not looking at me.

"I'm cold," I said.

"Yeah," he said, and kept looking not at me, but at the ceiling.

He found a blanket. My body hurt from Toucan pushing down on me. The Fat Man put the blanket over me.

"Can you tell Gert I didn't have anything to do with this shit?" the Fat Man asked.

I pulled the blanket closer around myself and pulled my knees close to me and rubbed them until I stopped shivering so much.

The Fat Man started going back up the stairs. They creaked under him. Then he stopped walking and came back down. I could hear the Grendels, growling somewhere I couldn't see.

The Fat Man came over and stood above me.

"Shit," he said. He knelt down. His knees cracked. "I'm going to leave the back door open. Okay? You listening?"

When I did not say anything, he gave my arm a squeeze.

"Hey. You need to listen to me."

"Please, don't leave me," I said, even though the Fat Man wasn't part of my tribe. Now I was holding on to him as much as he was holding on to me. His eyes were watery. "Please help."

"You just go upstairs and turn left and then go out the back door. There's a gate in the fence. You go through there. Okay?"

He touched my arm and then I felt my body get tense and shake.

"Wait ten minutes. And then you can go out there. You understand?"

"Yes," I said.

The Fat Man got up. His pants were hanging down below his waist so he pulled them back up. He walked up the stairs and did not look back.

chapter thirty-four

do not know how long I waited, except that every time I tried to count to sixty seconds I would forget how many times I had done it. It took me a long time to stand up. My pants were wet and so I did not want to wear them anymore. The wet was burning my legs. Somewhere in the darkness of the basement, the Grendel was growling.

I closed my eyes and told it to be quiet, to be quiet, and I said it out loud: "BE QUIET."

I went up the stairs slowly, trying not to make noise.

Toucan was talking to someone in the living room. I walked the way the Fat Man told me, out into the backyard, then started running to the fence where the gate was.

When I got to the gate, I saw AK47's car. It was parked out front. She had found me.

She had come to save me, and she was inside with Toucan and the Grendels.

I sat down on the ground and held my head and told everything to SHUT UP, all of the bad things that had happened. And I thought of the Viking woman in the grave who had become so legendary that now a thousand years after she was dead, people were still talking about her.

I went to a window and tried to look inside but could only see through a crack in the window. When I put my nose to the glass I could see AK47 in the living room and Toucan with her.

The Fat Man came up behind me and tried to take my arm. "Are you crazy? I told you to get out of here."

"My friend is inside," I said, pulling my arm away.

"What do you think is going to happen if he finds out you're gone?"

"I need to save her. Will you help me?" I said. "You can help me defeat him."

"You need to get out of here, is what you need to do." The Fat Man shook his head, said, "Man" again, and started walking away.

My legs still burned with the pee, and my stomach hurt and my face from where I had been hit. Everything had turned out wrong. And I was scared, more scared than I had ever been in my entire life. I remembered being scared of Uncle Richard when he hurt Gert with the beer bottle and yelled at him.

But I was tired of being scared of the Grendels, and of villains like Toucan and Uncle Richard who want to hurt innocent people.

Even without my Viking sword, which was inside somewhere, I decided I would fight and save AK47 and Gert and the World.

Standing up as tall as I could, I whispered, *"Skeggǫld, skálmǫld, skildir ro klofnir,"* a Viking battle cry, and told Tyr, the Viking god of war, that I needed strength and courage.

ᛯ

I went into the house, through the back door, and then down the hallway, toward the living room where Toucan and AK47 were arguing. I passed through the kitchen with the empty brown beer bottles and cigarettes in the sink and pot in bags and playing cards spread out on the table.

As I got closer I could hear Toucan and AK47 talking. Then I saw them. AK47 was standing across from Toucan.

She was holding Gert's gun in her hand.

"Where's Zelda?" AK47 was yelling.

Toucan did not have his arms up. He was still smoking and said he had no idea where I was.

That was when AK47 saw me and said my name, lowering the gun so that it was not pointing right at Toucan anymore.

That was enough time for him to attack.

Toucan was very fast and before AK47 could protect herself he hit her the way he had hit me, and then he took the gun away from her. My brain started speeding and I picked up the ashtray and threw it at him. It bounced off his arm and fell to the ground.

"Get away from her!" I shouted.

Now he was distracted by me, and AK47 tackled Toucan just like Gert tackled other players in football. She threw herself into his stomach, and the air went out of his mouth and he fell like a tree.

"Go!" AK47 said, crashing on top of Toucan.

It did not take long for Toucan to push her off. He held her down by her wrists and then punched her again and called her a dyke and a slut.

I did not run. My feet had become glue.

AK47 made a sound like an animal that was being squeezed too hard.

"Bitch," Toucan said, and then hit her again. He pushed AK47's head into the carpet and then there was blood. He hit her again and then he picked up the ashtray and hit her with that too.

Her eyes closed and her mouth opened at the same time like a fish.

The Grendels were scratching from under the carpet and inside the walls. The whole house was becoming a Grendel.

I saw the Viking sword. It was under the couch. I don't know how it had got there.

Maybe Odin had put it there for me, to use to save AK47, who was being hit again and again, and then Toucan had the gun and was using it to hit her face. He was hitting and the Grendels were shouting louder, and then I blinked and Toucan had turned into a Grendel who was going to devour AK47 inside of his giant mouth.

The Grendels were the voice of Uncle Richard hitting Gert and yelling, the voice of his fingers on my skin, the voice of Hendo saying I was ugly and stupid and retarded, the voice of the cancer cells in Mom taking over everywhere inside of her body until there was nothing but cancer and death.

The voice of the Grendel said that I was not going to be a hero, that there are no more Vikings anymore, and that AK47 was being hurt and it was my fault. Everything was my fault.

Then I heard the voice of Dr. Laird. He said that it was not my fault. And the voice of Dr. Kepple, saying that sometimes life finds us, and when it does we have to rise to the occasion, even when we are scared.

"You are a hero," his voice said. And then AK47 tried to punch Toucan, even though she was small and bleeding underneath him, and that was the most heroic thing I ever saw.

I took the Viking sword and yelled a Viking battle cry with the sword in front of me.

I did one of the attacks I had practiced, which is called the slash, and I made the sword cut into his skin on his arm, the one that was holding the gun.

"You're going to stop," I shouted, louder than all the Grendels in the world.

His arm was bleeding and he held it up and said, "Motherfucker."

He started walking toward me and then stopped, as if he had hit a wall in front of him that was invisible. His eyes became very big and wide.

"Ah," Toucan said, and behind him I saw that AK47 had the gun and had shot Toucan through his back and into his stomach.

I waited for a very long time, not able to move, before taking AK47's cell phone and calling 9-1-1.

chapter thirty-five

At the police station they asked me lots of questions about what had happened. The police officer who gave me the card was there and asked if I was the one who had put the Viking sword into Toucan's arm. I was having trouble speaking. Inside me things were exploding, but none of the words wanted to come out. They stayed stuck. Every time I thought something the thought would stick to the words already stuck in me, creating a big ball that got bigger and bigger until I thought I was going to throw up.

My heart felt like it had stopped working. But when I put my finger to my neck to feel, it was still beating.

The policewoman told another police officer to take me to the hospital and to stay with me. They were worried that Toucan's friends were going to get mad and then try to hurt me, or try to hurt AK47, who was asleep and not waking up.

"It's just precautionary," the police officer said.

I sat in a waiting room in the hospital, with a police officer standing at the other end of the room, reading a magazine. AK47 had been taken to the emergency room by an ambulance while I was at the police station. When Dr. Laird showed up in the hospital, it was the first time

I had seen him outside of the office. He was wearing a brown overcoat that went to his knees.

He saw me and said something to the police officer, showing him an ID from his wallet. Dr. Laird walked over to me and before saying anything he handed me the stress ball. I didn't want it.

I stared at the wall behind him, where there was a picture of a beach and the summer. More than anything in the world I wanted to be there with Gert and AK47 on the beach and under the palm tree.

"I know how you must be feeling," Dr. Laird said. "I came as soon as I heard."

I also wanted to continue being mad at him, for calling the police and getting Gert in trouble. But I could not be mad. He was not only my doctor, he was also my friend and a part of my tribe and the Wise Man in my legend. Sometimes people in tribes have to do things that hurt at first in order to help the greater good.

"I feel like a shit-heel," I said.

Dr. Laird held out the stress ball. "You sure you don't want this?"

This time I took it and squeezed.

He stayed for an hour, listening to me, letting me cry. He did not write anything down and had a package of tissues that he gave me so I could blow my nose. I told him all about Toucan, how he had died before the police arrived. I was supposed to feel mighty and heroic. But I did not feel either of those things. Toucan had tried to talk to me while he was dying and bleeding from the hole where the bullet had gone. He put out his hand and I had held on to it and it reminded me of Hendo's baby, Artem, wrapping his baby fingers around my one big finger.

Toucan could not hold on to my hand for very long. It became me holding his hand, until his hand let go and I let go and he was a corpse, not a person anymore.

"I forgot that he was a villain," I said. "He was a person who was dying, and AK47 was trying to pull me away from him and then she started dying too, and I didn't know what to do."

"Sometimes life isn't as simple as heroes and villains." Dr. Laird came close to me, until I could see into his eyes, which were green, even though I thought they were blue. "But I want you to know that you were very brave, and that you are heroic. You could have run away from your problems. A lot of people do that."

"He made a noise," I said, and thought of the way Toucan's mouth had opened and then words didn't come out. Just the noise.

And then I started crying again.

"Okay," he said. "I know." And he put his hand, with his big wedding ring and hairy knuckles, on my arm.

We sat in the chairs in the waiting room, Dr. Laird with his hand on my shoulder, and I made myself into a little ball on the chair.

"Can we talk about something?" I asked.

"Like what?"

"Anything but what is happening."

He smelled like shampoo and like laundry right out of the machine, and he told me stories about all the interesting things his daughter was learning in school, like how butterflies taste with their feet, and how starfish are one of the only animals who have two stomachs, one that they can shoot out of their bodies.

"Gross," I said.

"Very gross. They use it to eat oysters like that."

He had never talked about his family before. I did not even know he had a daughter. It was part of our rules that we did not talk about him or his life or family. I asked him why he was okay talking about his daughter now.

"I guess this is different."

"Yeah."

Dr. Laird looked at his hands. "I don't think I've been helping you as much as I could. And I feel responsible for a lot of this."

I did not understand what he meant. He kept squishing his hands and starting to breathe like he was going to say something, and then stopping.

"I should have been more prepared, with your personal history."

"My personal history."

"Your family history, I mean. With your uncle."

"Oh." I played with my hands, since it was easier to talk to my hands than to Dr. Laird. "Uncle Fuck-dick."

"Yeah. Uncle Fuck-dick."

The doctor came out and said I could see AK47 if I wanted. Dr. Laird and I both stood up.

"Well," Dr. Laird said. He put out his hand. I took it and gave it a shake.

"Can we hug one more time?" I asked.

"Yeah," he said. "We can hug." And I hugged him. I tried to give him back the stress ball but he told me I should keep it. "Whenever you feel like you're going to burst, just give it a good squeeze."

꙳

AK47 did not share the room with anybody. The policeman who was watching me went with me and the doctor to her room. The doctor pulled back a blue curtain that hung from the ceiling and wrapped around AK47's bed.

The person in the bed didn't look like AK47. She looked like a dead person on the crime shows on TV. Her skin didn't have the glow it usually did, and you could see the little pink veins on her eyelids. A tube went into her mouth and the computer next to her bed made bleeping

noises that reminded me of videos games—like AK47 had become a
video game that the computer turned into sound.

"Is she okay?" I asked.

The doctor cleared his throat. "We're not entirely sure. She sustained
a lot of neurological trauma and lost a good bit of blood."

"What does that mean?"

"It means that we'll need to do more tests."

The doctor said I could sit with her until Gert arrived. He was still
at the police station. I asked the police officer how long it would take.

"I'm not sure," the officer said. "Shouldn't be too long now."

There was a chair by her bed and so I sat down in it. AK47's hand
was turned up and had tape holding a tube going into it. I put my head
on it.

⚡

I stayed with AK47 for an entire hour, talking to her like she was awake.
Sometimes she talked back in my brain, or at least words I thought she
would say came to me. The words asked me to pray for her.

"I know you are still in there," I told AK47. "I will find a way to
make everyone see."

Normally I would have prayed the way Hamsa and I prayed
together, him to the Muslim god, me to Odin and the rest of the
warriors in Valhalla and to the Norn sisters, asking them to make a
different day for AK47 to die. But I was not sure I believed in any of
that anymore. I was not sure whether to believe in Odin, and I was
not sure I believed that good people could go to a place like Valhalla
after they died. AK47 was a good person and it had turned out very
badly for her, just like it had turned out very badly for Toucan, who
would never be alive again.

Maybe it was worth it to pray, even if I didn't believe it anymore.

"Odin," I said, and closed my eyes. "PLEASE HELP AK47 TO WAKE UP. I PROMISE I WILL BRING HONOR TO YOU AND TO HER AND TO EVERYONE IN VALHALLA."

I must have been saying it very loud because the nurse came in and asked if everything was okay.

"I heard shouting," she said.

"I was shouting my praise for AK47," I said, and since the nurse probably didn't know I called her that, pointed to AK47 to show that it was her that I was shouting praise for.

"Okay," the nurse said. "Maybe we can keep the praise to a level below shouting. We have other patients who need rest." She smiled and I said that was fine, I already did my praise shouting for the day.

⟨

AK47 did not have any family, and she had chosen Gert as the person to say when it was okay to take her off the machine that was helping her breathe and eat. We were in the hospital, standing all around her. Gert was not arrested. But he had to go back to the police station after, because he was a very important part of their plans for other people like Toucan.

Gert was talking to the doctor, who was saying that AK47 might not wake up. The tests they had run came back and the results were not good. Her brain had been hit very hard by Toucan, and blood had gone into it and that was very bad.

"But her body is alive," I said.

The doctor said he would leave us alone to talk, closing the door behind him. AK47's machine blipped and bleeped. Gert and I stood side by side, watching over her. Just outside the window, beside AK47's bed, was a tall office building. I could see a lot of people moving around in it. They reminded me of ants. I wondered if they were looking out and seeing us and asking themselves what we were doing that made us look so sad and depressed.

"Fuck, fuck, fuck." Gert walked to the window and pressed his face against the glass.

One of AK47's feet stuck out from under the sheet. Her toes still had bits of silver nail polish. I had brought a nail clipper with me, since in *Kepple's Guide to the Vikings* when a warrior dies, the nails need to be clipped off so that they can't be used to build a ship called Naglfar to bring Ragnarok, the end of the world.

I went toe to toe. "What are you doing?" Gert asked

"Saving the world by ending it," I said.

AK47's nails weren't long anymore. The nurse must have cut them. But there was enough to cut, and I kept the pieces of nail in my hand. When I got to her hands I felt her fingers. They moved whatever way I wanted them to. There was no AK47 telling the fingers to go one way or the other.

He came over. "Can I do some too?"

I handed him the nail clippers. "Be careful," I said. "She doesn't like them too short."

Gert went around AK47, very carefully. There were five fingers for him to do, and he kept her nails in his hand.

I thought about Toucan, how now he was a corpse, with horse eyes. The thing that scared me most was the way his mouth had opened and it was like he was screaming, only nothing came out. There was no more soul inside of him.

All at once Gert jumped back. "Holy shit," he said.

AK47 was blinking.

"What are you freaks doing?" she said. Her voice was not her normal voice, but it was the voice of a person who was alive.

chapter thirty-six

Gert stopped going to summer school. He said that it was impossible to concentrate on making up the credits that he'd missed with AK47 in the hospital, and he came to visit her. Sometimes they fought and I waited outside, and when I came back in they were in the hospital bed together, holding hands, Gert's head on her shoulder with his eyes closed.

I visited AK47 as much as I could, which was not every day since I was working more and more at the library.

At first she had to use a wheelchair, because her brain didn't know how to talk to her legs anymore. Then she taught the brain to speak, with the help of a physiotherapist who made her practice first moving her toes and then her legs.

"You ever hear people speaking Japanese?" AK47 said. "Well, that's what it's like. My brain's speaking Japanese and my legs can't listen."

One day she was able to walk with a walker, one foot at a time, very slowly.

Gert and I cheered when she showed off her walker, which folded up, and then when she could take steps without the walker, with just a cane made of metal, I sung her praise.

She was able to go back to her own apartment. Gert wanted her to stay with us. She said that it was important that she do things on her own, which made Gert mad at first.

Then he started going back to summer school. "You should be worrying about that, not me," AK47 told him.

One day she phoned the library while I was at work and said she needed to talk to me.

"Come alone," she said, and I thought that Gert's birthday was in less than one month, and she wanted to plan a gargantuan birthday party for him. Maybe we could order the Viking stripper for Gert again, as a joke. I said I would be over after work, and took the bus and walked across the park from the bus stop to her apartment building.

AK47 buzzed me in and when I came to her door she yelled that it was open. I came inside and saw that there were suitcases, black ones with wheels, sitting by the door.

She came out of her room with a backpack over her shoulder, using her cane and moving one foot at a time.

"You want to help me with this?" she asked, and I ran to take the backpack. She told me to put it with the suitcases.

"Are you going back to the hospital?" I asked, because sometimes she had to go back to spend the night and had to bring a bag filled with things she'd need.

"Not exactly." She sat down on the couch, very slowly, and began massaging her leg.

"What does that mean?"

"Sit," she said, pointing her cane at the chair across from her. "I want to talk to you."

I sat down. AK47 set her cane between her legs, leaning her chin on the end, where you hold on with your hand.

"I'm leaving," she said.

"Leaving what?"

"Leaving the city. The state." She smiled. "Probably not the country, but maybe the country. Depends how I feel."

I blinked, trying to understand what she was saying. When I started to talk, she held up her hand. "Listen, I was thinking about all of this stuff, about Gert and being in the hospital. There are some people I need to see, from my own family."

"I thought you didn't have a family. I thought they all died in Arkansas."

"Arizona, actually. And I know I said that, and to me they've been dead. Not *dead* dead. Just . . ." AK47 took her chin off the cane and started slowly spinning it like a top. "I've been meaning to go and see them, I guess."

"Are Gert and I going with you? Because I need to request the time off work and Carol would like at least one week's notice before I can take time off and get approved."

"Oh, Zelda, I know you'd go to hell and back for me. But I'm going solo on this one."

I felt a ball in my throat.

"When are you coming back?"

Instead of answering, she told me to bring her something. "It's in the bedroom. I wanted to have it out before you came, but I didn't have time." She patted her weak leg. "Limpy over here makes things difficult."

"What is it?"

She stuck out her cane and poked me with it. "Hey. Stop asking questions. All will be revealed. It's an envelope. On the bedside table. Bring it in here."

There were clothes all over the bed and floor. Inside the closet, empty hangers hung from a metal rod that stretched from one side to the other. There was an envelope on the bedside table and on it AK47's handwriting said ZELDA.

I brought it to AK47, who said to open it.

The envelope wasn't licked closed, so all I had to do was pull the flap.

Inside there were some folded papers, and when I unfolded them I saw a key attached to the front one with Scotch tape.

"Here's what we're going to do," AK47 said, stretching out her hand for the papers and the key, which she pulled off and handed to me. "This is the key to my apartment. I'm going to have to get another one made for the front door, but for now there's a code you can memorize. It's not too hard but it works on the front door. It's written here." She held up the papers and tapped the top corner, where she had written 2-6-0-8. "Now, these papers here." She flipped the pages over. "There's a place down here where you need to sign."

"Sign?"

"Correct. Your signature. The one you've been practicing."

I told her I didn't understand. AK47 leaned forward, and I leaned forward so that our faces were almost touching.

"These papers will transfer the lease to you. I've cleared it with the super of the building. He knows you'll be taking over the apartment for me. You'll need to get him a copy of a pay stub from the library, showing that you have an income, but you'll be able to afford it. I've paid the next few months in advance already, so that should give you time to get used to paying the bills. Electricity is covered, Internet isn't. I've sent you an e-mail with the details, but for the most part, you'll sort it out."

I sat back and stared at her, then at the apartment, which was very big all of a sudden.

"What does Gert think?" I said.

"To quote my favorite person in the world, which would be you: Gert is not part of this legend. I want *you* to have the apartment, not you and Gert."

"Why would it not be for Gert too?"

She put her arms behind her head and sank into the couch. "You know, I had a lot of time to think. About what happened back there, about how you saved me, and how hairy things got with that scumbag."

I looked at my hands. "I still have dreams sometimes about him."

"God, Zee, me too. And it's not fair. None of it is fair. But here's what I think. You've been cleaning up Gert's messes for long enough."

"I don't clean up any of his messes," I said. "He's very clean."

"I don't mean literally. I mean in life." She sighed. "You can't save a person who doesn't want to be saved. God knows I've tried to save him. And you have too. Sometimes the people we love are also the monsters, the—what do you call them? The Grendels?"

"Gert isn't a Grendel."

"Maybe. Maybe not. But he's not going to be good for you, or good for anybody, until he's found himself."

I turned the key over and over in my hand. It was silver and bright and as I turned it light from the metal shone on the walls and ceiling.

"He needs to write his own legend," I said.

AK47 smiled. "Exactly."

"I don't know if I can have my own apartment."

AK47 stood up, using the arm of the couch for balance. "Why not? You can always call me, and I've already told Big Todd, who is going to set up check-ins and help. Plus Dr. Laird. Besides, I might come back in a week and throw a wrench in this whole plan." She held out her fist. "The point is you're willing to give it a try. That's what makes someone a legend."

I said I needed some time to think about it. "When are you leaving?"

AK47 stood by her suitcases. "I'd say about now."

I wanted to stop her from leaving, but I didn't. She was crossing things off of her own list of things she needed to do.

We hugged and she walked out and I stood at the door. She got on the elevator and held up her fist, and I held up my fist, and from across the hallway we did a dab, even though we were too far for our fists to actually touch.

chapter thirty-seven

Every Viking home needs to be blessed, and the best way to do a blessing is to celebrate the home with all of your friends. Hamsa came, and Yoda too. Hamsa brought his uncle, who wished me a happy home and did a thing with his hands in prayer.

Marxy and Sarah-Beth came to the party together, which did not make me mad. I was very happy for them. Marxy had found someone who understood him and loved him.

His mother hugged me too. "I know your mom's not around, but I think she'd be proud of you." She brought me a special Norse rune to protect the house. "You're supposed to put it by the door. Good luck and all that." She stopped by the letter from Dr. Kepple, which I had printed out and hung on the wall and put in a picture frame, which you can get from the Dollar Barn for a dollar and fifty cents.

"That is very special," I said, standing beside her. "That is from Dr. Kepple, who is an expert on Vikings. People think that only men can be powerful Vikings, but they're wrong. Women like us can be powerful too."

Pearl smiled. "We definitely can be powerful, Zelda."

Big Todd brought his boyfriend and helped me with the Internet bill and showed me how to create an automatic deduction for the rent to come out. Carol from the library also came. She brought two book-ends so that when I started my own library, they could sit on the ends of the books and stop them from falling over.

I also invited the Viking stripper from my birthday party, who it turns out was gay and who Big Todd and Noah thought was super hot.

I showed them my Viking sword, and a new outfit that I had ordered from the Internet that was for female Vikings.

Dr. Laird came too, which I did not expect. He hadn't responded to my e-mail inviting him.

"You came," I said.

He was wearing his big coat and he had his wife with him. I knew it was his wife from the pictures on his desk.

"I thought I'd make an appearance." He looked around at everyone else at the party and smiled. He introduced his wife, who shook my hand and said it was an honor to meet me. I told her it was an honor to meet her.

"This is a nice place," Dr. Laird said.

"Thanks," I said.

He asked if Gert was there, and I said he was invited but hadn't come.

Yoda came over with a drink for Dr. Laird and his wife. "I am the official drink-bringer," he said. "And if you would like me to take your coats." He held out his arms and took the coats to the bedroom, where the coats of everyone who came were on the bed.

"Do you think Gert will come?" I asked Dr. Laird.

"Maybe," he said. "Maybe not. But even if he doesn't, you've done a very good thing. I'm proud of you."

He said he wanted to talk to me alone, and his wife gave him a kiss on the cheek and told him that she was going to use the ladies' room.

"Do you remember the Viking article I gave you? The one about the woman Viking?"

I said I did.

"Do you know why I gave it to you?"

"So that I could become a hero," I said.

"Everyone is a hero in their own lives," he said. "That's by default. But I wanted you to see that sometimes the world thinks something is not possible, but it turns out that they can be wrong. Even fancy scientists can be wrong."

"Sometimes the most important things don't fit on lists," I said. "And sometimes those are things we don't expect. Like this apartment."

Dr. Laird smiled. "Sometimes the most important things don't fit on lists. I like that."

"Me too."

We dabbed again.

⤸

I kept waiting for Gert to show up, but he didn't. We had not seen each other very much since AK47 had left. She did not tell him in person that she was leaving, which I did not like but also understood. Gert could get very angry and I know she did not want to have to fight with him. At first I wanted them to fight so that Gert could convince her to stay. Now I was glad she did not get convinced.

People from the party started going home.

"If you talk to Annie, tell her we miss her," Big Todd said, and we hugged and I said I would.

Dr. Laird said to call him to set up an appointment whenever I needed.

Once everyone left I started cleaning up and was almost finished at 10:12 p.m. when there was a knock at the door. Through the peephole I saw Gert standing in front of the door.

"You're very late," I said, opening the door.

"Too late?" He smiled and leaned in the doorway.

I shook my head. "You are welcome."

He started walking into the house and I cleared my throat and pointed at the RULES FOR ZELDA'S APARTMENT. Gert saw the sheet of paper and stopped.

"Okay, okay," he said, and took off his shoes. "I like the place."

Gert put his hands in his pockets. He had not shaved in a long time and I knew that he had been drinking beer from how he smelled.

"Thank you."

I made him not coffee but tea. One of the things that I learned is that I don't like coffee, not as much as tea. I also do not like carpet, because dirt hides in it and it gets ugly and smells.

He sat on the couch and picked at a thread. I brought over the tea.

"How are you holding up?" he asked.

"Fine. How are you holding up?"

He shrugged. "Not bad." He cleared his throat. "Have you heard anything from her?"

I had heard from her and told Gert that she was doing well. He kept picking at the thread of the couch. He asked where she was now—if she was in Arizona.

AK47 had asked me not to tell Gert things like where she was. I could tell him she was okay and safe. "But don't tell him anything else," she wrote in her e-mail.

"I'm not sure," I said. "But she is okay and safe."

Gert looked around and then rubbed his neck. "I'd really like to talk to her," he said. "So if you know how to get in touch with her . . ." He trailed off and stopped rubbing his neck. "She's not answering my e-mails."

He had not touched his tea.

"She is on her own quest," I said.

"Yeah."

He took my phone from me. "Gert. Stop."

"What's your password?"

When I didn't tell him, he threw it at the wall, where it bounced and fell onto the ground, making a chip in the wall.

I crossed my arms. "You need to leave now," I said, pointing to the door. "That is the most important Rule of the House—no yelling and throwing things."

Gert picked up his shoes and walked to the door. He wiped his nose on his sleeve.

He went into the hallway and punched the wall before starting to walk, holding his shoes.

At the end of the hall he stopped and said, "Can you just come home?"

"This is my home now," I said, and even though it was the hardest thing I have ever done, harder even than facing Toucan, I went back inside and closed the door.

I put the last dishes from the party into the sink and turned off the music and went to my room, where it was quiet and filled with shadows.

I knew, though, there were no monsters in the shadows, no Grendels in the walls. Just my breathing in the dark, and outside a bright moon hanging in the sky.

⌐

When I woke up the next morning and began getting ready for work, I saw that there was an envelope underneath the door. I bent down and picked it up and saw that the envelope had my name on it in Gert's handwriting, which is big and with a *Z* that looks like the number three.

Inside was a paper that had been folded three times. It was Gert's scholarship essay, the one he had written for college and did not want me to read.

I pressed it flat on the coffee table.

To the Rivergreen College Scholarship Committee:
My name is Gert MacLeish. I'm twenty-one years old, don't have a high
school diploma, and nobody I know has ever been to college, either.

  I'm not very good at writng essays, so the only way this is going to work
is if I write like I speak.

I frowned. Gert spelled *writing* wrong. He should have used spell-check. I took a pencil and corrected the word before I started reading again.

Some people are made to go to college, some people aren't. I always thought
I was the second kind. I played football. My grades weren't great, but
you can probably see that from my transcripts. Football was supposed to
be my ticket. When my knee blew up, so did every dream I had of ever
being someone.

  My sister Zelda never really knew our Dad. She was young when
he left. When Mom died of breast cancer, we ended up living with our
Uncle Richard, a really bad dude. Zelda's into Vikings and villains and
heroes, and if there's one villain, one dragon blowing fire on the world,
it's Uncle Richard.

  She doesn't really know how bad things got with him, how abusive.
Men aren't supposed to talk about this kind of stuff, and I don't know
why I'm mentioning it right now, except that the instructions say to talk
about "mitigating circumstances." Uncle Richard is the definition of
a "mitigating circumstance." Zelda is always talking about Grendels,
these evil monsters who hide in the shadows and come for you in the dark.
The longer we stayed with Uncle Richard, the more I realized that he was
the one she was afraid of, the monster that came in the dark. And since
Zelda couldn't defend herself, it was up to me to defend her—to get us

out of there. I'm not the type of person who asks for help, but that's what I'm doing with this letter.

At the start of this I said there were two kinds of people, and how I was one kind—the kind that most people probably think doesn't belong in a college classroom. Well, my sister, Zelda, she's the other kind. Our mother was also a big drinker, and even though she got sober in the last few years before she died, she wasn't sober when she had us. While I turned out okay, Mom's drinking was poison for Zelda's brain and she was born on the Fetal Alcohol Spectrum. They said she would probably never be able to read, and that she'd probably have other people taking care of her for her entire life.

They were wrong about both of those things, and she's the reason I'm applying for this scholarship. Maybe if I can do this, she can do something like it too. The world looks at Zelda and sees someone weak and defenseless. One of the things I'm most ashamed of is seeing her that way too, and not seeing how strong she can be—stronger than me, even. If I had half her strength and determination, I wouldn't need to beg for a scholarship. In a universe that was fair, she'd be the one going to college, not me.

It's been forever since I've written an essay, and this is already more than the 500 words I'm supposed to use to convince you that I belong at Rivergreen. One of the rules I remember from English class is that you should alway start with a thesis, so I guess I'm breaking the rules again and putting it right at the end.

Here goes anyway: there are people around the poker table of life whose hands aren't perfect and they see what they have and fold right away. They don't even bother playing. I feel like I've been that kind of person. But even if I don't get into Rivergreen, even if you turn me down for the scholarship, I'm tired of folding, knowing that my sister's the kind of person who would play her hand, no matter how bad the cards were.

While I write this she's listening to an audiobook about Vikings, writing down important notes. For her the world is a place where courage and being part of a tribe means more than anything else—where we are all Vikings paddling together, to the beat of the same drum. And that's the thing—all this time that I've been trying to protect Zelda, she's been the only one in our tribe paddling. It's time I got in Zelda's boat and took a turn at the oars.

Yours,
Gert MacLeish

When I finished reading I ran to my phone and called Gert's cellphone number, and when he didn't pick up I left a message saying that I did not want to close the door on him forever and that I loved him and that we will always be paddling together. My skin exploded in goose bumps when I thought about Gert thinking I did not want him in my life.

Then, from somewhere else, I heard his voice-mail sound. I looked around and dialed the phone number again.

A phone was ringing at the end of the hallway. When I followed the sound and opened the front door, I got a good bad feeling.

Gert was sleeping outside the door. His body was very small, like a ball, leaning against the wall and hugging himself. A door opened at the other end of the hall and a woman came out, dressed in clothes to go to work. Her keys jangled and Gert groaned but didn't wake up all the way.

"I didn't want to call the police," the woman said, walking by and putting her keys in her purse. "But he was crying all night."

I bent down. It was not a nice thing, to see the way Gert looked. He had pizza sauce on his shirt and he smelled like warm beer. It made me feel bad that I didn't want to be by him. I got up and went back inside my apartment and stood in the hallway. Then I went to my bedroom and got my Minnesota Vikings sweatshirt, which I had bought for myself with some money from a paycheck from the library (even though Gert likes the Patriots).

I went back into the hallway and touched Gert's arm. His eyes opened slowly. They were red and puffy.

"Hey," he said, sitting up and cricking his neck. "Is that a Viking sweatshirt?"

"Yes, because it is a team *I* like, Gert."

I gave him the sweatshirt. I helped him stand up. I told him he was at my home now and it was time for him to come inside.

acknowledgments

Like any good Viking saga, Zelda's story has an entire horde of people who made its publication possible.

First, many dabs to my superlative, indefatigable agent Grace Ross, who made magic with this book and saw its potential from the start. Big thanks as well to Markus Hoffmann, Joe Regal, and everyone at RHA.

Skål to the Scout tribe, especially my brilliant editor and powerful champion, Alison Callahan; my favorite double-doctor, Jen Bergstrom; the always-at-the-ready Brita Lundberg; and to Aimée Bell, Meagan Harris, Emi Battaglia, Stuart Smith, and the many publishing warriors at S&S who made Zelda possible. Special thanks to Carolyn Reidy, for believing in the book.

And thanks to the mighty Canadian contingent: Nina Pronovost, Felicia Quon, Kevin Hanson, and the rest of the team.

To the master, Larry Garber, who spilled the soup of his mentorship and good grace upon this humble schlemozzle. To mentors Edie Meidav, Sabina Murray, and Jeff Parker. Thanks as well to Annie Liontas for early draft feedback.

To my family, surrogate and otherwise: Mom and Dad, the Mitchells (especially L, an early adopter), the Maecks, Melissa Carroll, Beaker and George, and the Beckermans.

Wide-eyed love for Team Good Egg: Tim Alamenciak, Shannon Alberta, Shastri Akella, Amy Cunningham, Erin Pienaar, JoAnna Novak, Ali Ünal (note correct umlaut placement), Morgan Bruner, Catherine Stryker, Kathryn Pilkington, Margaret DeRosia, Trenna Sharpe, Julia Kramer, Arielle Bernstein.

And many, many others, to whom I tip my hat and open my heart. You know who you are.

Thank you to the Toronto Arts Council, the Ontario Arts Council, and the Canada Council for the Arts for much appreciated financial support.

To learn more about Fetal Alcohol Syndrome, to donate, or to get involved, please contact, in Canada, The Canada Fetal Alcohol Spectrum Disorder Research Network (https://canfasd.ca/), and in the United States, the National Organization on Fetal Alcohol Syndrome (www.nofas.org).